KEOTA — 1

WALKING BACKWARDS — 18

CREATION STORIES — 38

COYOTE SONGS — 43

CROSSING OVER — 51

VEDAUWOO — 69

THE LANGUAGE WE LEARN - 86

POLE VAULTING THE PERIMETER - 90

IN MEDIAS RES - 96

SEEGER - 112

THE COLONEL'S LIMOGES - 115

DRIFTWOOD - 128

BROKEN WINGS AND DAMAGED SOULS - 131

MIGRATORY PASSAGES - 144

TRANSITION ZONES - 150

VIRGINIA CITY - 159

WHERE'S HOSS - 164

UP ON THE ROOF - 170

ROUGHING IT - 180

HELL WINDS AND HURRICANES - 190

THE BATTLE OF WORCESTERSHIRE FLAT - 194

CONFEDERATE DREAMS AND TEXAS SCHEMES - 206

PICTURES AT AN EXHIBITION - 215

COLLECTING DUST - 224

DENOUEMENT - 228

AFTERGLOW - 229

Published by:
Powder River Publishing LLC
1014 Black Mountain Road
Thermopolis, Wyoming 82443

Copyright © 2022
ISBN: 978-1-956881-04-2
Printed in the United States of America

The Leaving Time

www.powderriverpublishing.com

Introduction

The book you are holding in your hand is a true story. All of the people, places and events contained herein, save those necessary for extending the narrative, existed and/or occurred as written. No names and/or events have been changed to protect the innocent.

Where changes have occurred, they've been made in order to protect what the reader should discover for themselves; the land and what it means to walk it; the interconnectedness between people and place and the spirit contained therein while discovering for themselves what constitutes truth and what doesn't in an increasingly disingenuous world.

To search for the Holy Grail.

May you find it.

As with all books, thanks and kudos in no particular order to John Steinbeck, Kurt Vonnegut, Richard Brautigan, Edward Abbey, Wallace Stegner, Ivan Doig, James Galvin, Mark Spragg, Sherman Alexie, Mark Twain, Jack Kerouac, James Hilton, James Michener, Frank Bergon, Harper Lee, John McPhee, George Frison, the East Texas Historical Journal, the National Archives, the Arthurian Legends, William Butler Yeats, Ralph Waldo Emerson, Lao Tzu, Chief Seattle, John Ford, Frank Capra, Mary Chapin Carpenter, Pete Seeger, Gerry Goffin and Carole King, the Drifters, the Byrds, Kevin Costner, Gary Farmer, John Trudell, Richard Farnsworth, Robin Williams, 1950s Hollywood, Franklin Gearing, Mike Daggett, Big Sur, Virginia City, Colorado, Wyoming and the Eastern Sierra as well as special thanks to Dan, Skylar, the Greatest Generation and my parents, Tunkasilla and every Native American storyteller both living and dead as well as Caleb.

Their influences should be obvious.

KEOTA

A hundred miles beyond the point, the farthest point, the most distant point on the horizon. Out beyond the Buttes, layered and stratified like two leftovers from Monument Valley and furrowed like the brow of an old mans eyes, creased and wrinkled, the corners stretching in crows feet covered in chalk dust, sifted and filtered into corrugated steel stock tanks by the prairie winds where a solitary magpie does the backstroke alongside a dead something or other, it's body no longer identifiable and reduced to an amorphous blob of feathers and goop, swimming as it does so in an otherwise rippleless water not yet turned green by the late summer algae, the constant drip of the failing windmill is the only sound one hears in an otherwise empty landscape.

"Walking in balance is the hardest dance you'll ever do."

Caleb Cutbank. A riddle wrapped in a conundrum. They say he'd always been there although he claimed he was born in 1911, the day that Shoshone Mike was killed out near Winnemucca, or maybe around the time Ishi appeared in California like some malnourished enigma outside Oroville.

1911 was an eventful year.

It was said that he shared Mike's spirit, or at least that part his killers didn't steal.

Said he was just another Ishi.

Like Mike, he seemed to have been everywhere and nowhere, always showing up when least expected and always on foot. Always with a story. Always the same.

Immutable.

Like Ishi, he was a person out of context. A being from a

different era. A different time.

To the Lakota he was Tunkasilla, grandfather, but to me he was just plain Caleb. The old man who, like Mike, said he walked from Idaho to California and back. Not once, but twice mind you.

When, he'd never say. How, he'd never tell. He simply did it.

Some things were better left unsaid. Some stories left untold. Some things you needed to learn for yourself.

Walking the two track between a sea of pebbles, prickly pear and tomatillos, the crushed alabaster chalkdust of a thousand years billowed in puffs at our feet as they passed over and into it. Tiny mushroom clouds stuck in a twentieth century sky, as limitless as the prairie space they exploded into. Stuck in another era, stuck in another time. An era of compressed dinosaur bones and eroding bison teeth, crumbling strata and encroaching cheatgrass where the occasional lance point'd stick out from between dessicated piles of dehydrated cowplop and sage.

"Notice how the one side is still salmon colored, shiny and clean, it's surface reflecting the sunlight in it's crystals and how the other side is kinda dull and rust red, the color of dried blood? That means it's been where it was broken, one side up and the other down for a hundred years or more. Maybe from the time of Lindenmeier or McKean. Maybe longer. No matter, it wasn't a missed shot. It was intentionally broken, you know. You can tell by the break in the middle where it was snapped. Hasn't been worn. It was a sacrifice. Somebody or something died and it's lived in the light of day ever since. It's spirit was free."

Damn old man. Why didn't I see that? And just what in the hell was he talking about anyway?

Out past Keota, eastward where even the railroads couldn't sell the land for all the dry wheat farming and sugar beets west of Nebraska, the skeletal remains of what'd once been a homestead, a Scandinavian dream gone bust, hung low on the horizon, the wood as yet unstolen for fashionable homes in Boulder. Two cottonwoods, one on each side of the remaining frame stood broken limbed, but otherwise intact. A testament to survival in an otherwise overgrazed landscape.

"You have to walk the land in order to understand it. You have to feel it with your toes, through the soles of your shoes. You have to walk with the seasons. In the years. In your time. In the time of those who've gone before..."

Riddles. Caleb was full of 'em.

And so it was that forty years after he sent me chasing after him over the Kelly Wire, passing between or underneath the barbed strands as either time or age would allow, I too would learn to walk the land. To listen to it's stories and hear of what'd been as well as what would be. To learn to speak it's language and listen to it's songs. But most importantly, I'd learn how, to him, it was all the same. Yesterday, today, tomorrow. There were no words in his language for the difference.

And it'd take a lifetime.

By late August, clouds'd scud southward across an otherwise trackless sky, a sky like every John Ford movie ever made. Movies where it'd hang suspended across the land and stretch limitless to ever decreasing points on the horizon. Suspended in space and time, unbound by what lay beneath it, the land and the furrowed arroyos beyond.

Coulda been a scene straight out of Cheyenne Autumn and maybe in a sense it was. After all, It'd been theirs once. Maybe it still was.

Multi headed sunflowers drooped in the arroyo bottoms where occasional shade and remnant moisture permitted. Like supplicants in an outdoor cathedral they prayed for the Canadian rain that headed southward out of Alberta.

"Coprolite."

Say what?

"Coprolite. Fossilized Dino dung."

The brown sausage shaped sandstone cast sat beside the two track oblivious to the horned lizard that ran for cover nearby. Each a remnant of a bygone era still alive in the present. Both from another time.

What one misses, another sees.

"Wonder if it came from a cat?"

Wonder if the dehydrated cow plop around us'll look like a

coprolite in another thousand years?

Space and time. Limitless as the sky.

By mid afternoon the scudding clouds would become flat bottomed and look like cotton on top afterwhich they'd turn gray, then black as they sucked up what little moisture they could find from the Shortgrass Prairie below. Not long after they'd form a southerly wall and advance across the cobalt around 'em like an invading army from Alberta. Lightning strikes would follow, then the boom.

Ten seconds. Five seconds. Three seconds away.

Looks like we're gonna get wet.

"Old Man That Grumbles."

Yep, just like you.

"We used to call 'em that you know. The Thunder Beings. Sometimes all talk and no action. Like old crows they'd squawk but then disappear as soon as they did so. Big noise. Little impact."

"We used to run our ponies with 'em. Used to match their advance while off to the side. Not unlike hunting buffalo, ya know. Always close enough to touch, but just out of reach. They didn't seem to mind, but hated being taunted."

In less than a minute both Caleb and I were soaked clean through.

So much for taunting.

There's no place to hide on the prairie when you screw up. You gotta suck it up. Roll with the punches.

Five minutes later and we'd be dry while Old Man That Grumbles would roll on toward Denver.

At least it wasn't hail and the sunflowers enjoyed it. Within no time at all their heads were up and their supplication was answered.

Life moves forward. Celebrate the moment or you'll lose it.

Continuing easterly as it had been the two track meandered, sometimes pointing us towards Nebraska, sometimes towards Julesburg, but always with the Buttes in sight.

Caleb picked up a piece of broken glass.

"Know what this is?"

Nope.

"A knife point."

Say, what?

"By the 1870s, what the homesteaders threw away became useful to the people. It was getting harder to trade for obsidian out west and their quartzite and flint gathering places were disturbed. The horse herds were dwindling and the quarry sites were overrun. It was often easier to go through the white mans garbage piles than to search for what we once had. Even old Red Cloud knew that when he gave Lupton his necklace down in Colorado. Coulda been a token of friendship, but coulda been a trade as well. No doubt Lupton gave him broken bottles in return, but at least he could camp where he used to and although the buffalo range was broken, he could get some beef."

I held the glass shard in my hand and like Caleb'd said it was side notched and conchoidially fractured. Probably came from a medicine bottle. No matter what, somebody'd purposefully chipped the edges to make it sharper.

"Ishi had nothing on Old Red Cloud, ya know, and unlike Lupton, Kroeber was an ass. He used to sit in that museum in Berkeley all day and just chip away on bottles for the tourists. Said it reminded him of Yahi."

"They removed his brain anyway. Sent it to the Smithsonian."

On another occasion Caleb showed me an old horseshoe nail he carried around with him. It looked unused except for the burnished tip and rusty body. Musta never been pounded into a hoof. The head was clean. Don't know why he kept it, but he did. Said it had once been used to make arrowheads by Shoshone Mike. When I laughed, he showed me the polished tip and held it against an agate birdpoint he carried along with it in his 501s. Needless to say, the corner notches in the point matched the shiny portion of the nail perfectly.

"Once belonged to Mike, ya know, but he no longer has any use for 'em."

One mans junk is another mans treasure. Never waste what you can use.

"Ya know, after Sand Creek some of Chivington's boys found arrows with horseshoe and square nails stuck in 'em where the obsidian shoulda been. Made better arrowheads than the stone. Didn't break. Wonder if they came from Lupton's trash pile?"

Hmm.

After several more hours of walking, the two track continued eastward as it had and wandered in and out of the arroyos and gullies, sometimes at the beginning of one, sometimes at the end of another, sometimes cutting directly across both. Sometimes it meandered east by southeast, sometimes east by northeast, but as always, it kept the Buttes in sight. Seemingly never closer, nor farther away it would zigzag like a rudderless ship adrift in a sea of bunchgrass and soon to be fossilized cow plop where between washouts it'd continue in the same manner it had, sometimes narrowing, sometimes widening, as it made it's way across the expanse and into the horizon of a Nebraska summer.

Sometimes one track would be overgrown with bunchgrass, sometimes the other, sometimes both, but after passing alongside the corona ring of a prairie pothole with it's sunken declivity devoid of all things living, it'd soon disappear.

Prairie potholes. After the rains they'd fill with water. In spring the Sandhills and Whoopers'd find 'em and stop over for either a drink or a bath while winging their way south toward Nebraska and Kansas.

"Buffalo wallows." Caleb said breaking the silence. "We'd catch 'em there and run 'em into the arroyos."

"When they're empty you can hide in 'em and catch 'em grazing up top. Ya know a man can sit upright on a horse in some of 'em and never see over the edge. With the wind in the right direction the damn bison never knew we were there until it was too late, but then neither did the wagon running settlers until we stole their horses."

Yep, guess I'll have to try that sometime. Maybe I can sneak up on a .223 carrying militia nut. Sure gets tiresome seeing their garbage everywhere.

".44-70."

Say, what?

".44-70."

"Sharps. Buffalo gun. See the casings?"

Sure enough, two of 'em were lying in the chalkdust just feet from one of the potholes.

"Wonder if they got any?"

"See how the ends are pinched" Musta been a rich son of a buck not to reload 'em, but then I suppose he didn't want any Indians to either."

"Musta been a dude."

The little things. Even the obscure held a story for Caleb.

Needless to say, he was usually right.

After raining, the atmosphere would hang heavy while the remnant moisture would lay close to the ground until after warming, whereupon it'd rise again and form new cotton candy in the cobalt sky above while blurring the horizon below as if it were just another midwestern mirage. Just another scene in another John Ford movie.

When that'd happen, it always made the Buttes look farther off than they were and appear as if they'd been suspended above the badlands to float in prairie space.

Distance.

At times it could be disorienting.

Within another mile or so the land began to rise, at first with little notice, but then into an actual north-south running ridgeline. While not exactly a mountain range, after traveling for miles across a cracked tableland, it felt absolutely montaine. From the crest, the Buttes, once a vague apparition on the eastern skyline, now appeared close and well formed. But the big surprise was that the land between where we were and where they stood was a basin. A basin that was green from some unseen creek or stream and covered in Tallgrass and Cottonwood stands. A grassland that had either been irrigated or fed by some as yet unseen seep or spring where the water percolated up from the limestone beneath. Maybe the aquifer was closer to the surface at that point. Coulda been that the Ogalalla was easier to tap.

Strange though. No windmills. Guess there must be a

spring somewhere.

A solitary Redtail floated overhead. Searching. Ever searching...

To the north were the Chalk Bluffs, now clearly visible as well as they marched eastward toward the convergence of the Platte.

When we turned around, the Rocky Mountains, previously unseen from below, now stood out as a distinct line on the western horizon as well, clouds scudding over 'em and drifting in waves as they traveled the distance from Lindenmeier to the Cache La Poudre.

"A hundred mile view."

"Can almost see old Cody's place from here. Raised dancing horses, ya know."

Didn't know that.

"Sitting Bull did."

Once atop our summit the land changed quickly. Rather than the pebbly chalk and sandy bottoms we'd crossed, it'd become rockier and contained occasional outcroppings. The prickly pear, bunchgrass and tomatillo were gone, replaced by intermittent sage and stunted juniper. No doubt it caught and held more moisture than what we'd seen. The rocks provided shade and ground cover for plant life. The sandy bottoms didn't. There was no cheatgrass.

Nature didn't have to compete with a foreign invader.

"Damn if this whole place isn't covered with petrified wood!"

Sure enough, a huge portion of what appeared to have been rock from below was nothing more than agatized wood that ran the colors of the rainbow; from gray, to white, to pinkish, to mustard.

"Musta been a quarry."

Microliths and debitage were everywhere as were dozens of intentionally broken quartzite and agate cobbles. If it wasn't a quarry in the traditional sense, it'd undoubtedly been used as a collecting spot for source material which was then turned into neolithic tools and hunting implements. Probably by one or more of the tribes that'd roamed the badlands from Colorado to the Dakotas while following bison bison and bison occidentalis. What wasn't covered in debitage was covered in tipi rings, the long abandoned anchor stones of hide covered shelters where the hunters who'd fashioned their tools from the surrounding agate once lived. Whether Cheyenne, Arapaho, Lakota or otherwise, neither Caleb nor I could tell. Hell, coulda been the Pawnee for all we knew. After all, the Buttes were named after 'em.

Geologically speaking, it was as if our little ridge, aside from being a fault line or volcanic uplift in the middle of nowhere, had once been a tree covered island surrounded by an ice age sea. Maybe it had been. Or maybe it was just a "sandbar" in the same ocean.

Neither Caleb nor I knew enough to tell that either.

An island in a sea of bison. Gone but for an eccentric rancher named Goodnight who saved some of the few that remained down in Palo Duro and then sent 'em up north to Yellowstone where they'd breed with the few that remained there.

God bless the eccentrics.

"Look."

Now what?

"See that?"

See what?

"It's a hand ax."

Sure enough, a gray chunk of petrified wood which'd turned to agate about the size of a mans hand lay where it was seemingly dropped beneath a juniper. It still had the bark running along one side and it's color was that of dried blood mixed with a rather dirty bowl of oatmeal.

"Look at the one end."

"See how it's been shattered?"

"See how it's turned a different shade of gray? Whitish where it's been beaten and darker in the center? See how the morphology's changed as well? The rest of the ax's shiny and crystalline but the hammered end's dull and fractured. The bark portion neither."

Damn smart for an old shit. Yep, it'd been used as a hand

ax, but for what?

"No doubt used as either a hammer stone, or to get at the marrow of what was hunted. Maybe make some pemmican. No signs of bones though, so it was probably used to break rocks."

"You know, in a time when measurement as we know it didn't exist, everything was measured by either the length of a man's arm, hands or fingers. Whether it was an atlatl, an arrow-point or spearhead, everything was measured that way. Same with the shafts, bows, and tools we used. Everything was measured from end to end or from one side to the other or from one appendage to the other. Seems like the short guys shoulda had a problem, but they didn't. Probably made it easier to figure out who made the shot in some cases. Mighta even made it easier to figure out who got first dibs on the meat and hide. Made for a few odd sized bows though."

Damn if Caleb didn't see what I'd often miss.

"Nice day for a hike."

And so off we went, Caleb crow hopping like he always did.

Pretty spry for an old man.

You look just like Walter Brennen. Always swaying from one side to the other. Damned if each of your two legs can't keep up with the other.

Shoulda been a Warner Brothers cartoon.

Whether a cartoon caricature or not, he could still outrun me, sagebrush and stunted juniper not withstanding. It was all I could do to keep up.

From there we left the two track behind. Caleb spotted a lone Cottonwood so off he ran. Already turning yellow, he sprinted for it, bushwhacking the entire way.

"Don't know what's there, but we'll see. Different ways for different days and all that. We can sight the two track from above or maybe pick up another before we head back to Eaton. Either way, it's time to go. The Buttes can wait for another day. Maybe one where we start a bit closer than Keota.

Whatever.

Needless to say, it wasn't long before the sky was once again darkening and the hundred or so feet we'd gained from ascending our ridgeline disappeared while the blue bottomed mountains in front of us sank from view.

"Looks like Old Man That Grumbles wants another round or two."

Yep.

By the time we reached the Cottonwood it'd simply grown worse.

The tree looked old. Eighty or ninety years old. Over time it'd lost several limbs and was hollow inside, but it'd survived. Survived as a reminder, that even in a seemingly barren land, things can grow.

"Grew too fast. Couldn't bend with the winds and just snapped."

But at least it was alive and standing. Guess that says something.

Two crows scolded us from above, lost in the yellow.

"Kinda hard to tell if it's the color it is from age or lack of water. Maybe it knows winter's coming on or it's just plain old."

Late August on the Northern Plains. It could be summer and ninety one minute, three feet of snow on the ground the next. No matter what, by September all of the trees'd be turning and the nights'd become colder. After that winter'd only be a matter of weeks, if not days away. You could sense the change.

To one side of the old tree sat a concrete foundation, rather poorly made and crumbling. Farther off was what appeared to have been a rectangular concrete stock tank or trough, poorly made as well, it's Standard Windmill long gone and only a solitary rusted pipe protruding from the ground where the rotor shoulda been. Coils of barbed wire surrounded what'd once been a field of unknown origin, the furrows still visible and growing nothing but invasive weeds, the fence posts long rotted or stolen for firewood and the tank filled with broken Budweiser bottles and empty Marlboro boxes.

"Looks like someone had themselves a party."

Yep. Garbage.

A faint set of oversized tire tracks were still visible in the yard nearby.

"Kinda sad. All these people came out here for a hundred sixty acres and a mule and all for a railroad lie. The damn land wasn't irrigable, the water table too shallow or farther down than they thought and for what? A few good years and maybe a decent crop or two and then drought. Year after year. No way they coulda hung on. The topsoil's thin and rocky if it exists at all and without the bunchgrass to hold it down the wind'd simply carry it away. They coulda sucked mud over time from that well too."

"Add to that that those same damn idiots'd buy a plot on a hillside, plow in the direction of the prevailing wind or downslope, and what've you got? Another Woody Guthrie song and another Tom Joad. The land goes sour and everything that isn't tied down ends up in Boulder. Looks like some California transplant got their barn wood though."

The unused frame of a steel swingset sat idle below the Cottonwood, it's chains and corded seat long gone while a broken Buck Rogers tin car poked it's hood out from between the cheatgrass that grew nearby. 1930's America. From Texas to Oklahoma, to Eastern Colorado and the Dakotas, the dust bowl simply blew the land and everyone on it away. They never came back.

"Couldn't sell the land and leave it. Couldn't give it back to the banks cuz most of 'em were gone anyway, so when it was all said and done, the government'd get it for back taxes owed and turn it into BLM dead zones or cheatgrass habitat. National Grasslands for all the good that'd do."

Most of it was gone no matter what and only isolated parcels remained. Like our ridge, an increasingly rare find in an overused landscape. From Goodnight to Deerfield to Keota, the residents simply left, never to be heard from again.

Blown away.

Dust devils kicked up around the perimeter of the foundation while the crows squawked overhead.

Life moves on. Even if it's in the wrong direction.

"Apparently they didn't know much. Couldn't see the root stock for squat or the rocks for shit. Blind bastards. Got what they deserved, but still sad. All they had to do is what you and I just did, open their eyes and walk around a bit."

All Caleb could do was shake his head while I just felt empty.

"They coulda made it, ya know. All they had to do was take a walk around and look at it. This land wasn't meant for farming. Cattle, yes. Sheep maybe. But even with that ya gotta respect what you see. What ya feel. What ya touch. The bison knew that. The Indians too. Ya come and ya go. Leave what ya don't need alone and let it recover for the next time. Don't overuse it. Go with the flow."

Go with the flow.

Time changes most everything, but some things remain the same. The land abides. Adapt or perish. Learn or lose.

Choices made.

Another lesson.

Old Man That Grumbles'd be overhead soon and we had a long hike back to Keota.

"Don't remember passing any two tracks heading this way. Roads either for that matter. Better cut south and pick up our tracks or we'll get a soaking again. The sun's running low now too."

Yep. Time to move on.

Within an hour we'd reached the two track and found our footprints right where we left 'em. Four prints side by side pointing eastward. Eastward into the dawn now gone. One set made by a rather gimpy old man who was prone to walking on the outside of his feet while the other was made by a person who had Vibram soles on his boots and walked with a longer stride.

We followed 'em in reverse.

"Look."

Now what?

"Coal."

Where?

"Over there. See those rocks?"

What rocks? Didn't see any before.

"Musta missed 'em. Over there."

When I looked in the direction Caleb was pointing all I could see were several dun to black softball sized chunks of what appeared to be soft stone. They sure as hell didn't look like coal.

"See how everything looks kinda layered like the Buttes? Kinda like the petrified wood we found on the ridge, but with less defined rings? Kinda sandy and soft?"

Yep.

"Not all coal's black ya know. Around here it can be this color. Made from the same stuff as our agate, but older. Decayed trees, softer than the agate. While our petrified wood may've come from pines or Dawn Redwoods, this stuff came from either palms, tree ferns or some giant asparagus looking thing when this was still a swamp. Lignite."

"And look at that one over there."

"Looks like someone tried to burn it. Damn idiots. Doesn't burn well."

All I could see was a tarlike lump that seemed little more than an ill defined pile of rock hard goop and vaguely resembled yet another pile of the cow plop that seemed to be everywhere.

"Musta had a barbeque. Sure can't tell who by the debris though. Nothing to date. The glass looks newer, no embossed pieces. No coloring. No bone. Maybe 1920s-30s. Maybe a cowboy. No lead slugged tin cans though, so who knows."

"Ya know, they used to mine this stuff down in Erie and Superior. They say that in Marshall a whole shaft caught fire once and they couldn't put it out so they just filled it in. Someone died in that one I suppose. Over at the Columbine in Serene the Wobblies took over. Old Joe Hill and his union boys got the same treatment as Ludlow. Killed. Machine gunned down by the State Militia. Sand Creek all over again. A whole damn town there and now it's the Boulder County dump."

Yep. Bury what you don't like. Hide what you don't want to talk about.

History is what you make it, but sooner or later the truth comes out.

Ludlow. Serene, Sand Creek. Some places didn't want their stories told. Some you couldn't forget.

You had to walk the place to know the difference.

"What happened to the sun? Gettin' kinda chilly."

Old Man That Grumbles was directly overhead.

"Looks like we waited too long."

Boooooom...

Within seconds the Thunder Beings roared and the lightning struck. You couldn't count the seconds between the two. It was that close. Ever see the air turn blue just feet away from where you stood? That close. Ever felt the percussive blast outward from the impact? That close.

You could smell it.

"Shit."

"Now we're gonna get it."

And we did.

Hail the size of frozen peas. Hail the size of golf balls.

Ya can't run and ya can't hide when ya get caught in shit like that in the middle of nowhere. All you can do is hunker down, put your face between your knees and cover your head with your arms for all the good that'd do. Ya get pelted no matter what.

Ever hear pea sized ice rattle off the ground? You don't need a metal roof over your head to hear it, it does.

After a few minutes that felt like hours the storm moved on and headed like the one before it toward Denver. Five minutes after that and everything looked as if nothing had even happened.

Caleb and I were soaked and sore in every place that wasn't covered, but within a few minutes more that disappeared as well, except for the sting.

That'd take some time to dissipate.

Our homeward journey would continue west until it did, and then some.

Miles to cover. Burning daylight. Coulda been Red River. Coulda been another damn John Ford movie. No matter what, Montgomery Clift was calling. Best to get going.

"Ya know, in the old days when shit like that'd happen, the Lakota, or maybe it was the Cheyenne'd hide under their horses bellies to keep from getting pelted. Don't know if it's true, but somebody told me it was. Hell, if we were back at the Cottonwood we coulda stood underneath it and avoided getting beaned. The crows wouldn't a cared. For that matter we coulda stood to one side of that Norwegian place and kept from being pounded too."

No comment.

Yep, it'd been a long day and both of us were more than happy when we could see the pine covered hill behind Keota with it's twentieth century water tank in front of it.

Seems every Midwestern town in the middle of nowhere had 'em; they were the lone sentinels of the prairie. The mushroom gods of Flyover Country. Most had the name of the city painted on 'em, but in Keota's case it seemed somebody forgot. Only a few ranch hands there now, a few Mexicans and a squatter or two. Everyone else was gone. Gone with the wind. Gone the way of Goodnight and Deerfield.

A solitary magpie sashayed down Main Street as it swayed it's girlish tail from side to side in time to a song only it knew while a stray dustdevil skipped across a vacant lot between two abandoned buildings like the child it had never known before turning westward and heading for Virginia Dale. Both alone except for the brief commotion they caused.

Caleb and I headed for home.

"Eaton won't be too far off now and after that Fort Collins. No more dirt roads for awhile."

Yep, it'd been quite a day. In just under twelve hours Caleb and I'd dog paddled in a prehistoric sea, communed with creatures long gone and stood beneath Redwood forests that'd grown in Nebraska. We'd shaded under giant palms in Colorado and found agates that'd been fashioned into neolithic tools by some of the earliest inhabitants of North America. We'd run buffalo with the Cheyenne, talked to the Scandinavian pioneers who came afterwards and got rained on, hailed on and dried out all within a matter of minutes.

We smelled of chalk dust and wind, sage and sky.

We'd lived.

Although we hadn't reached the Buttes, they'd still be there when we returned. A bit more weathered perhaps, but not so anyone would notice.

Not anyone except maybe Caleb and me.

I never made it back.

The dance changed and what once seemed as immutable as the bond between space and time, people and place had it's continuity broken, it's circle squared.

The world had little use for dreamers and idealists let alone those who followed nondescript roads and dirt two tracks. It had a habit of breaking things and destroying the balance that'd been created.

It'd swallow you whole if you'd let it.

And it'd be a long winter.

Walking Backwards

Between when Caleb and I walked the Grasslands and our next journey into the void, life became cold, insular and inbound. Winter set in with a vengeance and each day became a dull repetition of the other; leaden skies and lumpy snow; not unlike staring at the same bowl of oatmeal day after day hoping something'd change.

Being stuck in Denver during winter was no treat. The oatmeal wouldn't stir for several months.

Before our parting in Keota, Caleb had said something about wanting to head west; get away from the snow he knew was coming. Go someplace he imagined'd be warm. Said he might like to look for Mike. Talk to him. Follow his path. Hell, he might even walk all the way to California if Mike'd let him. Maybe look for the Yahi north of the Feather River. He hated winter that much.

I knew I'd miss him. I'd miss seeing the things he did and the stories he'd tell. I'd miss our adventures.

He said he'd fill me in when he got back.

I looked forward to the day when he would.

Long about the third week of February, that singular week in the middle of snow season when the skies clear and the temperatures climb into the balmy thirties, the Chinooks begin to blow and the downslopes rush out over the prairies from their genesis atop Long's Peak and Mount Albion, casting as they do so the accumulated inversion layers and photo chemical smog that sits over midwinter Denver like a lid and tossing it up and over the prairie to somewhere in Kansas or possibly Missouri.

For one week you'd swear it was spring until winter'd inevitably return. After that it wouldn't leave again until sometime in April or early May if you were lucky, sometimes the Fourth of July if you weren't. You had to make the best of it. Do what you could while you could. Get out and see the land that had been cleared of the snow before it was covered over again. While it was a long way off till mud season, the land'd be open enough to travel on without Sorel's and hard enough that you wouldn't be buried knee deep in the inevitable spring goop that would stick to the bottom of your boots and add another several pounds to your hike.

Winter in Denver was like an unwanted house guest. A guest that'd never leave.

It was nice to kick him out once in a while.

And so it was, in typical Caleb fashion, that once again he appeared looking as if he'd never left.

Said he'd fill me in on what he'd done since our time on the Pawnee but that for the moment it'd have to wait. We were "burning daylight" and like in Red River, or at least the outdoor environs of Metro Denver, the land was calling and it was time to go. Despite the urbanity, no doubt there would be something to see.

All he had was a week. Said I'd hear about the rest within that time.

t's amazing the amount of ground you can cover when you put your mind to it. Being cooped up for several months only adds to the intensity.

It was time to get out.

You'd never know to look at it, but Denver expanded outward onto the prairie around it as if it were a child playing hopscotch, or had been the creation of one or more of the post World War I military geniuses in France, who after deciding the Germans were more than they could handle, built the Maginot Line. Where the housing tracts ended, whether in the city or alongside the plains, it was as if someone had erected a wall between the suburbs and the land. On one side would be the good citizens of Levittown enjoying their suburban dream, while on the other, the bad nasty Teutonic warriors of Flyover Country'd roam unchecked, unfettered and unbroken.

In between were the vacant lots, former ranches and failed

homesteads of a bygone era; places where, if the soil was left un-disturbed, little'd change in hundreds, if not thousands of years. Yep, you could stand in your backyard one minute, then jump over the fence the next and walk back the centuries.

From Denver to Adams to Jefferson to Larimer the story was the same. A land rich in history and only feet from your door.

The isolated exception was Boulder, but then that was only because those who had the money to do so bought up all the open space they could find and fenced it off. Where they couldn't keep people out, they simply created environmental easements to pro-tect what they had and added bike paths along their property lines to ensure it. Unfortunately, with isolated exceptions, no Huns were allowed anywhere and everything else was off limits.

Caleb and I, being the good Huns we were though, jumped fences where we could and explored the rest as the spirit called.

Somewhere Ed Abbey was laughing.

It was going to be a busy week.

In the time before the beginning, when the first humans were either running ahead of, behind, or into, the alternately advancing and retreating glaciers that covered the Great Plains from Alberta to Southern Colorado and Northern New Mexico, the rivers were the freeways and expressways du jour. From Clovis, to Folsom, to Avonlea, to McKean, every culture that occupied the northern plains used 'em to traverse the land between. In time, some would learn to plant maize and squash, whereas oth-ers would alternately fish the rivers and hunt. Some would camp along the way, while still others would build small settlements and towns. Cities such as Cahokia in Western Illinois would be built and populations would, like those before 'em, ebb and flow with the vicissitudes of climate, weather and time. Game would come and go. Mastodons would give way to the Elk and Deer we know today and Bison Occidentalis would give way to Bison Bison. Boreal forests would disappear as would the savannas and steppes the Columbian Mammoth knew. In the end it'd be the Short and Tallgrass Prairies we're familiar with today bounded by the Rocky Mountains, the Missouri and the Mississippi.

In between would be the other rivers, streams and watersheds that spilled their contents into the Mississippi and Colorado.

Along the Front Range from Denver to Fort Collins, the Cache La Poudre, Big Thompson and Saint Vrain flowed eastward. When combined with the smaller streams such as Boulder, Dry, and Clear Creeks, they became the routes in, out, and over the intervening divide. From the earliest inhabitants to the most recent, anyone who passed through the area did so by following 'em, but as had always been the case, they did so by following in the footsteps of those who'd gone before.

Each had their stories to tell and none were silent. In fact, they all had more than a little to talk about.

Because of this Caleb and I thought the rivers and creeks'd be a good place to start. Although some passed through the Maginot around Denver on their way to the Platte, both of us figured they'd still be largely intact. If not in one spot, then another.

Despite the cities, you could travel from the Rockies to the Platte in short order. From there, if you had the mind and the time to, you could still go all the way to the Gulf of Mexico.

Neither Caleb nor I had either, so from the mountains to the Platte would have to do. The rest could come later if and when we had a mind to.

It'd be an adventure no matter what.

"Walking backwards is best done with your eyes open. If not, you might trip over your feet."

Whatever you say.

When not on the rivers, we could walk the distance between.

Running eastward from the crest of the Rockies was the land. Beginning west of the Parks; North, South, Middle and Estes, it'd spill downward from one glacial range toward another, crossing as it did so between the scoured troughs of the rivers it'd created only to rise again, then spill downward once more as it made it's descent onto the prairie below. Along the way it'd create mountain ranges which'd be altenately eroded and repetitively scrubbed away whereupon new ranges'd be formed atop the old ones like'd happened in the Snowies, or simply disappear into the red and white sandstone hogbacks along the eastern front. Hogbacks that'd run from north of Fort Collins to south of Morrison and beyond. After that it'd be the bottomland, where after leaving the cottonwood groves and tallgrass behind, it'd rise one last time before fading away into the badlands of Nebraska.

It was an odd thing. When crossing the prairie you'd see no mountains one minute, a low ridge the next, no mountains after that, and then, wham, the Rockies'd appear. It could leave you breathless and was if the entire range'd risen from nowhere or been suspended over where ya stood. Coulda been an apparition, maybe a Phoenix. The same thing was true with Denver. Stand anywhere around it and all you could see was the top of the Xcel building near Larimer Square, but get a bit closer and what looked like a building only a few stories tall was significantly larger.

Like Keota, looks could be deceiving. What was seen wasn't always what was being shown.

You had to recognize the difference.

Sometimes ya had ta look at things not only with your eyes, but into what ya saw and use your imagination. It was as if the actual image were beyond your vision. Out of range. At times it could be both.

Vision could be a funny thing.

The Rockies didn't rise from out of nowhere and Denver wasn't hidden below the prairie.

It was up to the observer to understand the difference.

And so it was, that Caleb and I followed the boulders in the rivers and across the land between. Boulders that'd turn into cobbles, that'd turn into pebbles, that'd turn into the sand of long extinct interglacial seabeds after which everything'd be commingled with the bones of the dinosaurs, mammoth and mastodons that only imagination could envision.

We'd follow their red sandstone tracks along the hogbacks of the Morrison and climb both North and South Table Mountain after which we'd explore the mines and Indian camps on top as well as the grasslands below. We'd wander tthrough the ghost town of Marshall and stand where some of the earliest inhabitants of the region'd camped beside Magic Mountain. Still later, we'd walk where the Ute had followed the Saint Vrain into Boulder Valley and see for ourselves their tipi rings near Hygiene. Afterwards we'd find a split Cedar bark lodge farther up the canyon; a lodge that was still standing a hundred years later. We hunted with the McKean north of Denver and laughed at the Pillar of Fire where even those who believed in eternity didn't know what was just beyond their tower.

We walked back the years.

In Metro Denver there was the hundred year old wisteria that clung to life in a twisted mass where it had tethered itself to one end of a galvanized clothes line. Contained within the Maginot Line it stood as an anachronism to the tract homes around it. Where once there'd been a ranch, now there was open space and the wisteria'd been abandoned. Somehow, it survived.

The building that'd been alongside was long gone, but it's concrete foundation remained. Not unlike those we saw in Keota, remnants of what was and what'd been. Farther off were the same rectangular concrete watering troughs as well as the same line of hundred year old cottonwoods we'd seen. A brown glass medicine bottle stopper lay next to one. Rat poison.

Out of place.

Along the creek we found a Coke bottle, one of those old embossed types that'd been made before the war. Inside were several pea sized unglazed ceramic beads; Indian trade beads. Somebody'd been there, same place we were. Possibly before the ranch was built, possibly not. Yep, somebody'd been there and gathered the beads up, put 'em in the bottle and then either lost, or left 'em behind. Looked like someone else either lost or left 'em behind before that.

Who lost 'em each time, we couldn't say. That they were left by one or another of the Indians who frequented the area the first time around was all but certain. Whether they were Arapaho, Cheyenne, Ute or Lakota, we couldn't say. They all traded for beads. All were known to have traveled along our creek and each had probably stood where we were more than once. Flint and quartzite debitage was everywhere as was a rusty bottle opener, the old kind. Wire.

Was the debitage gathered by the same person who carried

the Coke bottle and then scattered where we found it, or had it been there before the soda drinker arrived?

A mystery.

Or were both the beads and the flint microliths in situ, more or less?

Unknown.

Needless to say, Caleb was of the opinion that it was the later as the beads seemed to hold more value to the Coke drinker than the debitage around it. To him, it seemed that if it'd been important then some of the flint shoulda been in the bottle. Given that it wasn't, the later probably came after the fact.

He was undoubtedly correct.

Different eras. Different times. At least three generations had stood where we did. One was a hunter gatherer. The second was more likely than not a child who drank a Coke sometime before World War II and we were neither.

We'd all stood in the same spot, saw more or less the same thing, and each left something behind.

Continuity.

Did the Indians who camped on the spot know who owned the ranch like Lupton and Red Cloud or did one of 'em either lose, or purposefully leave their broken necklace behind only to be discovered by a child drinking a Coke a generation later after which they'd be lost again?

Neither we nor the land could say. Like the mountains as seen from Keota, the answer coulda been as simple as our guesses, or more than what we saw.

History was never what we were taught and never what it seemed.

Sometimes ya had to relearn it.

Standing within what was left of the ranch, metropolitan Denver surrounded us. Where Caleb and I stood, centuries had passed beneath our feet. Centuries that had built upon one another and revealed as they did so what'd gone before. Events remembered and then blown away or reburied with time. Beyond where we stood, the modern world swarmed like locusts, oblivious to the knowledge the land contained within. It was like we were existing not only in a different time, but in a different world. Beyond the imaginary wall that formed the Maginot were the restaurants, movie theaters, houses and boulevards of Denver. Within our sanctuary, time stood still and was marked by the footprints of those who the others couldn't see. We saw their faces and heard 'em talk. Beyond the Maginot, the silence was deafening.

"Kinda makes ya feel like Christopher Robin doesn't it? Our very own Hundred Acre Wood."

"Now ya know how Thoreau musta felt while camping at Walden, surrounded by Concord and all that. Kinda sobering isn't it?"

"Not everyone is given the gift of being able to walk backwards, let alone see what was, is, and will be. Nor is everyone able to understand how each are related to the other. To look into the past and see the faces of those whose lives you've discovered and understand who and what they were. It's a blessing, ya know. A blessing given to you by those who gave it. You've been given a gift."

Silence.

And what of it?

Silence. It's power could be greater than the strongest wind across an open prairie. It allowed one to see within their soul as well as into the souls of others. People feared it, avoided it, hid from it and actively tried to drown it out.

I could do none of it and although at the time I had yet to learn the extent of the knowledge I'd been given, I seemed to know instinctively that it'd change me. Probably forever.

Between when Caleb and I hiked the Pawnee and February, I could already see it. The city bored me and I spent most of my free time imagining where our next journey'd take us. When outside I'd see things not only as they were within the present context, but as they'd been before and I began to see not only what belonged and what didn't, but to see how they musta been when centered in place, space and time. I learned to see, touch and feel the relationship between everything that was there; the plants, animals, rocks and the land itself and what it was to listen to a language that only Caleb and I could understand, let alone speak.

Needless to say, I was learning alot.

"You shoulda been born a hundred years ago."

Sometimes I wished I had.

"You're becoming human."

And so I was. Human in the knowledge of what it was I'd been given as well as the knowledge of what it was I'd taken on.

Responsibility.

I had been entrusted with the knowledge of people and place, lives and stories, myths and legends, love and loss, good and bad, fact and fiction. Over time it'd become my greatest blessing…and my greatest curse.

To carry ones soul is to become one with it. At times it was hard not to own it. At other times, it was hard to not be owned by it. It was often even harder to share it and then let go. Acting in partnership was never easy, but then, neither was living. You had to approach 'em with an open mind and see things with the eyes of a child. All innocence and wonder.

How soon we forget.

As such I learned to carry many souls and I was learning the art of dancing.

I was learning the art of balance.

After all, "Walking in balance WAS the hardest dance" ya'd ever do.

"So, which way now? We can follow the creek eastward until we hit the Platte, or go the other way and head for the mountains."

Flip a coin.

"Lets do both. We'll go west for awhile and see whether or not what we've seen around here is an anomaly or a pattern and if it doesn't pan out, we can always turn around and head the other way tomorrow. The day's still young and we ain't "burnin' daylight". Besides, I still owe you a story. Different ways for different days."

Different ways for different days. I liked that. Have to use it again.

And so we turned toward the ridgeline and followed the creek west.

"Ya know, in the old days, the Utes used ta cross over the mountains and head out onto the plains to hunt buffalo. Did so by following creeks like this. Plenty of water and game. Unfortunately, once the Arapaho moved into the neighborhood, the Utes got kicked out. They never got along. Seems it wasn't always the white man who'd steal everything. Sometimes it was the Indians themselves. But damned if nobody in the neighborhood cared much for the Utes, the Lakota and Cheyenne included until after the whites came along and built Denver. After that they'd come over and camp out in town and pretend they were white. Even went to some exposition and were given beaver hats. A bunch of Lincoln looking guys in tophats and vests smoking cigars. Bet the Arapaho liked 'em even less after that."

Probably so.

From that point on, Caleb became mostly silent, preferring to follow rather than walk side by side, or in front the way he had on the Pawnee. He wouldn't say much more until story time. Guess he figured I'd learned enough to see things for myself. As such we headed westward, Caleb grinning when I said something he thought was correct and becoming stoic when he thought I was wrong. The quintessential image of every wooden Indian Hollywood created. Fortunately, or unfortunately though, I knew the difference. We could read each other like a book.

Shortly after leaving the ranch the creek began to wend it's way uphill and six to eight foot banks appeared along each side. Where they'd dip to stream level, it'd then expand outward in elongated curves and ribbonlike bends that'd alternately swing either in the same direction, or just as often, the other, whereupon small islands and ponds'd form. Ducks swam in the shaded pools oblivious to anything but themselves and Prairie Dogs chirped along the banks above where they'd run for cover everytime we approached. Both cottonwoods and tallgrass grew in the bends.

A lone Redtail waited for lunch.

A wandering, aimless, nothing of a river was how Michener described the Platte when he wrote Centennial and here we were walking along a creek that coulda been the same.

A wandering, aimless, nothing of a creek. Sometimes shallow. Sometimes slow. Sometimes had water. Sometimes didn't. Sometimes wooded. Sometimes not. And yet, just like the Platte, it contained within its range the history of everything it'd seen; the story of the land and its people and the creatures who depended on it.

It made me feel like Pasquinel.

Hurry up, McKeag, we're burnin' daylight.

As the early spring breezes idled downslope from Mount Albion they'd skirt the neolithic rock cairns and game traps of a bygone era and then eddy around 'em while they continued their migration over Gold Hill and into Lefthand Canyon before drifting out over the hills and flats of Marshall Mesa and on through Niwot and across our creek. All the way to Kansas.

Within a week the weather'd change and winter'd return, but for the moment the bare cottonwoods could dream of spring and we could mark the passage of the season.

Life was good.

"Niwot. Arapaho for Lefthand, ya know. Killed by Chivington at Sand Creek. Jack Fitzpatrick was there too. Both lived in Boulder Valley. One was killed for doing so, and the other was expelled to Wind River for the same reason. Never mind that he was Broken Hand's son, it didn't seem to matter much. He was on the wrong side of history. Both probably knew this creek. Both mighta camped or hunted along it. Gotta remember or somebody else'll forget. They'll rewrite the story. Tell a lie. And just like Jack, they'll be forgotten."

The wrong side of history, but who's?

We walked on.

Needless to say, our creek was a rather amazing find considering where it was. Walk along it and it was as though nothing'd changed since time immemorial. Never mind that Denver was just a few feet or yards away. Follow it west and it'd been fenced off, but by the time we got there all that remained were piles of unspooled double strand and rotted four Xs. Set back from the creek roughly eight to ten feet, it was just far enough to keep the cattle and tractors out which meant everything in between where the fence'd been and the creek itself was left intact. Undisturbed except for the Prairie Dog towns that seemed to be every-where. Yep, someone cared not only for the creek, but everything around it. The cottonwoods were left standing and there was little sign of stumpage.

Couldn't say that about what was between there and the Maginot though. Most of that'd been disced and the furrows were still visible despite the intervening years. On one side the rocks and cobbles were either whole, or mostly so. On the other, they showed signs of having been repeatedly broken, mechanically dug up or looked like they'd been clawed and raked, not once, but over and over again. On the creek side stunted sage and prickly pear grew. On the other, invasive weeds.

The land could tell you alot if you had the ears to listen and the eyes to see.

Along one side was neolithic Colorado. On the other, the first homesteaders. Beyond the Maginot, neither.

Within less than a mile the fencing along our side veered off in the direction of Levittown but kept the same eight to ten foot setback it had as it followed a gully that ran from below the Mag-inot toward the creek itself. Where the two came together there was a small hill with the gully on one side and the creek on the other. In front of it the creek meandered in horseshoe bends and formed multiple ponds where both cottonwood and cattails grew. Perfect duck ponds.

As if on cue, several Mallards swam by.

It was a perfect place to stop and watch 'em. Maybe see an eagle or two.

After following the gully, the fencline cut across it where it narrowed farther up and then resumed it's course along the oppo-site side as it returned to the creek below. Prickly pear and sage grew in between as before, but unlike what we'd previously seen, there was more of it. Yep, the detoured fenceline saved a bit more of what'd already been there.

That in itself wasn't all that unusual though. Somebody was simply saving time and fencing material when they ran the fence the way they did. What we found inside, however, was.

Where the gully and the creek came together sombody'd

dug a pit. Measuring roughly eight or so feet across and four feet deep, it was shaped like an inverted bowl and was partially filled with windblow and weeds. You couldn't see any mounding around the top and nothing was visible from below. In point of fact, you could stand right next to it and not know it was there.

"Pretty well hidden wouldn't you say?"

Absolutely.

"Know what it was?"

Nope, but I bet you'll tell me.

"Soon Grasshopper, but let's look inside first."

When we removed the debris it was as if everything inside had been cemented in place. There was no sign of erosion and no loose soil sat in the bottom. In point of fact, it probably had been because everything around it was either fine gravel or loose sand. Add rainwater to the mixture and it'd simply form a caliche and turn to concrete. After that everything woulda been held in place no matter what, and barring any significant disturbance, woulda stayed that way indefinitely. It was the same from the fenceline to the bluff. Everything'd been cemented in place, even around dog town.

If there were no cows, nobody walking across the surface, and no erosion or heavy objects pushed into it, the soil, including the pit, coulda remained as they had been for hundreds, if not thousands of years. Hell, over time, even the dog towns'd be cemented in place.

Yep, old, unused prairie dog mounds could be found right next to the new ones. It was no wonder they were called dog towns. An entire area could look like a series of sub Saharan mud huts.

Nobody had been inside the pit for a long time.

Next to it we found a highly serrated birdpoint about the size of a thumbnail that'd been fashioned from red quartzite.

"Plains Woodland wouldn't you say? Possibly over a thousand years old."

Looks like it to me.

Could our pit have been that old? In theory it shouldn't have been. Too many years. Too much going on all around it. Too close to civilization. Too close to Levittown. But what if it was?

Hell, if everything was left undisturbed, there would've been little to fill it in other than cottonwood leaves and those shoulda formed a distinct layer on the bottom when they rotted. Needless to say, there wasn't any.

And what about the birdpoint? Was it left by the person who dug the pit or was it carried in by somebody else? And what about the pit? Was it used more than once? By the same person? By different people?

The pit couldn't say and the land wouldn't tell.

Hell, for all we knew the birdpoint couda been left by the same person who lost their necklace back at the ranch. Plains Woodland covered a lot of years.

No matter what, it was a mystery.

Either way, we'd seemingly found what'd been someone's duck blind. Outside was the proof. Inside was the proof, and yet there was the riddle of who, what, where and when.

And it'd remain unanswered.

After finding the birdpoint we found the broken base of a point that'd been side notched and was made of agate that, unlike the Plains Woodland point, couldn't have come from around our creek. It was the wrong material. Probably came from a piece of petrified wood. Yep, coulda come from Keota for all we knew. Coulda been brought in from Nebraska. Either way, it was't red quartzite and it didn't belong. Besides, it was a completely different style. Newer. Possibly by a hundred years or more.

We found nothing else.

Was our blind related to the beads in the Coke bottle? Probably so and possibly not. Again, it looked as though more than one person had been there and used it for the same purpose, but they did so at different times.

Did each person come from the same place or did one or the other come from somewhere else? Were they related or was it the land that drew them in...

Again, we couldn't tell.

Clearly at least one of 'em had traveled beyond the area. Whether or not the other one did, was anybody's guess.

It would be that way along the entire length of our creek from the mountains to the Platte. History, and the people who followed it repeated themselves, went to the same places and stood in the same locations over and over again across multiple generations and was if an unwritten knowledge possessed the land that only those who used it could understand. Each generation read the same sign, saw the same thing and lived within the same reality. Such was the ebb and flow of knowledge. Like dancing, it was always circular. Always came back to the same place for the same purpose. Always constant, but always moving forward.

Buddhists called it the "eternal present", and few, if any, indigenous languages I was aware of contained words, let alone concepts, for either the past, present or future. There was only the here and now.

It would take the coming of modern man to upset the balance.

As such, it seemed ironic that two such disparate realities could coexist side by side without either one knowing about the other, but they clearly did so. Metro Denver was only a few yards away but the years between where we stood and the city coulda been measured in the thousands.

The thought was staggering and the proportionality immense.

Walking backwards was never easy. Walking between two worlds even tougher.

And I was learning to do both.

After leaving the duck blind behind the land began to slowly gain elevation and changed while doing so. The cottonwoods disappeared and the creek began to straighten out where it cut a path between larger cobble and boulder banks. The sand became more course and the caliche was gone. Sage and prickly pear were absent. We were entering a transition zone.

Prairie Dogs still built their towns atop the bluffs, but rattlesnakes had co-opted many and while hawks still flew overhead, the signs of man grew farther apart and of lesser consequence. Except for a broken arrowhead that lay inside Dog Town, it appeared as if few beyond ourselves had even been there.

It was an isolated incident.

Rattlesnakes. We'd wasted too much time there and our day was over. Long's Peak was casting it's shadow and cumulus clouds were heading toward Kansas.

Once again we'd burned daylight and there was nothing left but to turn and go.

It'd been quite a day.

We could head for the Platte tomorrow.

We'd seen alot and like Scarlett O'Hara said, tomorrow'd be "another day".

A day that promised to be filled with as many technicolor memories as the one we'd had.

Needless to say, Caleb and I were out on the Turnpike before dawn, where, after mixing with the early morning commuters who were already headed into Boulder for their shift jobs at Celestial Seasonings packaging tea for minimum wage or OCLI for a wage that was little better, we'd point our car east and head into the sunrise. Yep, all around us bleary eyed workers were either applying makeup or reading the Daily Camera while others were drinking their coffee and all did so while trying to avoid crashing into each other with their Subbies and Chevys. It was the same all over America, an entire nation commuting to jobs they hated, to provide for a lifestyle they couldn't afford, and oblivious to anything going on around 'em.

Because Caleb and I knew the difference, we drove the other way.

"Different ways for different days."

And so it was, that Caleb, looking like Floyd Westerman and wearing his ever present Larry Mahan and I, looking like nothing in particular at all, headed eastward into the sunrise. Eastward into another Colorado dawn.

"Always good to have an Ethiopian along. No better way to start the morning."

I took another sip of mine and stared into the technicolor sky as it grew brighter beyond the windshield.

By the time we got to where we were headed the hawks'd be up and flying across the horizon in search of breakfast, prairie dog al fresco or whatever else they could find, and we could once again set out for wherever it was we'd end up at.

We envied their freedom.

"Our creek looks the same".

Guess we'll find out.

"Let's go".

Another day of dust and dreams, imagination and amazement walking across a land the commuters of Boulder'd never see, let alone tread upon.

Somewhere Robert Frost was laughing.

Unlike the day before, once we began heading eastward our creek resumed it's Micheneresque wanderings and became slower, warmer and more shallow than what we'd seen. More oxbows, horseshoe bends and floodplains.

A slow, meandering, nothing of a creek...

But we'd follow it anyway.

Despite seeing occasional bluffs, the banks grew lower while those we did see were just high enough to see everything around 'em if the cityscape didn't block the view. Prickly pear and sage grew on top like we'd seen but the bottom lands grew nothing except for a caliche that was even worse than the day before. Salt brine. Possibly selenium. Too much flooding over too many years. Too many failed oil wells that pumped up nothing but contaminated water. The fence lines were gone as were their posts. Only coiled and barbed wire remained.

Occasionally we'd come across a cottonwood stand, but otherwise what we saw was mostly barren oxbows, caliche and invasive weeds.

"Not very good land".

As if to prove his point, Caleb nodded in the direction of a broken windmill that sat nearby. It's Dempster rotor and blades had long since vanished and only the salt encrusted spigot remained. Remained as useless relics in a contaminated landscape while south of us the Pillar of Fire stood where it always had, safe on it's bluff where it's brown sandstone buildings were just beginning to turn pink as the sun boiled up from the Armageddon below. An Armageddon of dessication, invasive oil wells and depleted aquifers that not even the old Westminster University could save.

"Looks like one of our hawks lost a feather. Maybe breakfast put up a bit more of a fight than he planned on, or wasn't quite ready to go down".

As Caleb bent over he picked up the left forefeather of a Redtail and stuck it in his hatband.

"Larry needs some new medicine. A good sign".

I just smiled.

"You know, the people had nothing on old Lao Tzu".

Say what?

"Somewhere I read that he believed that "the way to do was to be".

I paused mid stride to listen to the impending dissertation.

"If a man wants to do good, he behaves in a goodly fashion. If he wants to follow the path and be content with his journey, he does that too. Old Tzu musta been indigenous, ya know. We've been doin' that for years."

It was all I could do to keep from laughing as I smiled again.

"That's why we always dance in a circle, always in the same direction. That's how life works. No matter where you start from, you always come back to the same place. Whether newborn, adolescent, adult, or old and in the way, it's always the same. The journey is the path. The path is the journey. Make yours a good one."

Damn if Caleb wasn't going Zen on me. Maybe read Siddhartha one too many times. Think I'll have to read the Tao Te Ching again myself though. Maybe take it camping.

Once we left the Dempster behind, the creek began to straighten out and the water flowed more clearly than before while the banks on each side rose again. On each side of us the land greened up and more sage as well as bunchgrass appeared. One could see cottonwoods in the distance.

We were nearing the Platte.

Before reaching it though, the creek narrowed one last time while the banks on each side became increasingly overgrown with vines and blackberries. After that it became all but impassable and there were few places we could get to where the overgrowth didn't reach all the way to the Maginot.

That was until the confluence of our creek and Michener's river came into view where it exploded one last time into a series of oxbows and Cottonwood stands, multiple channels and islands.

It was a perfect spot. A perfect spot for a camp.

Almost immediately Caleb bent over and picked up a quartzite arrowhead.

"Kinda small, but big enough to do some damage, wouldn't you say?"

"Looks like it was made yesterday, but it wasn't. Out of context with Denver."

But perfectly in context with where it'd been found. The cottonwood stand was perfect for hunting in. Probably always was until Denver came along.

It was the later that was out of place.

Very Zen.

We'd reached the Platte. Time to follow the opposite bank and return to our ranch.

Time to follow the other side back.

Even though it was essentially the same, with the sun striking the creek at a different angle everything seemed different as well. It was as if we were traveling along an entirely different waterway and we saw things we previously missed.

Caleb said that was a metaphor for life. Look at the same thing from a different angle and it'd change.

Needless to say, our perspective changed as well.

"Nothing's black and white."

"Always need to see things from the other side."

Caleb was once again going Zen on me.

"Look."

At what?

"Over there. On the edge of the bank where that small bluff is."

I looked where he was pointing, but saw nothing.

"Now you're gonna learn how I got my name."

"See that gray-black bowl shaped stain that the bank's cutting into?"

Yep.

"Well, the creek eroded that out. Probably did so after one or more of the floods. It's charcoal. A fire was built there."

Yep. Ol' Caleb was correct again. The stained portion was indeed charcoal and there were burned bone fragments inside as well as several broken McKean points.

"Cutbank, the place where you build your fire. Safe from the wind. Always below the cut. Doesn't blow out. Or maybe it's cut by the river and eroded by time. Either way it reveals the story behind what's come and gone, who was there and what they did. Unlike that Indian Alexie was talking about, Builds The Fire or whatever his name was, I started being called that because I was supposed to listen to the voices of those who'd gone before and pass their knowledge along. Everything that burns leaves its mark, ya know and it's now doing so in you."

Silence.

And then it was gone.

Within our week, we'd walked back a thousand years or more. We'd spoken with the McKean, listened to the earliest Plains Woodland tribes tell their stories of ducks and game traps, prairie winds and journeys. We'd stood beside explorers, adventurers, travelers and dreamers. Some had failed. Some flourished. Like Keota, all had their stories to tell, some quietly, some loudly. Some barely discernible above the din of the city. Some had lived, many had died and some possibly had met their fate in a violent fashion.

Such was life, but at least we listened.

We'd pass it on.

By the time we got back to the ranch the sun was once again all but gone and elongated shadows had returned to cover the land. Our day, and our week were over, Caleb still had his promised stories to tell and it was time to leave for home.

Creation Stories

In the time before the beginning, before the people came to know themselves as such, there existed nothing save Mother Earth and Father Sky.

Life was good, but they were lonely.

One day Mother Earth looked up at Father Sky and asked him, "What are we to do? We have created everything, but something's missing."

After thinking about it, Father Sky responded, "I'm not sure what you mean. Haven't we created the stars and the moon, the sun and the rain, the lands and the seas, the rivers and mountains as well as the Grandfather Stones?"

"It is true, you and I as husband and wife have created all that is, but why, then is it not enough? Why do I feel lonely?"

Perplexed, Father Sky thought about it and after many days responded, "We need life."

And so it was that Father Sky sent down the Thunder Beings to bring forth the rain, and between he and Mother Earth, they created all that existed above; the birds and flying creatures both big and small. They created all that was to be below; the animals, trees and plants. Then they created that which swam in the seas and existed in the rivers. Lastly, they created man and scattered his kind throughout the world to live with the rest.

All were equal in their sight, but Mother Earth and Father Sky attached a special fondness to man, with the understanding that he, and only he, must honor all that existed every day. Failure to do so was not only dishonorable, but showed an arrogance that was unbecoming of their creation. It would dishonor their creators and bring shame to their memory and the gifts they were given.

And so it was, that Father Sky ordained that all that was created was sacred, and as such must be honored and respected with nothing being harmed except as necessary. The Four Sacred Directions were created as were the Four Sacred Colors, Seasons and Stages of Life, East, West, North and South. Red, Yellow, Black and White. Spring, Summer, Fall and Winter. Child, Adolescent, Adult and Old. All were to be honored and celebrated within their time.

To do any less, could cast a people out.

Over the hundreds upon hundreds of years the people grew, each distinctly as their journey required, each following their own path. Each growing along the way. They sang, they danced, they celebrated, they honored.

Life was good and Mother Earth smiled upon her children as they grew while Father Sky beamed down with the sun each day to reward what he saw.

All was well.

Then one day, in one year, within the course of many, things began to change. The people of the Canyons and Mesas began to grow hungry. The rains stopped coming and the crops withered and died. The maize and squash grew scarce. The deer and other creatures began to move away. Stories from the North country spoke of other peoples on the move. The buffalo were moving as were the elk and other animals.

It was the same all over.

Had the people failed? Did they do something wrong? Was it a test? Was Father Sky angry?

Nobody knew.

And so it was that the People of the Canyons dispersed, some going south, some going east, others going west or north, while people in other places were doing the same.

All over the land the world had changed. Gone were the seasons of plenty and only drought remained.

The Kuzedika, as they later came to be known, were no different. Their crops gone, the game gone, the people starving, they had to leave or die.

But where would they go? Wasn't it the same all over?

And so they set out. Year upon year they wandered north by northwest, sometimes following rivers where they still existed, sometimes not. The land was empty and barren. Little grew and what did, barely kept them alive.

The people prayed and prayed to Father Sky, but he was silent. No Thunder Beings came to carry his messages, no rain fell and the sun was often hazy. The sky grew cold.

The people wandered.

One day, a young boy spotted a hawk. When he did so, he implored, "Little brother with eyes that can see far, take pity on us for we are lost. We need your eyes to search out a new land. To find a place we can call home."

Hawk took pity on the boy and began to screech and circle.

The people saw this and listened. As Hawk flew off they followed where he led.

After many weeks Hawk landed atop a mountain where the people could look down upon a large lake with even higher, snow-covered mountains behind it. Mountains that were bigger and taller than the people had within their memory seen. The place where Father Sky was said to live.

Shortly thereafter, they followed Hawk down the ridge and around the lake to a spot on the north shore.

Hawk was tired from his long journey and rested.

After a while he spoke to the people and said, "I have brought you to the home Father Sky intended, but I am weary. It's been a long flight and I need to rest."

Just then another hawk flew down and alighted next to him, saying as she did so, "Grandfather Sky has sent me to you. He is pleased that you have led his people here where he can be close to them as they have proven themselves worthy. I am to be your mate. His people have done no wrong. The time of the test is over and now, they too, must rest."

Mother Earth watching this, began to cry. She cried and cried until her tears ran down the mountains and streams and into the lake filling it with salt.

The people seeing this began to cry as well, their tears mingling with those of Mother Earth.

"So that you may never lose sight of the journey you have taken, and that the people have made, this lake will forever remain as it now is, filled with the salt of both your tears and mine so that you may always remember. As such, you must always think kind thoughts and honor all that is as you would Father Sky and myself. You must never forget that which you have been given."

Father Sky, being equally moved, decided to honor both Hawk and his mate by sending down the Thunder Beings, whereupon the two were turned to stone, Hawk surveying the lake and his mate, being eternally reborn from the egg she hatched, forever giving birth and renewal to the memory of what had been. Forever to be remembered alongside the Grandfather Stones.

And so it was that the people made their home within their circle where they honored the legends of their creation every day, the Lake of Tears at their feet and the Mountains of the Sky beyond.

In time, Father Sky would give them another home within his mountains to live so that they might dwell closer together, but only in season, and only when and where permitted. There too they would be surrounded by the Sacred Stones from where they could travel either to the Valley of the Little Brother, Hetch Hetchy as it came to be known, or back down to their lake east of the crest.

Thus the Kuzedika were created.

"Whether you begin in the middle of the dance or at the end, every story must have a beginning. Each life is born again every day. All that exists is sacred and to be honored and remembered. To fail to acknowledge this is to live in profanity. And so we dance in a circle, honor the four directions and sing our songs."

"I heard this after leaving you at Keota. Out west. It was told to me by Tenaya. He claims it was true, but even I don't have the wisdom to know whether this is so. He was a great man but the Californians ran him out of the Valley anyway. His failure would eventually cause him to be killed at the Hawk Stones by his own people and his body would be thrown into the lake while those same Californians who ran him out of Ahwhanee would dam Little Brother sending the water as they did so far away from

Mother Earth. It was said that Father Sky cursed them for what they'd done. In time he would send them fire and plague so that they would remember. I hope he does."

"Not long after seeing Tenaya, I met another man, an old Scotsman, Muir, I think his name was, who used to tie himself to trees above the Valley so that he might witness Grandfather Skies fury when and if it came, but when I did the same, all I heard were the Thunder Beings. They didn't seem to want me there."

"I never did find out if old Muir found what he was looking for, although he did somewhat honor Father Skies creation. The Valley is now a park or something. Too many hotels. Too many people. Too many smoke belching dinosaurs. Too many people not walking the land in a sacred manner. He blew it. Shoulda kept 'em out and only let a few in at a time. Mighta pissed Father Sky off a bit less."

Creation stories, and just what was Caleb trying to tell me? Was I the maker of my own creation? My own myth? My own legend?

And what if I was? And what did it all mean?

"Walk the path. You'll know where you're going when you get there. Every day is its own beginning. Celebrate the moment or it'll be gone."

As Paul Harvey said, it was now time "for the rest of the story…" and I was all ears.

Coyote Songs

"After leaving you at Keota I decided to cross over the Chalk Bluffs and see if I could find Venneford and maybe talk with ol' RJ Poteet and the boys, but I couldn't find it. Guess Michener musta moved it. After that, I went up Crow Creek and followed it for awhile. Then I crossed over below Chugwater and headed north to the old Deadwood Stage Road. From there I traveled to Fort John and went on up the North Fork of the Platte and turned south at the river La Ramee named for himself. Conceited bastard. Always was full of it. Followed that for awhile and after I'd reached the buffalo plains I headed for Elk Mountain. After that it was due west again."

"Old Jacques wanted me to stop and see his rendezvous, but he was gone. Probably off looking for beaver."

"Anyway, once I got to the red sandstone bluffs, I turned in the direction of the Snowies and got to thinking, damn if I shouldn't a just followed Crow Creek on up and over at Pole Mountain. Woulda ended up in the same spot anyway and wouldn't a spent so much time wandering around all over the map, but then I woulda missed some fine buffalo country, so what the hell. Jacques was gone no matter what but maybe I could hook up with him on the way back. Coulda left DA Russell and gone straight into Fort Sanders too. Oh, well. Stupid me."

Then what?

"After heading west, I picked up some wagon ruts north of Elk Mountain where they'd been carved into the sandstone and followed those for a bit. Sure looked like a lot of people went through there. Followed them for a while and then hit Bridger.

He was gone too. After that I moved on to the Weber, followed it down to Salt Lake and saw the last of the buffalo country along the way. Once out, I went north of the lake and headed for the Apache Caves at Promontory. You know, they were wandering around the country the same time the Kuzedika were. Seems they used 'em as a stopover along the way. Whereas the Kuzedika headed north, the Apache headed south out of Alberta and ended up in the very same place the Kuzedika left. Seems Father Sky had a sense of irony. Anyway, after that, I got to thinking about old Mike Daggett and how he wanted me to walk with him to California. Said he hadn't done so since back in nineteen eleven and it was time. So I headed for the Humbloldt and after that Little High Rock. From there Mike and I could continue on toward either the Pit or Feather and cross over into California. Unfortunately, Mike couldn't remember which one he'd taken and both Lassen and Applegate were of little help. Neither was Meek for that matter."

"So much for short cuts."

And?

"Well, as said, I met up with Mike and we both walked on through Little High Rock and on over the Warner's, but after that he lost his way so I said adios and turned south. Mike said we could meet up on my return trip and that he'd wait for me where the water boiled out of the ground east of the Sierra. Said I'd know the place because you could see old Peter Lassen's mountain from there. Said it was a fine view. Said he had some relatives there and needed to stay and visit."

"Needless to say, I headed south, keeping the mountains which were growing taller as I went, to my right. It was an easy trail to follow."

And then what?

"I'm gettin' to it."

Grump.

"By then I was thinking about visiting Tenaya, decided it was time we met, and since I was heading in that direction anyway, I could camp with him next to the Grandfather Stones where he said he was living. In the meantime, the land over my right shoulder continued to grow, while that over my left became increasingly barren. All the rivers and streams ran in the wrong direction. They seemed to always be disappearing into sinks and basins or simply played out. It was a strange land. Disappearing water and salt flats. No trees. To cross that land you'd either have to island hop from mountain range to mountain range or rush across the basins and hope for the best. Then again, woulda been better to just avoid it, but many couldn't, ya know. Their un-marked graves were everywhere."

What Caleb said rattled me. So many unmarked graves. So many husbands, wives, sons and daughters forgotten. It was if ev-eryone who'd traveled west either didn't care about 'em or simply threw 'em away, their memory lost. It was as if everything they'd stood for, said or done didn't matter. All their hopes, dreams, triumphs and losses were simply discarded; obliterated by time. I couldn't shake it. How can you remember a person if nobody's left to talk about 'em? How can you remember people if you erased 'em? And how can you remember a culture if you simply bury it to blow away with the next wind?

To me, it seemed we'd done that.

From the eastern plains of Colorado, Wyoming and Nebras-ka to the Great Basin Caleb was talking about, the story was the same. The lives and adventures of those who'd crossed 'em, or tried to but couldn't were gone and their memory was lost. Years later, I too would wander the Great Basin and find their graves. So many unmarked graves. So many lost stories.

So many forgotten dreams.

It made me sick to think about it.

I swore I'd be different. I'd remember. Offer a prayer where it belonged and unravel their stories where I could. After all, what was a memory if it wasn't remembered?

As Sitting Bull'd said, "A man who doesn't understand the past is doomed to repeat it."

I vowed I wouldn't do the same.

"Well, after several weeks of getting nowhere in partic-ular, I came across old Jim Beckwourth. Said he'd been where I was heading and that he could point out the best way to get there. Needless to say, I questioned his veracity as he was prone to story telling and exaggeration, but I listened anyway. After that he told me about a mountain, or rather a peak, that was just south of the pass he'd found across the Sierra and that I could see everything including the trail I needed to follow from there. If it was bullshit I'd know soon enough. If not, well, I got to climb another mountain."

"And so I continued south."

"Within no time at all I reached the mountain he was talkin' about and climbed it. Rather than bein' a peak, it was more like a promontory, and was just easta the Range of Light and slightly northa the trail the Washo followed when they'd head for the Lake of the Sky. Seems Old Truckee led John C and Carson over it and down the other side into what was then Mexico back in '46. Tried to stir up a war between the Mexicans and the Gold diggers, ya know. Even was with 'em near Sonoma when they hauled down their flag. Yep, it was a rather strange war. Almost no shots were fired. Same thing happened afterwards in Yerba Buena and Monterey. Sloat and Stockton just sailed in and the damn Mexicans just lowered 'em. Yep, ol' Trukeee was a Bear Flagger, ya know. Well, anyway, as I was sayin', the Mexicans did manage to scare ol' JC outa the neighborhood when he reached Monterey. Did so by chasing after him with their lancers. After that they ran all the way to the Gabilans's easta Salinas and climbed the highest peak they could find. The one just south of the stage road. Said they were on their way to the old Spanish mission in San Juan, but that was a lie. They were running away. Claimed they were in a running fight the whole time and that they even fought a battle on top of that mountain, but that too was a lie. A running battle that never was. Seems ol' Fremont raised an American flag on Gabilan Peak though, but it blew down during the night so he turned tail and ran all the way past the mission and headed for the San Joaquin beyond. He always was a bit of image over substance. Always let others do his fightin' for him. A strange war. Almost no shots fired. Both sides ran until the Californios finally got pissed off and kicked Kearney's butt outside San Diego. San Pasqual. In the end the Americans got California anyway and the Californios lost their land to condos and Hollywood. It hasn't been the same since."

"But gettin' back to the mountain. After climbin' it I could see that ol' Beckwourth was right. Lookin' south ya could see the trail Truckee followed when he headed west and ya could see the one I needed headin' south. After passin' through a meadow and into some low hills it disappeared, but I was sure it resumed on the other side. Turnin' around the other way I could see where I'd come from in the north and to the east I could see more mountains. Mountains where the people who lived there carved their stories in stone or painted 'em on rocks. Kinda like the newspapers of the day, ya know. There were stories of rivers and lakes, windstorms and sunrises, lizards and dragonflies, deer hunts and Big Horns. There were even stories of ol' Tamsen Donner and Breen. Carved their wagon wheels into the granite. Yep, ol' Donner and Breen, two more idiots who, after goin' in circles out near the Humboldt, tried to cross over the Sierra along the Washo Trail and got stuck in the snow. Truckee told 'em to turn back, but would they listen? Hell no. Arrogance was never a virtue. Seems they got a bit hungry after winter set in though. The Alferd Packer school of wisdom."

"So after checkin' out where I was goin', I headed back downhill and turned south, followin' the deer trails as usual. Well there I was followin' the sign and not payin' attention to anything around me, when damned if I didn't feel like somethin' was starin' at me, so I stopped. And damned if something wasn't. Yep, right there next to me was this coyote no more than a few feet away. Damn thing was just sittin' there lookin' like every dog ya ever seen. Just sittin' there and grinnin'. Seemed like he was sayin' "What are you doin' here? Where's my ball and why haven't you tossed me a bone or two." Well, needless to say, I was taken aback. It was if I'd been out for a leisurely stroll and old fido was simply taggin' along for the ride."

"Sure as hell wasn't threatenin' me and didn't seem sick. Just sat there watchin' everything I was doin', so I stopped and talked to him. When I did, he cocked his head first one way, then the other like he was listenin' to what I was sayin' but otherwise he just sat there grinnin'. It was kinda strange."

"Well, after decidin' he didn't mean me any harm, I turned

my back on him and walked away. Coulda attacked me if he wanted to, but he didn't. When I looked to the side, he was just trot-
tin' along. Again, like every dog ya ever seen, so I stopped and
talked to him again. Told him he shouldn't be so friendly because
although he wasn't threatenin' me, if anybody else saw him actin'
the way he was they'd probably shoot him. Needless to say, he
just sat there grinnin' like before. After that I walked on again and
pretended to ignore him, but he just trotted alongside me until
after a bit he got bored and trotted off. To this day I have no idea
where he went. It was as if he'd appeared from nowhere and just
disappeared back into it."

"Ya know, to some, Coyote's a trickster. To others he's a
prankster. Some consider him little brother to the wolf. To others he's the Creator of all that is and in some cases, the messen-
ger of the Great Spirit. I tend to think he's all of 'em. After all,
what good's a god that can't laugh now and again? What good's a
god that can't take a joke? Seems Kevin shoulda called his movie
Laughing With Coyotes or somethin', but then I guess it wouldn't
a sounded near as romantic as Dances With Wolves. Mighta been a
hit though. My coyote was sure as hell was a star."

"Needless to say, the whole thing was kinda special. Like
that time up out of Sanders when I was walkin' the Telegraph
Road. That time a crow followed me. Damn smart birds, ya know.
Well, there I was walkin' along, when this ol' crow comes up and
begins hopping from one telephone pole to the other in the same
direction I was headin'. When I started to caw at it, it did the
same back. If I cawed once, it cawed once. If I cawed twice, it
cawed twice. Same with three and four. It was as if he was tryin'
to talk to me. Maybe he was. If not, he sure was a good mimic, but
like coyote, he became bored after a bit and just flew off. Guess I
didn't have anything to say."

"Call and response. The oldest form of communication on
the planet. Wonder if the oldtimers talked to the animals. Bet they
did."

Quite the story teller, Caleb.

"And it's only just begun."

"Well anyway, as I was sayin'. After I left the coyote behind

I continued headin' south like I had been. Had to meet up with Tenaya. Had to see the land he was always talkin' about. Needed to see where old JC dumped his cannon up above the Walker somewhere in the Sweetwaters and needed to talk with the Washo. Needed to laugh at their stories of how the ol' Pathfinder and Carson got snowbound up in the pass south of the Lake of the Sky, Bigler, I think it was called then, and how they thought the people were just another apparition as they floated over the snow without sinking up to their knees. Yep, the Washo had snowshoes. Old Kit and Fremont didn't know about such things, but they were learnin'. After that, they too could float over the mountains, but not without the rabbits they'd been given by the Washo when they couldn't even catch their own. So much for the great Carson. Couldn't even snare a rabbit in the snow."

"After that, there were places where the water boiled out of the ground and creeks ran hot no matter the season. I walked with the animals and hawks and eagles showed me the way. I followed the Beckwourth Trail, that followed the Bonneville Trail, that followed the Walker Trail, the Fremont Trail, the Immigrant Trail, the California Trail and the Pony Express Trail, which in turn, followed the Numa Trail, the Washo Trail, the Mono Trail and god knows how many others where each was named after those who thought they'd discovered em' for themselves. Such is the story of man, ya know. We all wanta think we're the first at everything. All wanta name everything after ourselves, and yet, more often than not, somebody was there before us and followed the same path. Hubris. Vanity. What a waste. Today it's a freeway. Go figure."

I just laughed, but Caleb was right. We're a vain, self absorbed bunch. Never were able to walk our talk, let alone admit that anybody else beat us to the punch line.

"Twas ever thus."

Mr. Natural in all his glory.

R Crumb. Right again.

Some things never changed.

Where Caleb would walk, I'd follow.

We both traveled on.

"Well, after what seemed like days, I reached a point

where, once I'd ascended a ridgeline, I could look down on a salt lake and see the smoke from Tenaya's fire. The Hawk Rocks were clearly visible from where I was so finding him wasn't a problem. After that Tenaya and I met and talked a bit and you know the rest of the story."

I never found out if Caleb reconnected with Shoshone Mike, or whether or not they returned eastward together, but no matter what, it'd been quite a story; quite an adventure.

After which Caleb disappeared again and winter returned.

And like before, it'd be interminably long.

Crossing Over

Steam billowed in puffs as it rose from the storm drains tucked into the curbs along Larimer Square while yet another emphysemic Marlboro Man gasped his last breath and trundled his oxygen tank down the windrows along Sixteenth Street, it's wheels scouring a disseminated two track through the late winter snow turned yellow from too much piss, homeless drunks and displaced barflies cast adrift under a sky turned leaden and wishing they were still in the Brown Palace, drinking large and imagining they were something they'd never been.

Tossed by the LoDo wind, Marlboro Man's Stetson tumbled along the icy slick walks and out into the gutter.

A taxi passed by and was gone. Like Marlboro Man, lost in a sea of slush and slime. Both drifting aimlessly through the city.

Inside the bars and taverns a faceless mass of humanity lived out their dreams in happy hour smiles and phony discourse while wannabe gangsters spun their El Dorados out on the black ice that covered Colorado Boulevard, heading as always for another methamphetamine deal gone bust in Five Points or maybe Globe Town. Unaware that the road they were cartwheeling on was once part of the wagon route between Julesburg and Denver. Colorado's original highway.

Such was life after Caleb left.

Bleak.

Winter'd returned and I didn't care. If I wasn't at work, I'd be stuck at home where I'd stare out the window for hours and wish I were someplace else. Anywhere else. Winters in Denver could be that bad.

They sucked.

Even the birds hunkered down. You'd seldom see any unless the sun came out, and then it was only when they were looking for a place the snow'd retreated from after which they'd hunker down again, sometimes in the hundreds along the telephone lines, sometimes in small coveys under the shrubs where after finding a non frozen worm or two they'd hunker down once more and sometimes simply lost.

I felt like Tom Horn musta when he was waiting to be hung in the Cheyenne jail. Every day he'd just sit there and stare out the window. Always west. West to the Laramies. West to freedom. Free to be who he was. Free to be what he wanted to be. Free to roam the Sweetwater and Medicine Bow. Free to simply go where he chose. Free to run with the wind. Stand in the rain. Freeze in the snow. Free to live the life he chose.

In between, he simply braided horsehair lariats and bridles. Too much time on his hands.

They hung him anyway. Buried him in Boulder where all the PC people could wander over from Pearl Street and stare at his grave, remember the bad man he was supposed to be or imagine the man he may or may not have been, and all while wishing he looked like Steve McQueen.

Another Hollywood moment in the Rockies. Afterward they could wander back to Pearl Street and nosh on a tofu burger, grab a hummus salad and wash 'em both down with a Perrier or ginger pop.

Maybe they could visit the Mork and Mindy house afterwards.

Tom Horn. Sometimes I envied him.

At least he was free.

I had nothing better to do than just sit there and stare out the window, lost in my thoughts.

As the winter stagnated, I grew my hair out. Needless to say, it wasn't long before I began to look like Wild Bill Hickok, droopy mustache and all. When the sun'd break through the Denver haze I'd lace up the Sorels and head for the creek. Sometimes the snow'd be hard, ice packed and thin. Other times it'd be soft and deep particularly where it'd gather in windrows beneath the cutbanks and overhangs. In other places it'd form rime ice, whereas, in still others the wind'd simply send it someplace else. Where the windrows accumulated, I'd often sink up to my knees or higher and the Sorels'd be damn near useless. In other places I didn't need 'em at all.

Such are the vagaries one encounters while walking the land in winter.

A pair of Sorels only go so far, winter or not, but at least the snow'd be dry. Champagne powder. Come spring, it'd be corn and concrete. You could break an ax on it, bust a D Tool. After that it'd simply disappear and the color'd return to the land. Cottonwoods'd turn the sky white with the slightest of breezes and the land'd bloom, the streams and rivers'd run and the geese and cranes'd migrate south.

I couldn't wait. Come spring, the Redtails would drift above our creek as they'd always done and the crows'd chatter in the cottonwoods. Redwing blackbirds'd hide in the willows and Prairie Dogs'd perch on top of their mounds and chirp. In between, it'd be the fox and coyote who dominated the land. Their tracks were everywhere. Winter hunters. It was rare to see any man made prints. It was as if the creek mattered little to anyone beyond the Maginot, especially with snow on the ground.

If spring was peaceful, winter was silent. It was a whole different animal as the mountain men used to say. I never cared much for it, but I missed being able to get out. Winter blotted everything out. It hid things from view. It distorted what you could see. Distances were shortened. Definition was lost and everything was monochromatic, white, blue, gray or haze. It could be ugly.

But then again, it wasn't. Winter made you stop and think. It made you look harder, stand still. Remember what you knew was there, but hidden from sight. But most of all, it made you understand the power of silence.

Whereas Caleb taught me to see things that weren't by looking within and then extrapolating outward, winter taught me to simply shut up and listen. Not just with my ears, but with my soul.

Silence.

As mentioned, it was feared by almost everyone in modern America, yet it was the most powerful sound nature made.

If summer was Yin, winter was Yang. You couldn't have one without the other and both were interrelated and necessary.

Winter allowed time to slow and in some cases stop. It allowed you to refocus and adjust your balance. It allowed all of creation to rest for the journey ahead and the burst of energy to come.

It gave old men their stories and for the rest, a time to remember.

Silence was the loudest sound I'd ever heard. It taught me to be still.

Caleb, in his presence, had taught me to see life with my spirit, the spirit of new beginnings and rebirth. The spirit of a curious child. The spirit of summer days and spring. Now in his absence he was teaching me to listen with my heart, the heart of winter, solitude and silence.

The heart of quietude and reflection. The heart where the spirit resides.

The heart of the soul.

It, like the gift of inner vision, was a blessing.

I wished Caleb had been there to see it, but in a sense he was.

We were never far apart.

Beyond the Maginot, Marlboro Man continued to cough his way through LoDo and cars continued to spin out on Colorado Boulevard where the hard freeze of winter'd accumulated in the shadowed overhangs and gutters of the city skyline. Meth heads continued to make their rounds in and out of Globeville and slit skirted girls continued to let guys oggle 'em over beer and brats in the Brown.

And all while I hiked back the centuries.

Ever so slowly though, winter'd turn to spring, icicle season, mud season, then summer.

Icicle season. They'd only be an inch or two long at birth, but by winters end some'd be as long as a foot or more. So long that their size'd cause 'em to come crashing down, sometimes on an unsuspecting passerby and usually all at once.

Skewered by winter.

As they grew, the air'd become warmer, until one day, usually by late March or early April, it'd become so balmy that they'd crack and wherever their stalagtites weren't already broken they'd come crashing down all at once and form piles of fractured crystals underneath. Although too soon for spring, once they'd done so it'd be mud season and winter'd be gone, disappearing like Marlboro Man, only to reappear as a coughing enigma before it was finally over. After that spring'd be on its way and there'd be no turning back. The meth dealers'd have to find another excuse for not meeting their appointed rounds.

Although too soon to travel outside of Denver, it'd be time to lace up the Sorels again and head for the creek. There wouldn't be much snow come mud season, but there'd sure as hell be a lot of goop on the ground and the ol' Sorels could be a godsend when that happened. Beyond the Maginot, what wasn't a Slurpee, all slush and slime, would more often than not end up that way, slick as snot and deep as a mudflat. The kind of goop that'd take a 4X4 and render it useless until it's owner came back with a wench and another 4X4 and pulled it out. If not, it'd simply ossify 'till spring assuming another 4X4 didn't come along and pick it clean.

Not all buzzards had wings.

Once laced up, I went back to the ranch and sat beside the old wisteria on one of the crumbling concrete troughs. It was beginning to bud and the meadowlarks and robins were returning. The air was balmy and the clouds once again formed puffballs overhead. Where the prairie dogs had built their lookouts, some were venturing farther out while others were repairing the old ones. Still others were digging new ones. It always seemed odd to me that they seemed to instinctively know where to build 'em. Always away from the goop, but close enough to mire a predator.

Nature always seemed to have a plan.

Prairie Dogs. Ranchers hated 'em and did their best to eradicate 'em. Their holes caused cows to break their legs and horses to stumble while more than a few cowboys themselves ended up on their ass after coming across one. While no doubt true, it always amazed me that bison never seemed to have that problem. Maybe some of the ranchers shoulda exchanged their Herefords for buffalo. Mighta survived a few more winters as well.

If it wasn't the ranchers, it was the farmers. Like the ranchers, they hated 'em cuz they were said to eat up everything in sight, which in some cases may have been true, but more often than not seemed otherwise. Whereas it was true that the dogs'd eat alot, inevitably the only sign of prairie dog grazing would be along their runways or within a limited distance from their burrows no matter the size of their town. In point of fact, the only real problem I could see was that once the dogs ate the naturally occurring vegetation near their burrows, invasive weeds'd replace what the dogs consumed, and more often than not, that was because man was nearby. Get farther away from human interference, and the land'd recover no matter the size of their town. As such, man seemed to be the greater problem.

Couldn't blame the prairie dogs for cheatgrass and Scottish Thistle, but no doubt some tried. Both were far more damaging to the west than any prairie dog could be. Cows and horses couldn't eat either one. Couldn't digest 'em. Sheep couldn't either, nor could bison, elk, deer, or even jackrabbits for that matter.

Nothing'd eat cheatgrass. Not even the bugs.

Cheatgrass.

When a fire occurred, it'd burn hotter and faster than anything else in it's path and where once only minor, short term damage would occur, entire acres and multiple miles of rangeland'd become lost for a generation or more. Native grass seeds burned, but the damn cheatgrass seeds didn't. Short of incineration you couldn't get rid of 'em. Even chemicals didn't help and short of a flame thrower, nothing'd wipe 'em out and the land'd be ruined no matter what.

Add to that the fact that their burrs'd stick into almost everything they came in contact with, and you had a recipe for disaster.

Infected toes?

Got 'em.

Useless socks?

Yep, couldn't pull all the damn burrs out no matter how hard you'd try. Easier to throw the socks away.

Christ, they'd even stick into boot linings.

And if that weren't bad enough, cheatgrass could out compete every other form of prairie grass or plant it'd come in contact with for water and minerals. Entire ecosystems were being lost.

Couldn't blame the dogs for that.

Had to look a bit closer to home.

Cheatgrass. An invasive, imported problem.

Gotta look in the mirror, but then man always was a rather myopic creature. Too vain to see what's in front of his eyes. Too purposefully ignorant.

Too stupid.

Needless to say, I was on the side of the dogs.

Prairie Dogs, natures archaeologists. Seems every time they'd dig a hole, entire civilizations'd turn up. Caleb's Creek was no exception.

Needless to say, I've never been sure which came first, the Prairie Dog or Man. Probably man in some cases, given that the dogs often showed up after the later'd moved on. Despite all of his wisdom, man was pretty unlikely to camp in the middle of a prairie dog town if he had anyplace else to go. Unlike out west where Caleb had mentioned that it was common knowledge that the people of the Great Basin used ant hills near their camps to throw deer and rabbit hides on after skinning 'em so that the ants'd remove what their scrappers couldn't, it seemed to me that the dogs themselves served little purpose other than that of sentry, but then any animal woulda served the same purpose to a watchful people. That being said, it seemed to me that the dogs were attracted to places man once occupied by something he left behind. Coulda been that he served the same purpose as the bison, wherever he went he got rid of enough of the unwanted ground cover to leave a surface that 'd support more edible vegetation. The sage and prickly pear, which most nothing'd eat short of starvation anyway, would disappear and prior to the unwanted introduction of cheatgrass and thistle, species such as morning glories and short grass would appear.

In the meantime, the dogs could continue their exploratory digs.

That spring they turned up a spot where someone'd camped along the creek, built a bonfire and burned what appeared to have been a nineteenth century wagon. Partially burned wood, iron mounting pins and hooks were everywhere as were broken strands of Kelly Wire. Nearby a small hand blown medicine bottle protruded from the edge of the cutbank while a partially crushed Mexican War era army officer's button lay along the periphery. Everything inside where the bonfire'd been was either melted or fused. Several hand crimped Henry .44 rimfires lay nearby, their embossed H's and crimp markings still clearly visible on the bottom, as did multiple arrowheads. Some were broken. Some weren't. Some were Plains Side Notch yet others were McKean. Some were unknown. It didn't seem to add up. Beyond the bonfire ring pieces of broken furniture were everywhere and although most had been burned, everything was within feet of something else and with the exception of the McKean seemed to be of the same vintage. Other than the McKean, everything seemed related, but to what?

The place felt eerie. Something'd happened there. Everything said so and yet it didn't. After months of research I couldn't find anything out. Utes used the creek to travel along when heading out onto the plains to hunt buffalo and were well known to sport surplus military jackets as a mark of distinction. But then so did damn near every other Indian tribe west of the Mississippi. They were also well known to imitate the ways of the newly arrived white man and frequently used their wagons for travel when available. It was also known that they were in constant conflict with both the Arapaho and Cheyenne who frequented the area as well and that each were in conflict with the settlers of the region at one time or another. Either the Cheyenne or Arapaho, depending on whose history you believed, raided the Hungate Ranch outside of Denver and stole their prized Henry .44 after massacring the entire family while other parties could have once owned a Henry as well. As said, it didn't add up and yet it kinda did. Each side killed the other and one or more of 'em had been where I stood. The McKean were out of place no matter what, but had simply used the same spot for a camp before the dogs dug everything up.

Had a roving band of Cheyenne or Arapaho run into a party of Utes or had a settler, possibly a rancher or cattle herder been ambushed by one or the other?

And what about the McKean?

Caleb'd shown me that it wasn't unusual for people to camp in the same location for the same, or similar purposes, year after year, generation after generation, century after century so the McKean presence wasn't that unusual. Neither was the Arapaho, Cheyenne, Ute, settler, or possible rancher for that matter What was unusual, however, was that Denver didn't know about any of it. Didn't know what was there. Didn't know what happened. And all of it, just over the Maginot Line from their swimming pools and living rooms.

So what'd the dogs turned up? An ambush? A fight between two disparate groups of people? Had the Cheyenne or Arapaho attacked a party of Utes? Had either the Cheyenne, Ute or Arapaho attacked a white settler or settlers? The Utes were mostly at peace with the whites east of the Rockies around the time of what the dogs revealed, the Arapaho and Cheyenne intermittently so. The Arapaho and Cheyenne versus the Ute, not so much so. No matter what, I couldn't tell and the site didn't say, but one thing was certain, with the exception of the McKean, a specific event had occurred at a specific moment in time at a specific spot and everything I saw was related to the same and it appeared to have been violent.

Shots were fired. Arrows and bullets flew and a wagon with it's contents had been burned. A military coat'd had a button torn off and nobody hid what'd been done. Afterwards a bonfire'd been set and a celebration ensued. No bones of any kind were anywhere so nobody ate anything. Whoever was there mighta been drunk. The fused glass didn't say, but it's colors did.

Aside from the McKean, everything from the arrowheads to the Henry casings and Kelly Wire, button and bottle said something happened between roughly 1846 and 1876. A very narrow window within a very specific timeframe. One spot, one event. Isolated. The button was older than everything except for the McKean, but then it appeared to have been so when it was lost. It'd simply been an older item used in a newer time.

But what about the rest?

There were certainly few white travelers in the region between the end of the Mexican War and 1858. Most followed the north fork of the Platte to Oregon and California. Few went south other than those who followed the Arkansas to Bent's Fort and most of them were trappers. The land between the two was mostly a buffalo commons until gold was discovered along Cherry Creek in 1858 and Kelly Wire wasn't invented until 1868.

Seemingly whatever'd happened did so shortly after that. But when, I couldn't tell. Whatever happened probably did so before Custer passed through the area on his way to the Little Big Horn in 1876. Probably before the railroads made it into Denver in 1870 as well. More likely than not, probably sometime between 1868 and 1869.

A very short window indeed.

But then again, the years between 1864 and 1870 were ominous. Fort Sedgwick was built along the Platte in 1864. Fort Collins was built near La Porte along the Cache La Poudre in 1865 and Fort Sanders was built farther north the same year near the Laramie. By 1868 Fort Steele would be built farther north along the Platte and between those and old Fort Laramie, the People of the Blue Sky and their Lakota and Cheyenne cousins would be hemmed in. Hemmed in to stick to the land between the Dakotas and the Republican. Hemmed in to hunt the ever decreasing buffalo herds. Hemmed in to inhabit Flyover Country.

It was only logical that after being pushed out of the bottomland along the rivers and mountain front that they'd push back against the invading whites and push back they did.

Never mind that Black Kettle used to camp on the lawn in the front yard of the Molly Brown house in Denver. He'd soon be dead at the Washita and before that run out of Sand Creek even though he flew an American Flag over his tipi and had a peace medal given to him by the same advancing horde that'd destroy his people and cover the land. Chivington won and Evans had his mountain. Soon after Molly Brown'd get washed up with the Titanic and the buffalo'd be gone.

And what about Lupton and Red Cloud?

None of the Lakota cared much for Red Cloud by then. It was said he'd lost his way. Gave up the land. Turned white. Turned apple.

In 1865 a band of roving Cheyenne Dog Soldiers sacked and burned Julesburg after which they fled to either Sand Creek or Cherry Creek depending on who's story you believed. The same Sand Creek where the massacre occurred a year earlier. The same Cherry Creek Denver was being built on.

It all fit.

1867 saw the Union Pacific reach Cheyenne. By 1868 it'd reached Laramie.

In 1870 a spur line was built between Cheyenne and Denver and in 1868 the Cheyenne, Lakota and Arapaho fought the army once again at Beecher Island. Fought them next to the Kansas Pacific railhead.

They seemingly lost that too. Lost Roman Nose in the process.

Made one wonder.

Between 1865 and 1870 there were three primary roads running in and out of Denver. One ran southward from Denver to Santa Fe and north to Cheyenne while another ran northeast from Denver to Julesburg and the last ran from Denver to the north fork of the Platte near South Pass. Along the last one Fort Collins was built as were Forts Sanders and Steele. All to protect the southern immigrant trails and railroad.

If the People of the Blue Sky didn't feel hemmed in by that, then nothing'd make 'em feel that way.

All were freight roads. All had stage lines. All carried alot of traffic.

Dog Town and it's Mexican War button were just yards away from one and only a few miles away from the other two and all were close to Cherry Creek.

Again, it all fit.

More likely than not, the burnt wagon and whatever skirmish had ensued had occurred within that time frame.

1868-1869 were watershed years for the Arapaho.

More likely than not they simply pushed back.

It'd been a small victory.

It was eerie. In my mind I could see what happened, or at least much of it. How Caleb and I missed it that week in February, I never knew. How Denver'd missed it ever since 1868 or 9, was beyond my comprehension.

I'd once again walked backwards and was reminded of both the blessing and curse of knowledge.

For better or worse, you could carry it with you for the rest of your life. Carry with you the memory as well as the spirits and ghosts of those you saw. Memories of events and tragedy. People and place.

It could make or break you. You'd become a part of each other. Commingled souls.

The dogs'd done their work, Indiana Jones be damned.

A mustard color, double headed quartzite club lay in the dust where the mud'd disappeared on the opposite side of the creek from Dog Town, it's handle groove still clearly visible along the center of its plane, oblivious to the tract homes behind it. Oblivious to the concrete bike path just inches away. Oblivious to the Maginot.

Each out of context with the other.

Each out of time.

Life moved on even if sometimes time stood still.

After leaving Dog Town I decided to return to the ranch. I'd seen too much sadness. The ghosts were about and their spirits were restless. It left me ill at ease.

After returning I could sit next to the wisteria and think about what I'd seen. The cottonwoods nearby would be just beginning to bud and soon the sky'd be white with their fuzz. I'd seen too much and wished Caleb were there to talk about it. Maybe if he listened I'd feel better, but he was gone.

All was quiet except for the crows.

Guess they didn't like me sitting underneath 'em.

Years later I'd work at the old Stewart Boarding School in Carson where when not working in the museum I'd frequently take the motorcycle out and head for the Sierra, passing as I did so through the very area Caleb had described in his travels. Guess I was looking for the lost connection between us. Wanted to see what he'd seen and experience what he'd experienced. Once out, I could follow him any number of places.

On one such occasion I passed over the first ridge of mountains east of the Sierra and into a valley just west of the north-south trail he'd talked about when he was looking for Tenaya. Although it was doubtful he'd been where I was, he'd gotten close. I was sure I was seeing something he hadn't. It was a beautiful place and the road I was following looped around and through it as it revealed both grasslands and wooded vistas depending on where you were as well as an open meadow and several creeks in between. Needless to say, it was idyllic.

Unfortunately, by the time I'd completed the loop, the Thunder Beings decided to move in and Old Man That Grumbles began to grouse while lightning flashed all around me. It was just like it'd been in Keota. You could smell the ozone. In the middle of the meadow I cut the engine and got off the bike. The storm moved all around but avoided the center and was as if I'd landed in the middle of an alien vortex. I didn't get wet or rained on and the wind blew all around except where I hunkered down beneath my jacket. It was weird.

Shortly afterward the Thunder Beings moved on and Old Man That Grumbles became once again silent, the sky turned blue and everything was calm.

I waited a few more minutes for the road to dry just in case, and then kicked over the motorcycle engine and headed for home. Needless to say, I didn't get far. Almost immediately I became sick to my stomach and had to lie down. My vision blurred and my head spun. I curled into a ball. A few minutes later and it was gone.

When I got to work on Monday, everything began as usual. "Where'd ya go? What'd ya do?"

Everytime someone'd ask me I'd tell 'em about the valley and the storm and everytime I did so I'd get the same reaction......

Silence.

And then damn near everybody I knew hit me up all at once.

"Know where you were?"

Not really.

"Know what you saw?"

Just what I told ya.

"See anything else?"

Only that it was like that time back on Caleb's Creek when I found the burned wagon.

Again, silence.

They were holding something back.

After that it was like someone'd opened the proverbial flood gate and the questions just poured out...

"Where'd he find out about that?"

"Who told him?"

Seems they were asking as many questions of themselves as they were asking of me and none of it made any sense.

"During the eighteen hundreds there was a massacre there. The valley you described was the summer home of several tribes before your people came along and took it for the gold and lumber they found. They built a fort there and Indians were killed. Those who weren't were driven out."

Like so much of history the story they described had either never been told, or had faded with the years only to be held in reserve by those with a direct connection to the loss. Nobody who'd built the fort wanted to talk about it and the Indians couldn't.

I'd never heard about it and subsequent research turned little up, but years later I'd accidentally discover that what I'd been told was correct. A "fort" had been built in the valley and "Indian fights" had occurred. Needless to say, the word massacre was never used, but what wasn't said, spoke volumes..."Indian fights...."

People were killed and those who weren't were simply driven out.

It was Dog Town all over again.

I'd seen and felt something that was unspoken and seemingly invisible.

I'd seen the massacre, felt the loss caused by either death or displacement and in a sense, I'd been there.

I possessed knowledge that no rational explanation could account for and it'd happen again.

Shortly after moving to Nevada I came across a campsite that'd been used by one or more of the tribes in the region around the time the first settlers arrived. Inside were the usual objects, basalt and obsidian debitage, square nails and glass shards, Prince Albert tins and hand soldered tin cans with lead slugs in 'em. But that wasn't the half of it. Broken Clorox bottles were everywhere. Clorox bottles that shouldn't have been there.

Something wasn't right and just like back at Caleb's Creek, it made me feel ill at ease and sick to my stomach all over again.

After returning to Stewart, the response was the same.

I'd seen something nobody wanted to talk about

Seems that once gold was discovered near where the campsite was, the newly arrived miners decided they wanted it for themselves and rather than creating another massacre as had happened just over the Sierra, they simply gave the Indians Clorox to drink and told 'em it was the best whiskey they'd ever tasted. Needless to say, those who drank it either got sick or died after which the site was abandoned. The Indians never came back and the miners got what they wanted. No shots fired.

A sense of place. All living things feel it. All living things know where they belong and where they don't. Even after leaving a place some carry it with 'em. Carry it inside. If they're human they carry it within their souls. Within their spirit. Carry it for a lifetime. It defines who they are, their humanity or lack thereof and what they think of themselves. It defines their commonality and shared identity, their individual and collective purpose.

Shared stories. Shared language. Mutual beliefs.

When driven out of their homes in the Northern Plains and into Oklahoma, the Cheyenne undertook the Long Walk and while traveling in winter with women, children and old people, they walked all the way back to Wyoming. Many made it, but most didn't, either way, they knew where home was and it wasn't in Oklahoma. They simply walked home.

Not even imprisonment in Fort Robinson could stop 'em. They simply broke free and continued on.

The Navajo did the same thing. After being forced out of Canyon de Chelles and sent to the Bosque Redondo and Fort Sumner, they too simply walked away and like the coyote that walked beside Caleb, followed one home.

Sense of place. Without it one can become lost. There's no reason to live. No reason to exist.

In places like Dog Town that sense could linger long after those who lived there were gone.

It wasn't supernatural. It was simple fact. Some see and hear what others can't.

Spirits linger.

It's all a matter of being attuned to ones surroundings and paying attention, to having an open mind and a receptive soul, but most importantly, it's about being able to connect the dots. To connect what belongs and what doesn't, to be in the moment and not someplace else and to blocking out the ever incessant white noise that seems to be everywhere.

Some places are happy, some are sad, and everyplace attracts those who identify with what they abstractly believe exists within.

The ghosts of Dog Town were restless for a reason. Place was important and theirs had been supplanted by those who either didn't know, care for, or were simply uninterested in anything that'd happened before their arrival, least of all their stories.

The spirits of Dog Town needed to be set free and what I'd seen had done so.

Someone remembered.

It reminded me of Seattle's speech...

"Yonder sky that has wept tears of compassion upon my people for centuries untold, and which to us appears changeless and eternal, may change. Today is fair. Tomorrow it may be overcast with clouds. My words are like the stars...

There was a time when our people covered the land as waves of a wind ruffled sea cover it's shell paved floor, but that time long since passed away with the greatness of tribes that are now but a mournful memory…

To us the ashes of our ancestors are sacred and their resting place is hallowed ground. You wander far from the graves of your ancestors and seemingly without regret…

Your dead cease to love you and the land of their nativity as soon as they pass the portals of the tomb and wander away beyond the stars. They are soon forgotten and never return. Our dead never forget this beautiful world that gave them being. They still love it's verdant valleys, it's murmuring rivers, it's magnificent mountains, sequestered vales and verdant lined lakes and bays, and even yearn in tender fond affection over the lonely hearted living, and often return from the happy hunting ground to visit, guide, console, and comfort them…

Every hillside, every valley, every plain and grove has been hallowed by some happy event in days long vanished. Even the rocks, which seem to be dumb and dead as they swelter in the sun along the silent shore, thrill with the very dust upon which you now stand (and) respond more lovingly to their footsteps than yours…

And when your children's children think themselves alone in the field, the store, the shop, upon the highway, or in the silence of the pathless woods, they will not be alone. In all the earth there is no place dedicated to solitude…"

1854.

Coulda been yesterday.

Place mattered. If nobody remembered, it'd simply disappear. After that it'd be forgotten.

Dog Town and the Valley'd been remembered.

Their spirits could rest.

It was as if I'd been hit by lightning when I thought about it. If one didn't form an emotional or physical attachment through the process of remembering, then a sense of "place" couldn't exist. You had to form an emotional or physical bond. Without that bond, there couldn't be any "place" and if place didn't exist, it'd simply be a collectivization of observable attributes. A "setting."

Place required active participation between that which existed and those who interacted with it. It required a kind of give and take. A sort of existential Yin and Yang of equal forces cooperating in harmony, each needing and benefiting from the other. When either didn't exist, or was destroyed, the balance that'd been created would simply vanish. There couldn't be any "place" without it.

Place required both active as well as passive participation from the participants. Without it there was no connection. No need. No bond. No attachment.

Koyaanisqatsi. Life out of balance.

Without balance, there could be no "place."

And we were living in a time of Koyaanisqatsi and almost nobody was paying any attention.

Somehow, during those few hours after leaving Dog Town I'd crossed over a bridge. A bridge between being merely an observer/recorder and that of being an active participant.

And it'd mark the rest of my life.

I'd journeyed home.

Vedauwoo

The Wicasa Wakan stands in the middle of the bunchgrass meadow holding a twisted braid of sage and sweet grass in his right hand. With his left, he removes the sweat stained Larry Mahan from atop his head and sets it upside down in the Sherman loam between two clumps that'd been cropped so close, that at first glance they appeared as if they'd either been mowed or attacked by a herd of goats. Maybe a Massey Ferguson, possibly a John Deer. Maybe a Nanny. Never mind that it was simply a matter of elevation.

The grass always grew shorter higher up, besides, the Sherman loam wasn't exactly conducive to producing any viable topsoil.

The Redtail feathers that'd been tucked into the rawhide band twisted in the breeze but stayed in place. It was important that they stayed that way, so the holy man carefully placed the hat upside down with the feathers well above the soil. Larry could rest propped up against a stunted sage bush. Kinda seemed appropriate.

His crown wouldn't get crushed and the Redtails'd stay clean.

"Gettin' kinda old ol' hoss. Gonna have to replace you someday. You're getting' kinda beat up."

The Stetson remained silent.

"You're the wrong brim for this country anyway, too narrow, and your crown, well, it's pinched in the wrong place. Not high enough for these parts, but then, Larry, nobody knows who you were anyway. Coulda been a goat roper for all they know."

"Yep, You're kinda like me. An extinct species."

"Old and in the way."

After checking the direction of the wind, he pulls a match-box from his shirt pocket and removes one, unsnapping and then re-snapping the pearl button as he does so, after which he strikes it with a thumbnail.

Time to light the braid. Time to see the smoke.

He thinks about Niwot and how all the trees in these parts tilt eastward. Too much wind, too much of the time, he thinks. Always coming from out over the Medicine Bow. From over the Fourth Ridge, the place of the setting sun.

"Makes sense you look eastward", he says to the trees. Always important to remember where ya came from."

Looking in that direction, the hoodos, aspens and Lodgepole pine around the meadow begin to burn golden in the late spring morning.

The Wicasa Wakan stands in the sunlight.

A beaver tail slaps the surface of the pond in front of him as its owner pulls an aspen branch loaded with new leaves down into the water behind it.

"Breakfast, I suppose. Gotta think of that soon too."

He ignites the sweet grass, smells the sage.

After waving it in the air for a few seconds, it catches and smolders, sending a blue gray tendril of smoke in the direction of the stunted trees, always eastward. Always into the dawn.

The Wicasa Wakan then bathes in the smoke as the sweet grass and sage smell washes over him, permeating his hands, hair, face and skin. After doing so he turns to face each of the four directions, east, west, north and south waving the burning braid over his head as he does so.

The scent of the gods, he thinks. It serves Wakan Tanka well.

After moving his lips wordlessly while observing the horizon, he offers smoke to the earth and then to the sky. Once done, he snubs the twist and after cooling, places it back in the right rear pocket of his 501s.

He then removes a tobacco pouch from his other shirt pocket and offers what's inside in the same manner, talking silently as he does so.

"Red Man. Funny name for tobacco isn't it. Shoulda called it Kinnikinnick."

"Guess the Wasicu couldn't pronounce it," he giggles while shaking his head.

"Ah, ho." Time to think about breakfast.

"I knew you'd be here."

The voice carried across the meadow to the west of Potato Chip Rock and into the parking lot where I stood.

Caleb?

"I knew you'd be here. You had an epiphany, ya know. In case you forgot, we talked about this place and the power of language and remembering. You made a moonwalk, ya know. You were another Armstrong or was that Collins? Can't remember. Maybe you can tell me. Yep, ya took a giant leap and grew ten feet in the process."

I watched as the speck in the distance bent over, picked up a hat and stood erect, albeit, somewhat stooped.

I could see the hawk feathers in the Stetson as they flickered in the Vedauwoo breeze and thought I saw a smile.

"You've changed."

I suppose I had. Since last seeing Caleb I'd grown my hair, taken to wearing pinch visor baseball caps and seemed to've developed what Hollywood called, that "distant look in my eyes."

I always seemed to be someplace else and everyone I knew in Denver called me Pasquinel now. It was as if they were expecting yet another Micheneresque story about somewhere beyond the Maginot every time I'd see 'em. Someplace they'd never been but could only imagine.

Someplace just over the lost horizon...

It was a strange sort of power. The power of knowing something others didn't. Something they couldn't understand.

It was as if you'd been to a foreign land and'd returned to talk about it, not that anyone cared anyway. Coulda gone to the Serengeti for all they cared.

Reminded me of the X Files.

"The truth is out there."

Yep, but ya gotta look for it. Doesn't just come up and bite ya in the ass, ya know. Doesn't sneak in over a cuppa Joe and bagels.

Gotta get out and see for yourself. Lazy bastards.

After awhile it got to the point where seemingly everybody I knew was waiting for another story over an Ethiopian and Lox.

Funny how reputations are made.

"Whatcha got this time, Mulder?"

Reputation. Mine was becoming something of a cross between a character out of a Michener novel and an actor in a cult television series. Coulda been worse though. Coulda been just another nine to fiver hell bent on accumulating unaffordable junk and sitting around a Denver Coffee shop listening to bullshit all day while dreaming of a weekend in Glitter Gulch.

Yeesh.

Perish the thought.

But then, Caleb was right once again. Not only had I changed, or was well into the process of doing so, but so had Colorado and the Front Range with it.

What was once open range had turned into housing tracts. Stapleton'd been shut down and DIA was built. While it was supposed to be well removed from the city in order to handle more air traffic, it simply created an area for Aurora to expand into. More tract homes. More Californians. More of everything I couldn't stand. Levittown was on a roll. If Stapleton was surrounded by housing, now DIA was merely the eastern edge of a city that had morphed outward at breakneck speed.

DIA. "Dead Indians Again."

Although it was never proven, DIA was supposedly built atop an old Cheyenne burial site. Colorado had, like the ghosts of Caleb's Creek, become restless, but these spirits, rather than wanting peace, just seemed to want ever more of what they couldn't have.

And they destroyed everything they touched.

Greed was killing 'em and the land was swallowed wholesale. Boulder County, ever the uber liberal bastion it was, got fenced off and turned into a play land for the granola crowd and their California buddies where no heathens were allowed beyond Pearl Street and Castle Rock became the mega middle class shopping destination it is and everything else became, well, white bread and spam.

From Adams, to Larimer, to Jefferson and beyond, the story was the same.

Tra, la, la. Let's go to Aspen.

Skippy, skippy, LoDo's calling.

Overnight the land and the funkiness that'd been Colorado disappeared. Gone were the beat up Jimmy's and Blazers with cane broomsticks sticking out of their load beds. Gone were the ancient V Dubb buses and even more ancient IH Scouts.

Gone with the wind.

All hail the conquering Range Rover. God bless the Saab.

It was a new world.

Where oil and gas wells had long been abandoned, wellheads were once again being uncapped and drilling rigs moved in. Moved into Weld, moved into Adams, moved into Larimer and Jefferson. Hell, they even moved into Boulder County. Yep, they were going up everywhere. Even in the middle of the Saint Vrain River.

Unfortunately, the Saint Vrain flooded several years later and sent the well pad downriver to Firestone. Sent it's toxic sludge there too.

Collateral damage.

Flyover country.

NIMBY.

After that, a house in the same neighborhood got blown up and the occupants killed because of 'em. If it wasn't oil, it'd be methane or natural gas. Either way, the well pads that'd gone in and the directional drilling they allowed for created a situation where property lines meant nothing. You could set a gas wellhead right next to one with only a minor setback and after doing so, simply drill underneath it. Drill right underneath the house. Directional drilling. Fracking made it even worse. Frack the shale substrate and voila, cash'd flow. Unfortunately the chemicals would as well. Yep, when combined with directional drilling, fracking would leave many a new Colorado homeowner caught in an antiquated 1872 mining law nightmare of property vs mineral rights where the owner had none and the extractive industries had every.

Mining trumped property rights every time.

Colorado. Buy a home. Get a Methane well.

Welcome to the Front Range.

To this day, the laws've never been amended. Even in Boulder.

The Western Slope fared little better and both the Roan Plateau as well as the Flat Top Wilderness Area were opened for drilling and gas exploration. Never mind the pristine, isolated land that was prime habitat for deer, elk and bear. They were expendable. Collateral damage.

Flyover Country.

Even Rulison, where an underground thermonuclear explosion was set off in 1969 became fair game for the wellheads and drill pads. Never mind that what wasn't either fused or sealed by the heat and radiation from the blast was shale, sandstone or coal. Never mind that all are porous materials. Never mind that each was a previously distinct layer and that the very same blast'd fracture everything beyond what'd been bonded, creating as it did so even more fissures and cracks. Cracks between the layers. Fissures running between one layer and another. Intersecting cracks. Contiguous fissures. It all sucked.

While some rock was indeed fused and sealed, the surrounding layers would simply have more cracks than before and new ones'd be created. Yep, the shock waves created by the blast'd fracture the rock well beyond that which was fused allowing not only radioactive water to migrate away from the site, but the fracking chemicals that were used in the subsequent oil and gas drilling as well.

Fused rock won't stop radiation. Not without any lead around it, and to my knowledge, Rulison didn't have any. Cesium 137, Uranium 220, Americium and whatever else was in the mix'ld simply pass through where they'd contaminate not only the underground aquifer, but the streams and wells of the communities and ranches that depended on 'em.

And it did.

At ranches outside Rifle, calves were either stillborn or so badly deformed at birth they'd be put down. At least one had it's water supply contaminated to the point where, when a Denver news crew came out to report on the issue, the rancher simply lit the well on fire. There were enough fracking chemicals in the water to ignite its contents. Needless to say, the ranch was abandoned. And then there were the chemicals themselves. They were proprietary and as such not regulated by the EPA. That meant that not only the manufacturer of the mixture, but the driller of the well as well as the owner/operator didn't have to reveal the chemical content of the water and therefore couldn't be sued over environmental concerns. They got off Scot free. Colorado shrugged and the US Government blinked.

The lawsuits were thrown out.

Collateral damage.

Flyover Country.

So much for fracking and individual property rights. Between directional drilling and the injected fracking fluid and the entire ranching operation became non viable. Mining laws trumped water rights every time and once the fracking fluid was used, it'd simply be re-injected back into the ground where it'd percolate up once again.

Either way the land'd been ruined and ranching was useless.

I could think of another, similar word to "frack" and to my way of thinking, Colorado'd done that.

It'd "fracked" us all.

And it'd never be the same.

Despite Keota, Caleb's Creek and so many other places I'd grown to love, Colorado no longer felt like home. I'd seen too much and seemingly everything I cared for was either being destroyed or thrown away.

It felt like I was living at the end of an era.

The land was disappearing and it's history with it, vanishing forever under a sea of concrete, houses, extraction and abuse.

The things we throw away.

Out in Keota and around the Buttes the story was the same. Wind turbines were going in. Turbines with hundred and twenty foot blades that'd been designed to extract electricity from the constant easterly blowing wind. Designed to assuage the newly minted PC crowd in Boulder and Denver, who although they claimed to believe in green energy and despised the oil and gas expansion in their midst, were more than happy to kill off every raptor and migratory bird in sight of their poorly placed rotors. Rotors that chewed up everything they came in contact with. Birds, bats, small planes, no matter. The turbines would spit 'em out like so much detritus. A poorly sited turbine farm was deadly. Equally bad within it's own right and range as the oil and methane wells the Greenies professed to loathe.

If the conservatives and the fossil fuel industry they built were guilty of planetary crimes, then the liberal Greens in their zeal to electrify the world were equally so.

Paper or plastic? What's the difference if you can't simply make do with less.

When not building Wind Farms, those same Greenies'd build Solar Farms. Farms that'd be so big you couldn't see from one end to the other. Farms with roads where none'd been. Farms with generator plants and relay stations where none existed previously. Farms with megawatt transmission lines. And for what?

Mega mansions in Boulder and Windsor, Genesee and atop Lookout Mountain? Mega mansion owning, RV loving, perpetually vacationing, heated swimming pool in winter using, Suburban and Range Rover loving phonies.

Never mind the endangered Sage Grouse or Desert Tortoise.

Collateral damage.

Flyover Country.

There was never any viable conversation from either the right, or the left about addressing the over consumption and acquisitive nature that both possessed. Never any discussion about placing solar panels on top of homes and businesses. Never any talk about localized wind farms. And they were both guilty. Guilty of facilitating the irreplaceable destruction that was occurring around 'em.

Seems making do with less was never a part of the equation, but then neither was quantifiable logic.

It was enough to make a thinking person ill.

We lived in different worlds and what I cared for, they didn't.

I couldn't look at the Buttes, the Front Range, or for that matter the Western Slope without seeing what it'd been and what it was turning into. What'd been lost and what'd been thrown away. All the remembering in the world couldn't change it and when it was gone, it was gone. Only the fading memories of those who passed before could keep what was from vanishing completely.

The things we leave behind. The things we throw away. We never miss 'em till they're gone.

Progress. But who's and at what expense?

Keota and the Buttes were lost and now so much of the rest of Colorado was as well. If the land and what was on it suffered, so what. It was the same old story. These new settlers were a different breed. They hated what they found while at the same time claiming to love it. They destroyed everything they touched and were well into the process of turning everything into just another San Francisco or Dallas.

Another Bay Area nightmare. Another Texas delusion.

They destroyed everything in their path and hated most of it.

I drifted north.

At the Terry Bison Ranch, everything'd be different. If you looked toward Pine Bluffs there'd be bison on the range, even if they were farmed and came from Goodnight stock.

You could still look east and see what it musta looked like when ol' Beckwourth saw it outside of Carr. It fit.

The land between the North and South Platte was still relatively pristine, it's features mostly untrammeled by the Rocky Mountain invasion.

It contained distance, rolling hills, an endless sky and vistas as far as the eye could see. No houses, no oil pads, nothing but an occasional fence line.

Simply space.

Space to be what I'd come to realize I was. What I needed. The last of a vanishing breed. Someone who needed to feel the earth beneath their feet and see the clouds pass overhead, to feel the wind, sun and rain on their face. To jump fences and simply head off for points unknown. Someone who needed to dream the dreams of those who had gone before and walk in the ever present that unbound time allowed for.

A world without clocks,and probably always would be, if left alone.

Free to walk the land.

Vedauwoo was simply a logical extension.

I smiled when Caleb and I met again.

It felt like coming home.

We shared one mind, one soul, one spirit.

I'd forgotten how much I missed him.

Vedauwoo.

The "Land of the Earthborn Spirit".

To the newly arrived People of the Blue Sky it was as sacred as Noah-vose was to the Cheyenne and the Paha Sapa to the Lakota. Before their time the Clovis people had passed over and through the Sherman canyons that encompassed it on their way to camps in the Shirley Basin and Dent. The Folsom would make theirs along the southern edge at Lindenmier where they would hunt mammoth and camel. Within the meadows and Grandfather Stones of Curt Gowdy, Pole Mountain and Blair-Wallis the Dalton, Besant, Pelican Lake, Avonlea and McKean people would hunt bison, deer and elk, trap beaver in the high meadow ponds and possibly grow maize in the lower elevations. The influences of both Hopewell and Cahokia would travel up the rivers that flowed into the Mississippi and bring their lifeway and technology with them leaving their distinctive spade shaped projectile points everywhere. After the Hopewell, the Shoshone would arrive, dividing as they did so into the Comanche and eastern bands we know today. The Comanche in turn would migrate southward toward

Texas, driven out by the Cheyenne. Then came the Arapaho. Relative newcomers in the scheme of things. Apache and Dine' would emigrate through the area along the eastern front of the Rockies and possibly over South Pass north of Vedauwoo before turning southward and moving into New Mexico, Arizona and Southwestern Colorado. To the east, the Lakota would roam the plains as they always had.

South of Vedauwoo was the Cache La Poudre. To the north was the Platte. The Laramie bordered the west and buffalo country, the east. Multiple creeks and streams ran in between.

As such, it was the center of the universe for generation after generation of people who passed through, or lived within the aspen groves that spread out along the canyons and creeks within. For at least 9,000, and possibly as long as 13,000 years, one people or another had prayed, lived, camped, hunted, fished, harvested, and died within sight of Vedauwoo's hoodos. Possibly the oldest, continuously inhabited spot in all of North America and here we were, Caleb and I, standing at the center.

It was truly inspiring.

Standing at the center of the universe, Lindenmeier, Dent, Shirley Basin, Powars II and the newly discovered Mahaffy site in Boulder radiated out from Vedauwoo like the spokes of a medicine wheel and ranked as some of the oldest inhabited archaeological sites in North America. All were close to each other and all were within eyesight, more or less, of Vedauwoo. All were less than a hundred miles away, and all were a two to three day journey apart on foot. As such, the Land of the Earthborn Spirit had attracted man since the beginning of time; from when he first crossed over the Bering Straight during the last ice age in search of Mammoth to the present. Possibly even longer. Certainly since the last of the ice had retreated to Alberta.

The sense of place that emanated from every corner was overwhelming and Vedauwoo was at the center.

If place was defined by a person or people remembering and telling their stories as they did so, then Vedauwoo contained alot.

They were everywhere.

Take Grenville Dodge. Ol' Grenville passed through the area

in 1865 while scouting possible routes for the newly proposed Transcontinental Railroad and got into it with the Arapaho in Vedauwoo.

They kicked him out but by the end of the decade he'd be back.

Back to work for the Union Pacific as their Chief Engineer, where he'd run the rails up and over the Sherman Grade into the mountains. Run the rails all the way to Promontory Point where he'd have his picture taken shaking hands with his Central Pacific counterpart.

Between 1865 and 1868 the Union Pacific'd try to undo everything humankind from Clovis to the Arapaho had honored in Vedauwoo. They'd split the Great Plains buffalo herds in two as well as divide the Arapaho and Cheyenne into northern and southern bands. After the tracks were laid, hunters'd sit safely inside their Overtons and bang away at everything they could see and entire herds of buffalo and antelope would disappear. Pyramidal mounds, sometimes higher than a man could reach, would then appear along the UP right of way, outside Fort Sanders and around damn near every other military post and town along the way where the bones of hundreds, if not thousands, of bison and pronghorn would be stacked like so much cordwood to have their pictures taken.

It was a tragedy of epic proportions. Most of the meat'd be left to rot and even the once valuable hides'd become nothing more than homes for blowflies and fleas.

It was slaughter plane and simple, government sanctioned, commercially authorized and industrially executed. Sanctioned by the man who'd lend his name to the Vedauwoo granite. Authorized by the same commercial interests that'd within a few years bring a nation to its knees and cause an enabling presidency to damn near collapse and all while allowing every damn redneck from Omaha to Salt Lake to kill anything and everything they saw fit.

Sherman.

Durant.

Ames.

Some things never changed.

With the coming of the railroad, Fort DA Russell would be built near where Crow Creek entered Vedauwoo. Fort Laramie would go up where Fort John once was and be expanded. Fort Collins would be built in La Porte before being flooded out and moving to where it now sits and Fort Sanders would be built outside Laramie. Once completed, Vedauwoo and the Sherman hoodos'd be surrounded, and all for the Union Pacific and westward expansion.

Manifest destiny.

If the rocks could talk, no doubt they woulda said they felt like Atlanta. Sherman and his cohorts were on a roll.

Needless to say, even though the Arapaho kicked old Grenville Dodge out of the area in 1865, the People of the Blue Sky were kicked out themselves only a few years later. 1865-1868 weren't good years for the people.

By 1876, Custer's supply train'd pass through Fort Russell on its way to the Little Bighorn and in 1903 Teddy Roosevelt and Wyoming Senator Warren would camp on the land between Russell and Laramie. Vedauwoo'd become a part of the Warren Livestock Company, and Roosevelt, being the ever present "westerner" he thought himself to be, would head west for where the Virginian gunned Trampas down in Medicine Bow. Teddy couldn't wait to hook up with old Joe Le Fors and ride with him to Cheyenne. Couldn't wait to meet the man who captured Tom Horn and who'd hang him in Cheyenne.

1903. Coulda been yesterday.

Another era would come and go and the military, after changing the name of Fort Russell to Warren, would then use both Vedauwoo and Pole Mountain for "target and maneuver drills", obliterating as it did so part of the former senators ranch in the process. Never mind the hoodoos. They were simply targets.

Flyover Country.

In 1876, the Arapaho along with their Cheyenne and Lakota cousins would exact revenge on Custer while he was visiting Montana, wiping him out in the process.

By 1901 Roosevelt and Buffalo Bill would include prominent members of the Arapaho, Lakota and Cheyenne tribes in their publicity tours, photo ops and parades.

Custer made good publicity.

The Indians too for that matter, but only when being used as a sideshow act.

Eventually, like so many tin wind chimes cast eastward on the prevailing wind, the senator's ranch'd disappear and leave behind their "Warren Livestock. No Trespassing" signs to clatter in the breeze between the double strands, while in true Ed Abbey fashion, I'd ignore most of 'em and continue to "corner jump" where I felt like it. The military'd abandon their bombing range to the Cold War and rock climbers and the parks we know today'd be created.

Like the Arapaho at the Little Bighorn, Vedauwoo would abide. The Sherman Granite would continue to be lifted upward and everything else would simply erode away. Trees would still grow from the cracks and what wasn't upright would continue to tilt eastward.

The hoodos and spirits carved into the pinkish brown granite by the wind, rain, sleet and snow'd survive, continuing as they always had to rise from the earth, a bit more damaged, but mostly intact, and as always, guarded by the beaver, fox and deer.

The railroad town of Sherman would turn into a ghost and blow away leaving nothing behind but rusty square nails and divets and the Ames Monument would be built commemorating the two brothers who financed it's construction, only to be vandalized by a person or persons unknown at a later date. Handax peeled line shacks and cabins would go up throughout the area, only to collapse under their own weight with the passage of time and then, they too, like the bones of the bison herds before 'em, would have their pictures taken by tourists searching for the American West.

Crumbled and lost. Fading into the land that supported 'em.

An abandoned tin army canteen of Indian War vintage sat where it was dropped atop the Sherman loam, its chained cork stopper and US insulated white wool cover missing but otherwise intact.

A railroad spike which'd been removed from the UP right of way was left at what'd probably been an Arapaho campsite miles away from the tracks, its head mushroomed around the edges and one side cupped where it'd rubbed against the rail. Reminders of what'd come and gone.

"Standing at the center of the universe, the sky bends backward as if an inverted bowl had been placed over the land, over the hoodos and spirits of those who've gone before and forming as it does so a perfect dome, azure blue during the day and coal black at night when it'd become filled with a myriad of pinpricked light and swirling gauze. Occasionally a shooting star would track across the ark and Grandfather Sky would send his messengers to the people below. When walking at night, the starlight alone'd be enough to see where one was heading. On the nights when Sister Moon would appear, the hoodos'd speak and the animals would turn restless, wandering about in search of whatever it was they were looking for. When that happened the people would dance and celebrate within the aspen groves and around the hoodos, and strips of trade cloth would be hung from the branches of the trees and objects of value placed within the cracks of the Grandfather Stones or along their bases to remember those who'd gone before."

"In prehistoric times the hoodos woulda simply be prayed to and the voices therein remembered."

"Standing at the center of the universe one can see all that is, was, and will be. When at the center, one can look to the West and see the Medicine Bow and Snowies, the backbone of Mother Earth. Follow the backbone north and you can travel all the way to Canada. Follow it South, and you can walk all the way to Tierra del Fuego. Mankind did that, ya know. Look East, and you can see where the people came from, the land where the sun lives. If you're Arapaho or Cheyenne, you can see all the way to where you came from. To where you were born. Into your history. All the way to Minnesota and the western Great Lakes."

"Minnesota, when the People of the Blue Sky lived there they were farmers in the tradition of Cahokia and the Plains Woodland cultures of the Mississippi Valley and Ohio. They planted maize and would cross over the Missouri and Mississippi into the buffalo lands to hunt. Their trade routes extended from the

Rockies to Canada and down the rivers into Texas. They'd gather wild rice from the lakes and pick both blueberries and strawberries from the land about 'em. They'd trade red pipestem chert from their quarries back east for exotic goods such as dentallium shells and obsidian out west and they'd travel onto the plains to hunt, but that was before the Ojibwe came along and formed alliances with the Americans, French and English who in turn drove the people out. Same with the Cheyenne, Nakota and Dakota. Displaced. Two found homes with their cousins, while the others found new ones. Two called the Paha Sapa home, one Noah-vose, and the other Vedauwoo. All found a place where they could recount the stories of their people."

"All beings must find the center. All must walk in it. To do any less is to not exist. Without center, one is lost."

"Turning and turning in the widening
gyrre
The falcon cannot hear the falconer,
Things fall apart, the centre cannot
hold;
Mere anarchy is loosed upon the
world,
The blood-dimmed tide is loosed,
and everywhere
The ceremony of innocence is
drowned;
The best lack all conviction, while the
worst
Are full of passionate intensity."

As Caleb spoke I couldn't help but thinking of William Butler Yeats and "The Second Coming." Although he'd written it in the aftermath of World War I, he seemed to have been thinking about the People of the Blue Sky, Vedauwoo and the place where Caleb and I were standing when he wrote it. Some thoughts and feelings were universal, unbound by the constraints of time and space.

"Seems the Lakota were right, Mitakuye Oyasin. We are all

related. Seems Mr Yeats musta been indigenous."

Maybe so, but then everything that existed was related, even if others never seemed to get it. They'd destroy everything they touched and they'd take pleasure in doing it.

Needless to say, Yeats was right, "The best lack all conviction, while the worst are full of passionate intensity."

And so the newly minted Greens would continue to build their mega mansions within sight of Vedauwoo and all that encompassed it while those on the other side of the political spectrum would either dig it up, blow it up or contaminate it so badly that nobody wanted it.

In the meantime, Caleb and I would walk at the center.

Vedauwoo was indeed sacred space. Even the rock climbers seemed to feel it. Most climbed 'em free hand without the use of pitons and stays and damn near everyone followed the cracks and crevices within. Whether they knew it or not, by doing so they could not only feel the Sherman Granite they were ascending with their fingers and toes, but be guided by that which existed within the granite itself. The spirit of the stone. Needless to say, most followed its path.

Almost nobody left any form of garbage. It was the cleanest place I'd ever seen. Again, those who visited Vedauwoo seemed to understand instinctively that one doesn't despoil a cathedral.

They'd been given sanctuary from the forces around 'em and they respected it.

After watching several freehanders ascend the Nautilus, Caleb and I wandered in and out of the hoodos for the rest of the day after which I continued to do so over the next five years, spending almost all of my free time there.

I never saw it all.

After running into Caleb at Vedauwoo, he'd leave once again, although this time, instead of going away for weeks or months, he'd do so for years.

He never said where he was going.

The Language We Learn

"If a tree falls in the forest and nobody's there to hear it, does it make a sound?"

Although I probably heard it in college, it mighta been the sixties. Possibly in a comparative religion class. Been quite a while ago. The mind forgets things after a while.

"If place is defined by people talking about and remembering it, then more likely than not, those stories and remembrances are formed by language."

"People define place, but language defines people. Without one, you can't have the other. As such, the sound of a falling tree, whether making a sound, or not, is "heard" differently by each person reporting what it sounded like. One may imagine it. Another may actually hear it. Likewise, one may report it as sounding like one thing, whereas someone else may hear it differently. It's not simply science or a psychology experiment, or even religion for that matter. It's how one hears, interprets and responds to the world around 'em. To understand what it sounds like to one person, ya gotta stand where they did and in the same context, and ya gotta listen within the same parameters as the original person did. Ya gotta "walk in their shoes" so to speak. Same with sight, taste and touch. We all experience 'em differently and respond accordingly. It's more than nature vs nurture, ya know. Again, ya gotta look at things the way the first person who saw it did. Ya gotta use their frame of reference. Most people can't do that, they just talk past each other and form their responses before the speaker's even finished. Ya gotta process the information using the same world view as well, use the language the event was based on. It's all about how we see things. How we process that experience and how we make sense of it. But it never works. Time changes everything, language included and knowledge changes both. So does technology for that matter. And so we cross talk, talk past each other and never understand what the other one's talking about anyway."

"Ya gotta really listen to hear that. Takes practice. You're not born with it, ya know, but you're beginning to get it."

"To listen, truly listen. Without bias or prejudice or predetermined answers based on half heard information is tough. As said, ya gotta walk in the shoes of the person you're listening to. Ya gotta stand where they did and think in the same manner, but you're learning to do that too. The land's been teaching it to you, but now, like in that other movie Costner made, ya gotta "go the distance". Ya gotta connect the dots, build your own "Field of Dreams" and complete the crossing over you've already begun.

"It's all about subjective vs objective language, ya know. One is pre-industrial and circular in logic and is based on context as well as everything else that's experiential in what's being talked about. As such, it doesn't require a lot of words because what words're spoken speak of many things simultaneously, not simply the object, place or thing at hand. The other is an industrial creation. A creation that requires ever more words to describe what's being talked about because it does so in a linear fashion. A is B, followed by C and D. One requires contemplation and oratory. The other avoids not only those practices, but tends to cut to the chase, but that in turn requires even more words to describe what's being talked about because it only speaks to one level of sensory input. With one ya participate in the language through imagery as well as the other senses, whereas, the other, it's simply words. They're no experiences. No sight, sound, sense or smell. It doesn't require imagination. Ya can't touch 'em. Sometimes it seems that those who created it did so simply to hear themselves talk. Or maybe to move on to other things to talk about. No imagination needed. No personal knowledge or experience."

"Take the word Vedauwoo. You already know that to the Arapaho it meant "Place of the Earthborn Spirit". That says a lot with one word. It allows the listener as well as the speaker to visualize through their own knowledge that which was said. Each person understands the other, but interprets the meaning differently. As such, language becomes a personal experience. We all get it, but we get it differently. It's common, but it's also singular. Takes practice to communicate that way. In your language, Vedauwoo is simply a place, a turnoff on the highway. It means little. No experience needed. It doesn't even exist. It simply is."

"it's no wonder we cross talk. We never really hear what's bein' said."

"Take Lao Tzu. Said "The way to do is to be.""

"Ya wanna understand the people, their stories and the land? Ya gotta be one with 'em and walk in their way, in their time, and on their terms. Same with the other side."

"Walking in two worlds has never been easy, and most fail. Hopefully you can straddle that river and cross that bridge without getting wet. It's tough."

"Take Tatanka, Wakan Tanka and Wicasa Wakan. In your language they simply mean buffalo, Great Spirit or Great Mystery and Man of Mystery or Medicine Man but to the Lakota they embody all that which makes each the supreme manifestation of what's being said. A buffalo isn't merely a buffalo, but a creature which is the ultimate manifestation of all things that define, "buffaloness"— size, shape, everything. Tatanka is all that makes a buffalo a buffalo in the best manner possible. To the anglo, it's merely a word, a thing. Same with Wakan Tanka. Wakan Tanka to the Lakota is not merely the Great Mystery or Spirit, but rather that which contains all that encompasses that same spirit or mystery. As such, Wakan Tanka is everything that exists in it's perfect form and is holy. With Wicasa Wakan, it's a man who carries with him all the knowledge that Wakan allows for and as such is more than simply a "medicine man," but rather a holy man versed in the knowledge that mere mortals cannot understand, fathom or use. They're not merely words, but entire belief systems. It's up to the speaker as well as the listener to visualize what they believe."

"The Lakota, like their pre-industrial counterparts worldwide understood something you've forgotten in places like Denver and San Francisco where technology reigns supreme. It doesn't take a lot to say plenty. Look at what we just covered. In Lakota we said a mouthful with less than four words. In your language, It took an entire paragraph to say the same thing."

"Subjective vs Objective language."

"You're walking through places that not only have stories to tell, but are doing so with the language the people who told them understood, not the one you were born with. We should all do the same. We might understand things better."

As before, all I could think of was Seattle's speech and wonder why nobody listened. Why we seemingly could never hear what was being said.

In Seattle's world, quite a few trees had fallen and he knew every one. He remembered.

I wondered if we would.

POLE VAULTING THE PERIMETER

Corner jumping, the act of diagonally crossing from one parcel of public land to another where they intersect with an equal number of private parcels at the point where they come together to form an X was considered illegal by the state of Wyoming unless the person or persons doing so were using the public portion to hunt or fish on. Anyone else was considered as trespassing on private property and as such, subject to prosecution. The Federal Government, via the BLM, took that a step further by declaring that corner jumping between Bureau of Land Management holdings, aka public land, and private parcels in the same manner was guilty of trespassing on private property, no matter the reason. Therefore, given that the majority of public lands in Wyoming were managed by the BLM, a person could be shut out from the use of that land and in turn their right to access it under the term "public" for any reason whatsoever, or none at all. Private property rights trumped public property rights even with regard to the usage of the latter in Wyoming and indeed much of the west despite the former receiving disproportional advantage. As such it'd become a flash point across the American West from the Rockies to the Sierra with no resolution in sight, particularly in states like Nevada where the Federal Government owned most of it. And it'd play out over not just hunting and fishing access, but over public rights of access on hundred year old two tracks that crossed modern era private holdings as well as mineral rights on private land and grazing fees on public. It'd become a war, a "Sagebrush Rebellion." A rebellion that'd cost a BLM employee his arm in Nevada when he opened a mail bomb in Carson City and a rebellion that'd incite an anti government standoff outside Vegas. A stand off that shoulda never happened. One that happened because someone refused to pay their fees for grazing cattle on public land. And all because someone thought the land was theirs and theirs alone.

Later, some of those same idiots would end up in eastern Oregon and seize a Federal Wildlife Sanctuary outside Burns where they'd dig latrines into what'd been archaic Paiute campsites, disturb the archeological record and destroy what'd been considered sacred in the process. And all because yet another anti government rancher refused to pay damages to the Federal Government for range fires they set on public land.

Yep, another standoff occurred and those who created the problem in the first place were simply given a day pass. Unfortunately, unlike in Nevada, someone got killed. And all because public meant private by right of prior acquisition, use and manifest destiny.

Never mind the Paiute who were there first. They could have the Paisley Caves. Maybe Harney Lake.

Maybe someplace in Flyover Country.

Public land was meant for private use and screw the rest.

The public didn't know what to do with it anyway.

To those who supported these theories of land usage, access and public rights, the term land only applied to them and what they in turn wanted to use it for. Public wasn't public and nothing should be owned by and/or regulated by the government. In short, be they individuals or otherwise, those who supported such interpretations simply wanted the land for themselves. As such, land usage could be manipulated to the advantage of those who felt entitled to it whether legally or by force. Needless to say, more than a few weren't above resorting to gun play and/or using the US government and military to advance their cause when it suited their purpose. Unfortunately for Wyoming as well as Vedauwoo and throughout the west in general, the impact would be disproportionate.

In Wyoming, the self proclaimed "Equality State," equality and land usage were fungible realities, each independent of the other depending on the era and/or context. Never mind that the basic premise seemed to be the same in every case no matter the point in history. In almost every instance, the players would remain the same, sometimes even coming from the same families.

During the mid to late eighteen hundreds the railroads and cattle barons were kings of what was then considered public in Wyoming. Where the former had used "right of way" laws in order to promote public projects by seizing huge and virtually unnecessary tracts to create towns on or sell to unwitting settlers, often for spurious farming and unsustainable ranching use, the later'd continue to graze the "open range" free of charge. In doing so, the railroads, their investors, and those in congress who backed 'em'd reap huge profits, cause the stock market to crash and come damn near to bringing down a presidency. In the case of the the cattle barons, they'd continue to use the "open range" as they'd always done, create yet another class of millionaires, some of whom didn't even reside in the good ol' USA, and each'd do so with little or no cost to themselves. In the end both would control the land and the benefits associated therein for free.

As with Owen Wister's The Virginian, barbed wire and fencing were anathema to the open range, whereas to the railroads, they were a boon. No fence, no farm, no small ranch, no city lot. The stage for conflict was set, promoted by divergent self serving interests and an often witless, if not corrupt government.

When the railroads and federal government opened the former Indian lands to settlement and homesteading, the non ranchers swarmed in. Never mind that most of the newcomers immigrated from Germany and Scandinavia, where for a possibly worthless 160 acres and a mule, they'd settle, throw up a soddy, fence off their parcel and then attempt to grow winter wheat, sugar beets or corn while running a few head of cattle or a small herd of sheep in between, but they'd do so without understanding the language or the dynamics that'd been in play before their arrival. In short, they'd upset the status quo and threaten the livelihoods of those who'd benefited from the free ride mentality that'd been in place.

The cattle barons'd lose their land and their right to graze freely wherever they chose and the railroads'd overextend their credit at the government's expense. In the end the range'd be fenced off no matter what and the so called English lords and

Eastern conglomerates who'd previously considered everything theirs by right of prior appropriation, would become infuriated.

Cattle would be reported as having been stolen by the new-comers and "long ropes" would supposedly be thrown, whereupon Stock Detectives would be hired and "wars" would be declared. Associations would pop up overnight and sodbusters'd either be lynched or killed. Gunfighters would be brought into Johnson County from Texas and Stock Detectives would be hired to police Sweetwater. Whether any of the sodbusters actually threw "a long rope" or not, homesteads would be burned and entire sheep herds would be slaughtered as had happened near Tie Siding. Afterwards crops'd be destroyed and cattle'd be reappropriat-ed, and all because the newcomers were on land the associations wanted for themselves. On land that'd been legally homesteaded. Before it was over those same associations would call in the US Cavalry in Johnson County to rescue their Texas gunslingers from annihilation by the County Sheriff and more than a few pissed off Swedish, German and Russian immigrants and save 'em from the very problem they'd created for themselves. And all because those same barons had unduly benefited from the government's largess to begin with and were wealthy and politically connected. Never mind that it was the same government who'd issued the Swedes and Germans their homesteads. Never mind that it was public land they were located on.

And all because of fencing and public vs private property rights.

When it was all said and done, it'd be the cattle barons who'd throw up the wire. If they couldn't keep the range open, then they'd lock everyone else out. Corner jumping and trespass-ing laws'd be enacted and bent in their favor and public land'd either be surrounded by what was now private or the public'd simply be locked out by property lines and sometimes illegally placed fences that were put up on public land. No matter the case, the cattle where free to graze where they had and all while legal-ly keeping any newcomers out. In coming years the oil, gas and mining industries would employ the same tactics. After that it'd be the trust fund millionaires, hedge fund managers and Holly-wood celebrities who'd move into the neighborhood and repeat the process. Yep, you could throw up a mini mansion, develop a trophy ranch or simply create your own private retreat by simply surrounding, encompassing, or blocking access to public land.

From the Bitterroot and Gallatin Valleys, to the Roaring Fork and Frying Pan the upshot was the same. No commoners allowed.

Before being murdered by the cattle barons in Johnson County, Nate Champion wrote, "Well, they have got through shelling the house like hail. I heard them splitting wood. I guess they think to fire the house tonight. I think I will make a break when night comes, if alive. Shooting again. It's not night yet. The house is all fired. Goodbye, boys, if I ever see you again."

And so the open range and what was once public land would disappear. Nate Champion would join Jim Averel and Ella Watson in heaven, if there was one, and Hollywood'd have a field day concocting an entirely different story than the one that occurred. In an age of immediate gratification we'd sit in front of our television sets and believe the later, while all the while failing to understand the former.

In the end, the very same interests that'd driven the millionaires in Wyoming and the Sagebrush rebels in Nevada to alternately either fence in or out what they felt entitled to had created a situation wherein the public would be left out of the conversation no matter what and what was theirs to begin with would be gone.

Charity Valley out in the Sierra would have it's BLM trailhead blocked and a trophy ranch'd go up in the meadow where the trail began its journey along a small creek that ran between there and Grover's Hot Springs and in the process part of what'd been the old Carson Fremont Trail'd be lost. Lost to public access. Gone with the wind. I never knew what happened, but I'd heard there'd been a land swap between the new owner and the Feds. Probably swapped for land in Flyover Country. Land nobody cared for.

Land nobody remembered.

Unfortunately, I did. I'd hiked it. Hiked it before some special interest or another took it away. Saw the trout. Skirted the granite. Saw the grinding rocks. Yeah, I'd even hiked up to the old petrified forest on the ridgeline.

I remembered.

Fences served a purpose, but they could also be obstacles. Sometimes man created both simultaneously, sometimes not. Sometimes he switched roles. Seldom did he think of the unintended consequences of his actions. Sometimes what he created did more harm than good. Sometimes he was just plain mean and selfish. Sometimes I simply wanted to get away from it all.

Due to the checkerboard nature of the land around Vedauwoo I'd continue to corner jump. After all, I was a part of what was public, and where both public and private interests met at a fixed point wherein neither held dominance, I felt I was at least as worthy as the other in sharing what was on the public side. To me, those who held property rights on the private were no more, or less, entitled than I was to share in the same. After all, we were in the "Equality State" and there were no longer any cattle barons.

Public was public and private was private. I respected both and I felt they should as well. If the private land owners didn't want the public touching their land at the smallest conceivable point possible in the least destructive manner known, then they should grant an easement. After all, why should they be allowed access to what was public when I was denied it?

Weren't we both the same under the law? Why should they be afforded greater rights to the land than I was? The days of the cattle baron were over and the 1872 mining law was obsolete.

Somewhere Ed Abbey was laughing.

We all needed to respect the rights of the other.

Corner jumping. If you touched it or crossed over it you were trespassing. If you didn't, you weren't. Guess you could always parachute in. Maybe bungee jump. Maybe fly in by helicopter. It was a point I'd argue with the Albany County Sheriff more than once. In the meantime, I'd continue to corner jump, or maybe, if all else failed, pole vault the perimeter.

In
Medias Res

I didn't know about Caleb back in 59. In point of fact, I didn't know much about anything at that point in my life, so he could've been right next to me for all I knew, but if he was, I didn't see him.

1959. Eisenhower's America. Smack dab in the middle of the post World War II expansion that saw Levittown sprawling like a cancer across a land flush with GI bills and low interest Fannie Mae loans. The returning Gobs and Swabs were procreating furiously and children filled every neighborhood with their din and commotion.

Eleven hundred square foot homes were the new American dream wherein you could raise a family of four in a two bedroom house with a detached garage, attached if you were lucky, cram the kids into bunk beds and then lull them to sleep over a three network, six channel black and white television set that they'd sit in front of for hours on end while watching the Mickey Mouse Club, Rin Tin Tin and every western known to man. By midnight the networks'd go off the air, but America'd be put to sleep long before that anyway so the drone of a featureless Indian head would mean little to anyone save an Indian.

1959. Nobody owned more than one car unless they had money to burn, and when not being driven by dad to work, it'd be traded with mom for shopping, errands or whatever else was needed. On the weekend, it'd be washed and simonized come rain or shine. The routine never varied. The kids'd either walk or ride their bikes to school as well as everywhere else and if you lived in the country, it'd be a long walk to and from the bus stop, followed by an even longer bus ride to town. Going to school was little different than ranch or farm work in those days, you still got up by four and were out the door before sunup, the only difference being that when you were in school you didn't have to do your chores all day long and you could see your friends. The chores could wait until you got home, or if not, you simply got up earlier in order to do 'em. There was no such thing as helicopter parenting and everybody pulled their own weight, even the kids.

Needless to say, it was a more self-sufficient era.

Add to that one dial up telephone on a party line where anybody could hear about what you had for dinner and who was screwing who, one television set and one Hi Fi record player if you were lucky, simply an AM radio if you weren't, and voila, you had what passed for life in a middle class neighborhood. If one were truly living the high life, you might even have a console with the AM radio and Hi Fi included with the television. It was an entire piece of furniture unto itself and more often than not, was the centerpiece in each home. As such, it was the entertainment center du jour. Living rooms were off limits to kids, pets and family unless accompanied by an adult and were only used to entertain guests over martinis and gossip. There was no FM radio and stereo had yet to be invented. Cable, WIFI, the internet and satellite anything other than Sputnik were pure science fiction. Only dad was allowed to touch the dials on anything having to do with it, while in many a household, it was a right of passage out of childhood when a son was allowed to do the same. Never mind the daughter, she had her Easy Bake Oven and hair rollers to play with.

If the later didn't work, she could always use an empty toilet paper roll or two. A lot did.

To many, the nineteen fifties were a dream time in America. To others, the story was much less so.

That being said, the story for my family was not unlike that of so many others no matter their circumstances or economic situation.

The American interstate highway system was in its infancy and what'd once simply been routes across America were now highways, with Highway 80 being the primary one. Yep, you could jump on 80 in New Jersey and within a few days you could be in San Francisco. Route 66 would become the stuff of legend and an entire generation would leave the East Coast, upper Great Lakes and Midwest for the land of opportunity; California. The place where anything was possible. Where the streets were paved with gold and the weather was mild. All of life was a Hollywood script and "Father" really did know "best". Never mind mother, her vote didn't count. Like Donna Reed, she was meant to be window dressing.

As such San Francisco and Los Angeles became beacons for every ex soldier and sailor who sailed from Long Beach and Alameda for the pacific during World War II, swearing as they did so, that like McArthur, they'd return, maybe not to Manila, but to the West Coast when their hitches were up. No more New York winters for them. No more Detroit hard freezes and lake effect Cleveland snows.

No more corn fields and cows.

No more Flyover Country.

They were getting out. It'd all be milk and honey from now on.

As such, Highway 80 was a dream come true for the new pioneers where it alternately followed the Oregon and Mormon Trails and the Union and Central Pacific rails.

A railway, that if you looked at a map from when it was platted revealed two things, the entire country from west of Omaha to the Sierra was either publicly held or government owned, and where it wasn't, the railroad owned the rest. Yep, the entire route stood out as a solid line running through nothing as it made its way across the plains where an entire region, fifty miles wide in some places, had been set aside for personal profit. Personal profit that'd include damn near every city from Omaha to Reno. Cities that paid fealty to those who extracted benefit from the land and it's people or the government owned; Crocker, Huntington, Stanford and Credit Mobilier to name but a few.

Cities who sent their profits to Nob Hill and Palo Alto.

And so it was, that flush with their newly acquired GI Bills and low interest Fannie Mae's in hand, the Greatest Generation headed westward. West into a state that hadn't seen an invasion like the one taking place since the Oakies invaded Bakersfield during the Dust Bowl.

Cities popped up overnight, schools were added on a daily basis and the Santa Clara Valley which'd previously been known as the Valley Of The Hearts Delight would disappear. Destroyed by IBM, Fairchild and Silicon Valley. Where the survivors of the Donner Party planted peaches, plums, cherries and apricots, tomatoes, garlic and onions, concrete, asphalt and crappy air would come to rule.

In short order, an entire way of life'd be gone.

In San Diego as well as over in the San Fernando Valley it was the same story; sprawl was eradicating everything in its path. Overnight the citrus and avocado groves disappeared and were replaced by row after row, block after block, street after street, of houses that looked exactly the same as the one next door except where the builders could reverse the floor plan. Entire neighborhoods as well as cities were being created in pop up fashion. Sherman Oaks was just another Levittown. A treeless expanse of tract homes, television sets, highways and cars.

Demographers would give it a new name. Suburbia.

Crackerbox dreams.

Where I'd once been able to walk to and from school with my Cowboy Bob hat and fill it with cherries, apricots and plums, Eichlers'd go up.

There wouldn't be any more apricot cobblers or cherry pies. No more braceros. No more mustard flowers and sourgrass shoots to suck on.

No more barns, fruit crates and packing houses.

Eichlers.

They were supposed to be state of the art, architecturally designed suburban homes which were built boxlike around a central atrium. Homes where every room'd either look out on, or into, a traditional backyard or courtyard, sometimes both. Floor to ceiling glass'd be everywhere and the roof'd be flat and pebbled. No shakes. No tiles.

They were supposed to be the latest in homeowner fashion.

Frank Lloyd Wright for the late nineteen fifties working man.

Talisien they weren't.

A new found American dream, they were.

Mass produced status.

In the fall when the packing plants and canneries were busy, the entire valley'd smell like a bowl of spaghetti filled with tomatoes and garlic. In the spring it'd smell like stewed plumbs, prunes and drying cots, but by the time the Eichlers moved in, the Valley of the Hearts Delight'd smell like toasted almonds (cyanide), and the once blue skies'd turn yellow brown and smell of photochemical waste and smog. Where once you could see the Santa Cruz mountains, nothing would be visible over a mile or two away and the San Francisco Bay, once clearly visible from Alviso, would disappear.

Gone like the rest.

Never mind the loss. We had semiconductors.

It was a new world.

Where the braceros once worked and tossed an ample supply of excess fruit into my cowboy hat, the land'd grow silicon foundries and defense plants and the country too, would change.

Tube radios and television sets would make way for transistors and ever smaller solid state components and nuclear depth charge carrying P-3 Orion's would fly in and out of Moffett Field to wing their way out over the Pacific where they'd track invisible Soviet subs. After all, it was 1959 and we were at war. Russians were everywhere and Cuba'd already fallen to the commies. Christ, Florida could be next! Maybe Guatemala. Maybe Honduras. Maybe even Ecuador!

For all of it's 1950's naivete, the Eisenhower era was a time of air raid sirens and fallout shelters. Shelters that were supposed to protect you if the Ruskies decided to drop a bomb. Air raid sirens were everywhere; atop telephone poles, alongside offices and even in the middle of damn near every downtown park in every podunk town in the middle of nowhere.

They were ubiquitous. As ubiquitous as a grain silo in Kansas or a water tower in Keota.

And then there was duck and cover.

Duck and cover drills'd be held regularly in school. Just like reading and math, they were a required subject.

Duck and cover.

Crawl under your desk when you hear the siren, then place your head between your knees. After that, cover everything else with your arms. If you're outside, forget the desk. Simply fall to the ground and pray.

Somehow that was supposed to save you from a nuclear attack.

"But what if you're at home, or shopping?"

Well, Johnny Cheesecake, if that's the case, you're vaporized.

Although it was never tested, Kennedy and Khrushchev'd try.

By the Johnson era they'd be all but gone, but the joke wouldn't.

In case of war, bend over and kiss your ass goodbye.

Welcome to sunny Vietnam. Enjoy your vacation.

But back to 59.

1959.

Tube testing stations were everywhere. Inside grocery stores, hardware stores, drug stores and gas stations. Even car dealerships had 'em. Sometimes they'd be next to the checkout counters, but more often than not, they'd be next to the door. Every one had a myriad of tube sockets on top, some big, some small. Some with a few pin holes. Some with a lot, and all with enough cubby holes underneath to put the tubes into that you could sink a ship. Yep, they were ubiquitous. As ubiquitous as the hardware man, the grocer, the car repair man and the television repairman. It was always fun to go in and try to figure out what you had and where it'd fit, especially when the damn numbers always seemed to be worn off anyway. Blew up more than a few. Always felt disappointed when the supposedly bad ones lit up. Meant ya hadda go home and do it all over again. Meant something else was wrong with the TV. Meant there'd be no Gunsmoke tonight.

1959.

And the times were a changin'.

Eisenhower'd be gone soon and with him the grocer, the milkman, the lunch counter attendant and the television repairman. Gone the way of the vacuum tube. Replaced by the supermarket, discount store and transistor.

Replaced by technology and a disenfranchised throw away culture.

There wouldn't be any more milk bottles with paper stoppers in 'em. No more empty bottles to be put outside in the morning and ice cream'd come frozen in the frozen food aisle.

There wasn't any WalMart in 1959, but its time had surely been foreseen.

Eisenhower would make way for Kennedy, black and white TVs would become Living Color, and Levittown family rooms would glow in the luminescence of the cathode ray tube where if you wanted you could watch Bonanza on Sunday night or hear about yet another war in southeast asia from Walter Cronkite and Huntley-Brinkley damn near every other night.

Never mind that those watching it had lived through Korea and World War II. Wars never changed. Seems we were always in one.

Pass the popcorn, please. Gotta see what life's like in the Mekong.

1959.

The Valley Of The Hearts Delight was gone.

As I recall it now, with the exception of the Russian, and soon to be Cuban menace, the times were simpler and less complex, but then hindsight is always "20-20" as they say and there's no complexity to a four year old anyway. All of life is an adventure. Nevermind the changes taking place around you. They were trivial, if they registered at all. Each day was a new experience, and mine was no different.

After loading the 1956 Mercury Monterey with everything that could be crammed into it, my father, like so many others before him, headed west. It was time to leave Cleveland behind. Time to follow the Lincoln Highway. Time to begin a new life and find a better place in which to do so.

He'd never return.

It was the American way.

Manifest Destiny.

1957.

By 1958, we'd settle in Watsonville and live south of town on a small hill called Loma Linda, or "beautiful hill" in Spanish.

Beyond being a world unto itself, it was unique in other ways as well; it had more kids than adults and it had more boys than girls. So much so, that an outsider woulda been hard pressed to find one. Seemingly every household was nothing but boys. Boys, dogs and their parents. Dad went to work and Mom stayed home, or when not, she'd simply run back and forth from one house to another, gossip, clean, do laundry or cook and all while the kids and dogs were left alone.

Left alone to roam.

None of the kids were out of high school and most were, like myself, too young to go to school no matter the grade.

Across the street were Butch Walden and his sister, the only girl on the hill aside from mine. He was in high school and could drive, but seldom seemed to.

On the end were the Opdyke's. Three pre school boys, equally spaced.

Down the street the other way were the Yamamoto's. All boys. Ben was in high school and could drive, but the rest were all closer to my age, pre school or slightly older. I no longer remember how many there were, but they were all spaced less than a year or so apart. Ben was significantly older. Years later I'd learn that Ben, like his parents, had been held in Manzanar during the war. Ben was born before and the rest after. They never talked about it. The younger ones were always happy. Ben was sullen and seldom smiled. It seemed the war weighed on him.

Despite the age difference we all spent most of our free time together, albeit, for Ben and Butch, it may have been a bit more grudgingly than not.

It was as if Harper Lee'd written To Kill A Mockingbird about Loma Linda, what we did and how we lived. There weren't any Boo Radley's or Ewell's in the neighborhood, nor a Scout for that matter, but in almost every other way, we were just like

Jem and Dill. We certainly behaved like 'em. The Yamamoto's at times were no different than Tom Robinson and my father acted just like Atticus Finch, or at least the Gregory Peck version of him more often than not. He hated guns, would read incessantly, and when not doing so he'd tip his glasses on top of his head and ahem the world.

Loma Linda.

It was a self made, blue collar success story, but then, that too was the fifties. Most of America would remain that way for the next twenty years or so until technology rendered even that an anachronism.

Ike Yamamoto was a Foreman for Bud Antle. Mr Walden, I never knew his first name, was a Yard Supervisor for the South-ern Pacific. Mr Opdyke, I never knew his first name either, was an architect, but he seemed to be out of place and tended to stick to himself, and my father was Vice Principal at Watsonville High. Something Butch and Ben were more than a bit conscious of. All of the other fathers seemed to come and go as workers usual-ly do, early to bed and early to rise. You seldom saw 'em except when they were either washing their cars or mowing their lawns and that was only on the weekend. In between they simply went to work. A forty hour week was an anomaly in those days. Most worked longer. Anything less, was unheard of.

Men in "Grey Flannel Suit(s)".

The women were straight out of My Little Margie.

The boys straight out of To Kill A Mockingbird.

All of our free time was spent outside where we could dis-appear at the drop of a hat and scatter en masse to wherever the moment beckoned.

"Different ways for different days."

Musta thought that up on Loma Linda.

We were everywhere and nowhere. Like the members of the Hole In The Wall Gang, the neighbors'd report that we were south of the hill, north of the hill, nowhere on the hill, or had simply vanished altogether. More often than not, simultaneously. We simply disappeared. As with the Hole In The Wall Gang, where Butch'd lead, the others would follow. We were just like baby quail. Butch's own little covey and we'd toddle along or run after him whenever and wherever we could. It didn't matter whether or not we could keep up with him. As long as we could see him, we'd try to, even if it meant our legs had to run twice as fast and work twice as hard as his. After all, he was our leader and we were his gang.

Caleb would always laugh at that. The idea of hiding in plain sight and being simultaneously invisible always seemed to amuse him. No doubt because he was so good at doing both.

As said, I didn't know about Caleb in 1959, but it seemed he was already there.

Hiding in plain sight.

Network TV was in its infancy then, but it'd already learned to be responsive to the era and the culture du jour. As such, most of the programming was family oriented or child centric. Where it wasn't, more often than not a child or two were thrown in to keep the kids happy. This was especially true with the ever present western.

The Lone Ranger, Rin Tin Tin, My Friend Flicka, Fury and The Adventures of Champion. Rawhide, Davey Crockett, Wagon Train and the Rifleman. Those were our role models. They were a boy's dream and many had characters who were our age, or close to it, and all were filmed outside where the TV boys were doing more or less what we were already doing, or dreamed of. It seemed like every boy on the hill wanted to either be a cowboy or wear a coonskin cap. In the end we had to settle for having the run of the hill and whatever lay beyond that we could reach. In between, there'd still be barbed wire fences to cross and cattle or horses to chase even if we didn't rope or ride 'em. Our bikes and trikes were our horses and we'd either ride 'em or drag 'em everywhere, even over, under, and in between the barbed wire.

We were the kings of our hill and ours was still a world where we could climb a tree, eat strawberries fresh from the vine or chase after cattle if we wanted to. We were little different than our heroes, but then we were little different from Jem or Dill for that matter; we explored what we wanted to and reveled in the experience.

Our parents were little different. Those who came home from Korea, or from the war in the Pacific would sit around their television sets night after night and watch Adventures In Paradise while dreaming of sailing the South Pacific with Adam Troy and Chris Parker. They'd go to the movies and watch Mitzi Gaynor and Rossano Brazzi sing about Bali Hai and listen to Arthur Lyman and Martin Denny on the radio. Quiet Village could be heard from every Hi Fi on the hill. They'd become fascinated with all things Michener and his Tales of the South Pacific'd be on every book shelf after which they'd dream of sailing to Tahiti with Thor Heyerdahl on the Kon Tiki or across the Atlantic on the Mayflower II. Ever westward. After all, ours was a society of dreamers and adventurers who after every war since Plymouth would set their sites on moving in a westerly direction once it was over. Westward where they'd find a better, cleaner land free from the corruption and disintegration of the old. I suppose it was in our genes. Part of our Euro-American heritage. After all, more than a few immigrants had already done the same. Unfortunately for my parents generation as well as those who'd made it to the west coast before 'em, once they went as far as they could, they stopped. They couldn't sail over the ocean, so dreaming of the Pacific and what lay beyond'd have to do.

They settled for the dream.

If you couldn't move any farther west when the urge to wander took hold, then it was time to look inward. Maybe there you'd find that mythical land of milk and honey, that better place, that special paradise. After all, ours was a nation of wanderers. It was in our genes.

We were always looking.

For the moment though, our hill was enough. Our parents could continue to dream of Bali Hai and sailing aboard the Kon Tiki. We had closer worlds to explore.

Keeping up with Butch was never easy, He was tall for his age, or so it seemed to me, and his legs were long. Mine were those of a typical four year old, short and stubby, but that didn't matter. I'd chase after him everywhere. If not by myself, then with the entire hill in tow.

I remember one time when he thought it'd be fun to chase the cows on the other side of the Aromas fence. Maybe throw a rock or two at a few. He had no fear, but then there were no bulls and they were dairy cattle anyway so there was little chance they'd turn and chase us. Either way, I was considered too small for doing what he intended and was told to stay home. Needless to say, I didn't. Butch jumped the wire, those older than me, but younger than Butch, squeezed between the strands and I crawled underneath. Once that happened, it was a scene straight out of To Kill A Mockingbird. After chasing the cows, tripping in and out of every gopher hole known to man and getting generally dirty, which was every boys dream in those days, we turned for home and headed for the wire. Butch once again jumped it. The middle-sized boys squeezed between the strands and I crawled under, or at least that was my intent. Needless to say, the backside of my overalls got caught on one of the barbs and I couldn't wiggle loose. Just like Jem, I simply took 'em off and ran the rest of the way home in my shorts. The boys thought it was funny. My mom, less so. I'd ruined a perfectly good pair of overalls. After that it'd be Lee Riders, but always at least two to three sizes too big. I could grow into 'em even if the cuffs were rolled to my knees. My parents remembered the Depression and nothing was wasted. Unfortunately, they underestimated the power of a fence circumventing four year old. I simply wore holes in the knees or cuff seams and the entire concept of frugality was useless.

On another occasion I thought it'd be fun to meet my father on his way home from work rather than wait for him to get home, pour a martini, and sit in front of the television and watch Walter Cronkite while pretending I wasn't there so I saddled up the ol' red Western Flyer and headed for town.

Down the hill I went and out onto the Monterey Highway. At the Aromas turn off I headed north and pointed my Flyer toward Watsonville. When I reached the halfway point between the bario of Pajaro and our hill, my fathers station wagon was heading south. Once he saw the Western Flyer and realized it was me, he slammed on the brakes, made a U turn and raced back in my direction. I could see him coming, but in true four year old fashion, I assumed he was simply coming back to pick me up.

Wrong.

After jumping out of the Monterey wagon, he pulled me off the trike, threw the Flyer in back and tossed me on the seat next to it, while all the while screaming "wait 'till we get home."

I guess he was angry.

Once home, out came the trike and me after it, but by then he'd calmed down.

"You know what your son did?"

My mother as usual shook her head from side to side. After all, I was part of the Hole In The Wall Gang and coulda been any-where.

"He was riding his trike down near Pajaro."

"He what?"

"He was riding his trike down near Pajaro. Just this side of the packing houses."

(Scowl)

"How come you didn't know?"

"How come you didn't?"

"He's four."

(Silence)

As I recall, after that they both just stood there and stared at me with their hands on their hips.

"How'd he know how to get there?"

"Guess he learned from all the trips into town."

"But it's four, maybe five miles or more."

Never underestimate the power of a child. They're often smarter than you think.

Soon after that, the parental finger pointing stopped and they just looked at each other. By then the expected belt whipping had vanished from my mind and I just stood there as well.

Shortly after that, it was once again just another day in Maycomb as I watched my father change into Atticus Finch. Up went the glasses onto the forehead, down came the hand, and after being snatched up and carried over to the Wingback, he plopped into it and sat me on his lap.

After that I was lectured on what was appropriate behavior for someone my age and riding the Western Flyer into Watsonville wasn't a part of it.

I never saw the belt or got spanked and I never rode my Flyer into Watsonville again.

1959.

My father built his own patio, garden walls and fence. Brick by brick, post by post, concrete bag by concrete bag. Sometimes he'd let me help, but when he did so, he usually ended up redoing everything.

I never got it right.

I couldn't even grade sand.

When not in his office or regrading the sand I ruined, both he and my mother would spend most of their free time with the Yamamoto's. Whether it was at our house or theirs, it didn't matter. Both families might as well have been one. We were always together.

My parents and the Yamamoto's were inseparable, neither locked their doors to the other and time of day didn't matter. We were constantly in and out of each other's houses.

After work Ike'd bring home fresh produce, and more often than not, include us in his haul whereupon bags, as well as crates of broccoli, artichokes, Brussels Sprouts and strawberries would show up in our kitchen, or miraculously appear on the back porch. My parents enjoyed every minute of it. Being from Ohio, we'd never seen an artichoke or eaten fresh strawberries let alone anything else that was considered fresh. Frozen strawberries were simply colorless and tasteless mush. Everything else was unheard of.

We ate a lot of strawberry shortcake after that.

Ike and his family had to teach us how to eat artichokes though. Being from Ohio, we assumed you ate the whole thing, thistles and all. We had to be taught otherwise.

To this day I can't get enough and Brussels Sprouts on the stalk are one hell of a lot better than when they're cut off.

And so out went the creamed corn. The creamed chipped beef on toast; "shit on a shingle" as the Gobs used to call it. The creamed salt cod. The succotash. The frozen this. The frozen that. No more canned anything. After Watsonville there was no turning back. Ohio was a distant memory and we were in the land of milk and honey. There'd only be fresh produce from now on. We were

Californians.

When not bringing over produce, Ike'd bring us fresh seafood from the trawlers in Monterey Bay, and my father'd come to think it was the greatest thing on earth. That and trout. He never could get enough of either. For the rest of us it'd be a mixed blessing. Needless to say, he caught the fishing bug and I'd learn to fish.

After that it'd be San Francisco, Japantown and Chinatown. My parents loved Stockton Street. Loved the smell, feel and touch. They loved San Francisco. Loved everything about it, but that was 1959.

In Chinatown the Yamamoto's introduced my parents to the Wong's and every weekend after that for almost a year we'd all cram into one car or another and head for the city where the Wongs'd order Chinese food from Chinese menus while speaking in Cantonese and Ike'd order Tempura and Sake in Japantown while speaking in Japanese. We'd haggle for fish on the wharf and shop in Cost Plus.

By the end of the decade my mother'd fall in love with all things Asian, Oriental furniture and Shoji screens and end up redoing the entire house in black lacquer and Tatami. Almost everything from Ohio would be thrown out and every table had either a Ming Dynasty horse or Kwan Yin bust on it. All that was missing was the hidden camera inside one of the Kwan Yins, but then my mother never was a fan of either Raymond Chandler or The Big Sleep, let alone Humphrey Bogart. Never mind Betty Bacall. She never had a Kodak moment anyway.

Once she was through with the house, she started in on the yard, afterwhich bonsai and bamboo appeared everywhere as did more than a few miniature Japanese pagodas.

Adios, Ohio.

Over martinis, my father'd continue to dream of Bali Hai and everything else'd remain the same. I'd continue to follow Butch, and the rest of the kids would be everywhere at once.

The Yamamoto's gave us California. I never knew exactly what it was we gave them in return.

Seemed we were always on the receiving end.

Years later I'd come to realize that things aren't always how they appear, and although we never gave the Yamamoto's much that was tangible, we offered them something far more important than all of the fresh produce and seafood Ike'd bring home could buy.

We offered them friendship.

Respected 'em for who they were.

Something their country denied 'em because they were different. Because they were Japanese.

We listened and we treated them like family.

We cared.

In hindsight, my father was little different than Atticus Finch. The Yamamoto's little different than Tom Robinson.

My father offered hope. The Yamamotos found respect in return.

Each found what they were looking for on Loma Linda.

As such our families remained friends for years, but as is often the case, the relationship faded after we moved away and was eventually lost.

Butch would be killed in Vietnam and we would never see the Walden's or Opdyke's again.

My parents would continue to move every other year or so for the rest of their lives looking for Bali Hai.

They never found it.

In time I'd leave California.

Like my parents, I'd continue to wander; always looking for greener pastures and jumping, if not crawling under fences. Still heading off into the unknown.

Different ways for different days.

In medias res.

Seeger

To every thing there is a season,
and a time to every purpose under
the heaven:

A time to be born, and a time to
die; a time to plant, and a time to
pluck up that which is planted;

A time to kill, and a time to heal; a
time to break down, and a time to
build up;

A time to weep, and a time to
laugh; a time to mourn, and a time
to dance;

A time to cast away stones, and a
time to gather stones together; a
time to embrace, and a time to
refrain from embracing;

A time to get, and a time to lose;
a time to keep, and a time to cast
away;

A time to rend, and a time to sew;
a time to keep silence, and a time
to speak;

A time to love, and a time to hate;
a time of war, and a time of peace.

By the time Pete Seeger came along, he'd turn the Book of Ecclesiastes into an anti war song and the Byrds'd turn it into a generational touchstone.

By the end of '65 you'd hear it everywhere anybody'd listen to an AM radio from Little Rock to Saigon. It struck a nerve, defined an era, and spoke to the nascent generational disillusionment over yet another Southeast Asian war, this time in a place called Vietnam.

And it marked the beginning of the 60s.

The beginning of the counter culture.

Eisenhower was gone. Gone the way of the Cold War and Wonderbread.

Gone the way of Kennedy and Camelot. Pillbox hats and Gidget, Berlin and the Bay of Pigs.

Gone the way of Dylan and acoustic. There'd never be another Newport.

It'd become an electric world and the kids were restless.

Another war was underway and the South was beginning to burn. Too many Freedom Riders. Too many Woolworth's lunch counters. Too many Hai Phong's and Na Trang's. Too many Mekong's.

By 65 it seemed as if a universal angst'd settled over the land. We were free from nuclear annihilation, but free to do what?

Nobody knew.

Free to change, I suppose.

Every generation does it. Always has, always will.

Change was universal.

And unfortunately, inevitable.

For myself, and seemingly everyone else in America who watched television and tuned into the Wonder Years two decades later, when we saw Kevin Arnold sit astride his Stingray in Sherman Oaks and look out across the neighborhood while Turn, Turn, Turn played in the background, each of us seemed to know instinctively what it meant.

Our childhoods were disappearing and Butch Walden had

died. Idealism was simply an illusion and we were growing up.

It was time to move on and either you accepted it, or you didn't.

If you did, there was hope. If you didn't, you'd end up bitter.

It was the end of the innocence.

When I was a child, I
spake as a child, I
understood as a child, I
thought as a child: but
when I became a man, I
put away childish things.

Our beautiful hill was gone and each of us has to sooner or later move away.

THE COLONEL'S LIMOGES

When driving north on 287 between La Porte and Virginia Dale, the mind tends to wander. Usually it's around Livermore, but sometimes it's just before you cross over the first hogback north of Fort Collins. Sometimes the cement plant triggers it. Sometimes it's the steam rising from the Rawhide Power Station. At other times, it's Ted's Place. More often than not though, it's Livermore. After that, the mind simply wanders until the old Presbyterian Church in Virginia Dale comes into view. Once past it, the mental grounding returns and the drive to Tie Siding is more often than not, uneventful.

Sixty-five miles. Plenty of time for the mind to wander. In some cases all the way back to 1959.

As with the winter Caleb left to look for Mike Daggett, it had been another long one. Even the treks out to our creek or along the Platte couldn't shake loose the cobwebs that'd accumulated, and wandering around in one's mind didn't make it any easier.

1959 was a lifetime ago. So was Loma Linda for that matter. Best to forget about it

Spring had sprung as I'd heard someone say, and after passing the sandstone hoodos just north of Tie Siding, life was once again good and filled with promise.

If the hoodos were there, Vedauwoo'd be there. If Vedauwoo was there, Caleb might be as well.

It was time to see both.

Within a few miles Laramie came into view and I was once again passing a cement plant. What it was about those things and why they were all over the Rocky Mountain west was something I never completely understood. Maybe it was the ever present lime-stone. Out on the plains it was the grain elevators and mushroom shaped water tanks that dominated the landscape, but up against the mountains it was the cement plants. What made it worse was that most of 'em were either past their prime or had long since been abandoned. Where they weren't, most everything downwind of 'em was either stunted, gray or dead. Too much powder coating for too long. It could be a bleak world. Needless to say, the cement plant outside Laramie was notoriously bad, not only because it was suffering from the later, but because it was surrounded by a boneyard of rotting and rusted train, truck and auto parts that almost always seemed to be awash in a sea of mud or covered in whatever southern Wyoming could kick up. Ironically the pronghorn and deer loved it. Fort Sanders never stood a chance.

After passing the local eyesore and under Highway 80, Highway 287 becomes Third Street. From there, if you continued north you'd hit Grand.

At Grand, I turned left and headed for the Union Pacific railyard where, if I was lucky, I could find a place to park in front of the Johnson Hotel. If not, maybe I could find one in front of Sweet Melissa's. After that, it'd be Muddy Waters and coffee.

Muddy Waters. Seemed like a rather ironic name for a coffeehouse in Wyoming given the small African American population in the state, but then again, maybe not. After all, Bill Pickett spent most of his time in Wyoming and he was black. But then ol' Pickett was a cowboy, so that made everything okay. Folks used to watch him in Cheyenne during Frontier Days and by some accounts he was quite the local hero. Quite the bronc rider. Couldn't say that much for Jim Beckwourth though, even if he was black and buried outside Fort Laramie. Jim wasn't a cowboy.

Muddy Waters.

Never knew why they called it that. Coulda been named after the blues singer, but then again, coulda been simply a pun on the coffee, or maybe on the color and flavor of the water in the Laramie River come spring.

Then again, it coulda simply been because of the rusty pipes that were in damn near every building in town.

Needless to say, I never found out.

No matter what, the coffee was good and it kinda fit. Laramie did seem to have the blues now and again and the pipes were indeed rusty. As for the La Ramee, hell, it was all too often more muddy than not and what was life without a little pun anyway. Especially after yet another Wyoming winter.

Whatever the reason, once inside, I could see the Ethiopian and hang with Los Companeros. Maybe swap a fishing story or two. Discuss hiking and packing. Where it was good. Where it wasn't. What to see. Where to avoid. Where people were. Where they weren't. All the things nobody much cared for in D Town.

Yep, we all had our favorite spots and loved to talk about 'em, but everybody, myself included, always seemed to hold something back. Something in check. Nobody wanted to give too much away for fear of losing what they considered theirs. It was kinda like when I used ta pan for gold on the Rubicon out in the Sierra, find a spot with color and tell someone about it and the next thing ya'd knew, ya'd be up to your armpits and asshole in gold seekers. Best to stretch the story a bit, tell the essential truth, but be vague about the exact location. On the other hand, it was okay to tell just enough so that the true soul who deserved to find the spot for themselves could do so provided they did it on their own. That was okay, if they could find it for themselves and were smart enough to connect the dots and read the sign as they say, then it was okay to be there. Otherwise, tough shit. They didn't need to know anyway.

Needless to say, I was no different. I guarded my special places fiercely and more often than not, was offended if someone, anyone else was around. After all, it was my spot and I figured it out on my own so they could too. We all felt that way.

The unwritten code of Wyoming and the American West. Be open, but never give too much away. If you did, you might lose it and then where would ya be?

As Caleb'd taught me, place was important. It defined who we were. None of us ever forgot it. We were more than happy to share our places with others, but you had to prove you were worthy of the knowledge and could learn from what you were given. If you weren't, well, you were just another interloper from someplace else and you didn't belong there anyway. Best be on your way back to where you came from. Back to the land of green and white license plates and D Town. Back to California.

Late March, and the sky over Scottsbluff hung like a damp woolen blanket, gray and devoid of form save the diffused ceiling light of the sun as it shone through the gauze pulled over my sleepy eyes. How many springs had come and gone? How many falls and winters where the rime ice would shatter and melt under the pressure of the trespassing Sorrel's? How many muddy tracks rich in eroded quartz and buffalo dung had been slung, curling and soon hardened with the passing of the seasons; the accumulated steps and transitory journeys?

The mind jumps tracks, skips over the memories, choosing what it wants to, and what it doesn't. Sometimes the thoughts are linear. Sometimes they change with the stimuli. Sometimes they mix everything together so that yesterday becomes today, becomes tomorrow, becomes forever. In memory there's no time. It simply passes and then's gone. Not unlike the cast off mud the Sorels'd toss, walking the land held everything together. Curled or not, the quartz'd still shine through and the onion ringlets'd remain where they were thrown. Sometimes for a season. Sometimes for a year. Sometimes until an as yet to be determined future took hold whereupon they'd break apart and become one with their surroundings again.

A remnant memory.

Moki Balls.

It was time to head for Jacoby Ridge.

I could park next to the golf course or turn north and park on Crow Drive. After that it'd be an easy amble across the hogbacks and blowouts that bordered the aquifer and only a matter of a few minutes before I hit the patchwork of BLM and Warren Livestock lands. It didn't matter. Different ways for different days. I'd done both.

The Laramie aquifer; to the west were the hogbacks. To the east, Pole Mountain and Vedauwoo. In between were the sandstone and limestone deposits of ice age seas and creatures long gone that'd either been alternately deposited, lifted, fractured or cracked and then laid down again to mix with the ever present shale and granite that seemed to be everywhere.

And it'd happened over and over again. So much so that it was sometimes hard to tell where one epoch ended and another began. Hard to tell one zone from another.

A geological mess.

A mess that was randomly covered with cottonwood, some solitary and some in groves, stunted juniper, willow, bunchgrass, an occasional aspen, lodgepole pine, sage and prickly pear as well as ferns, coral bells, lupine and sunflowers. A true transition zone.

A transition zone of seeps, springs, gullies, arroyos, bench lands, alluvial fans, conglomerates, sand bars and sinks.

Deer, antelope, fox, bear, chipmunks and coyote.

Hawks, eagles, falcons, red wing blackbirds, crows and meadowlarks.

And before the coming of the railroad, bison.

Where the ancient streams that'd created the arroyos would widen, bend, or hit bottom land, the still older seabeds would deposit limestone, sandstone or shale alternately mixing with the others to form cut banks, small islands, spits and alluvial fans of varying sizes. Over time, grasslands'd take hold above and below the limestone and where the funnel shaped arroyos would narrow, they'd create cliff walls and overhangs. Overhangs where the seeping and dripping water of a thousand years'd cut the banks from underneath, creating as they did so homes for Coral Bells and ferns that'd hang suspended from their slickrock sides. Even in the middle of winter when the temperatures on the benches above'd hit twenty below, they'd grow in semi-tropical contentment oblivious to what was going on above 'em. Their leaves never curled and their fronds never turned brown, while everything above, stunted Lodgepole and Juniper included, were ever beaten eastward, their scraggly canopies flat to the west and bushy to the east. The wind never stopped in that part of the country and seldom bothered to change direction.

Over time, some of the beaches'd settle and then compress and cutbanks'd form. Cutbanks that'd show where man had been and reveal the charcoal stains of ancient fire pits where prehistoric bison hunters made pemmican and roasted buffalo hump du jour.

Two bison teeth and a hoof would be exposed. A toe bone. The remains of the hunt.

A yearling.

Possibly shot from above, or driven into the maze of arroyos below where it'd been trapped and killed.

Sometimes the cutbanks revealed an entire layer of charcoal staining that extended well beyond what a bison roast would've created.

The remains of an ancient grass fire.

The same depth below the cutbank as the fire pits, but always at the mouth of one or more of the arroyos. Nothing farther out on the grasslands or inside the gullies. It was as if the fires were set intentionally.

Probably were given that the arroyos were used as both game traps and blinds. Drive a herd into any one of 'em and light a fire at the end to either block their escape or drive 'em further in, and voila, one could have buffalo hump for dinner. No need to make camp farther out when dinner was right there. Just dig a pit, light a fire, and voila, you had a bison roast.

Hopewell, Besant, Avonlea, Dalton, Pelican Lake and McKean people had each used the arroyos as game traps and blinds while hunting the abundant deer, antelope and bison that drank from the springs and seeps inside. Their sign was everywhere. Shoshone and Arapaho did the same thing afterwards. Once the buffalo were gone, the same Shoshone and Arapaho would use 'em as trenches and converted the blinds to rifle pits where they'd engage in random skirmishes with both the army as well as any unwitting railroad employee stupid enough to wander inside. That too was obvious.

More likely than not, both Clovis and Folsom people had been present in their time as well. The land held enough to tease that possibility out.

A gray white quartzite Cody Knife lay broken in the sand midway between the hogbacks and Pole Mountain, its blade snapped at the point where it would've been hafted. Afterwards a stunted juniper had grown from the cracked limestone beside it, it's roots gnarled and exposed to the Vedauwoo wind. Whether the blade had been broken accidentally or not, it didn't say and as usual, I couldn't tell. No matter what, It'd served it's purpose and belonged where it fell.

It blended in with its surroundings.

After that the juniper continued to grow, widening the crack in the limestone as it did so and the blade remained where it'd been. Where a juniper grew today, it's grandfather's grandfather grew yesterday. Life moved forward, but as always, it was rooted in place.

Everything had the power to change what was around it, but only if it adapted to what was there.

After crossing the aquifer and pole vaulting the perimeter into Warren Livestock range, I could follow any number of deer tracks through any number of arroyos and make my way toward the ridges above.

If I was lucky, I could find the spot where ol' TR, Warren and Le Fors had been in 1903. The spot where an entire entourage of hangers on, military personnel and more than a few token reservation Indians had followed the Telegraph Road over the limestone between Laramie and Cheyenne to DA Russell so that Teddy could see the west, or what was left of it. Never mind that most of what they saw was either on the road itself or on Senator Warren's ranch, Warren could show it off and TR could have a "bully" of a time afterwhich ol' Le Fors could brag about how he captured Tom Horn and chased Butch Cassidy all over the west. Never mind that the Hole In The Wall Gang was always one step ahead of him. Facts were fungible and everybody loves a bullshitter, unless, of course, you were someone like Beckwourth.

Whether made by the iron wheel rims of Conestoga Wagons, early twentieth century Maxwells or the subsequent Firestone and Goodyear tires of later day ranch trucks, where man had crossed in and out of the arroyos in any manner other than on horseback, foot or rail, the two tracks were obvious and the underlying limestone'd either be worn down, polished or burnished. You could spot their course long before you hit their tracks. They always moved in the same direction, east to west or vice versa. I never saw one that moved any other way.

West of Laramie Conestoga's had worn ruts into the underlying sandstone.

While some could've been deepened by TR and the boys as they wandered around Wyoming, more likely than not, they'd been made by the successive flow of emigrants as they headed westward for the California gold fields and Oregon apple orchards.

Year after year they'd follow the same route. Two legged deer leading oxen and mules into the sunset, their unmarked graves extending from Fort Kearny to Sutter, the Willamette Valley and beyond.

Dreamers.

When not following the arroyos and deer trails I'd follow the two tracks.

Needless to say, it wasn't long before I found what I was looking for...

A bronze Scovill army button from the front of a field jacket lay next to the trail. Looking the same as the Great Seal on the back of a dollar bill, it was easily dated. It was bronze instead of brass and the star pattern on the back indicated when it was manufactured.

1902.

And then there was the campfire ring...

Although it appeared relatively new, something was amiss. There wasn't any modern garbage around, Nothing old for that matter either. No modern cans or sardine tins. No beer bottles or pop tops. No cans with lead slugs in 'em. The charcoal wasn't loose, but neither was it caliched or overly compacted. In point of fact, it was a shallow, rather poorly made, single use, simple stone rimmed campfire. Small chunks of singed wood were inside and nothing appeared to have come from a place nearby. What wasn't burned hadn't decomposed and there was no windblow covering it. No dirt, no dust, nothing. Next to it was what appeared to be a broken dowel pin. A dowel pin that'd been painted with red stripes. A broken flint arrowhead lay nearby.

Strange. No Indian I ever heard of made their campfires with stone rings around 'em. More often that not, they were simply pits. Stone rings were a white man's invention and usually modern to boot.

But what about the dowel pin? That certainly wasn't Indian made, or was it?

The broken arrowhead was a bird point. Late Plains Side Notch. Speckled agate. Same material as the one I'd seen at Caleb's Creek. Late nineteenth to early twentieth century.

But what about the dowel pin?

And why was it painted in stripes and with what looked like red house paint?

And why was it the same diameter as the base on the bird point?

To me, it seemed obvious...

More likely than not it'd been part of the foreshaft on a compound arrow.

Compound shafts were pretty common out west. Same thing down in South America. Why should they be so strange in Wyoming even if I'd never heard of one?

A bird point woulda been too small for hafting on a typical shaft and the same shaft woulda been too heavy for small game. If you fired a smaller shafted point from a heavier bow you'd either snap it in two or it'd simply be too light to travel far. A compound shaft, being smaller and lighter, could simply be inserted into the end of a standard one and then have the bird point attached. Once fired, the two'd more likely than not separate and the lighter shaft'd still be enough to keep any animal from going far. Besides, in a land where everything large had already been hunted to extinction, an arrow with a standard shaft woulda been pointless. Too many jackrabbits all over the area now and the prongs were hard to shoot.

As such, the explanation seemed equally obvious.

While nothing I saw mighta been related to either TR or the button, the dowel pin was out of place within the context of where I'd found it and everything around the campfire was out of context with everything else. But that being said, both the dowel pin and bird point could've existed within the same point in time. Hell, the Arapaho used square nails for arrowheads at Sand Creek. Why not use a dowel pin for a compound shaft in Wyoming? Either way, it appeared to have been painted with red commercial house paint and nobody painted red stripes on dowel pins anyway.

I stuck it along with the button into my pocket.

It was time to look for Caleb's crows and follow the Telegraph Road out of the arroyos and head for the high country.

Maybe they could tell me what it all meant.

Within a few miles the limestone benches gave way and I was once again on terra firma. Actual dirt underfoot. Bunchgrass was more abundant and the road was actually turning into one. I could see telephone poles in the distance.

One last limestone outcropping and I'd be on my way up and over the ridge and into the Crow Creek watershed. After that it'd be a downhill run to DA Russell.

One last stop and clear sailing.

Looks like someone's been here before ol' hoss...

Too much broken glass and a broken Morey Mercantile bottle to boot.

1900 to 1910.

Same age as the Scovill.

This was getting weird. Too many coincidences. Too many things popping up where they shouldn't be and all along the same trail.

And what's that?

A Limoges plate.

Again, 1900-1915. And just what in the hell was a Limoges plate doing smack dab in the middle of the Laramie Range? Limoges porcelain was fragile and a far cry from the heavy Tunstall ceramic crockery one would've expected to find from the same period.

It was delicate, hand painted, gold trimmed and extravagant. Extravagant in a land that shouldn't have even known about it beyond the environs of either the Gem City, Cheyenne or Denver. Beyond the ranches of the wealthy. Beyond the TR's and Warren's.

And what about the Scovill army button? All were made sometime between the turn of the century and WWI.

And why was there a neolithic birdpoint next to what appeared to have been a compound shaft?

To me it seemed like they were all related.

Just then something shone in the dirt near the broken plate.

It was a brass washed Colonel's Eagle that woulda either been pinned to the collar of an army field jacket or onto it's shoulder lapel or onto a hat. It'd been broken in two and the pin was missing, but one wing as well as the head and tail were still intact. But that wasn't the half of it. Where each came together a sorta notch'd been formed that was the same size and diameter as the basal notch on the bird point I'd picked up. If you held it with the wing pointing up and the head and tail pointing down, the dowel pin woulda matched perfectly. In point of fact, the broken eagle was the same size as nearly every damn bird point I'd ever seen.

Hell, If Ishii could make arrowheads from broken glass and the Arapaho could use square nails for the same purpose, then why not turn the cast off eagle into the same thing?

Talismatic medicine.

Takes a bird to catch a bird.

One man's junk is another man's treasure.

Maybe I was imagining things, but it all added up.

TR was a Colonel. Both Roosevelt and Warren were wealthy. They traveled with ranchers and politicians who were wealthy and they all lived luxuriously even when "roughing it". They had a military escort. TR loved Indian ways. He liked to be seen with famous Indians. If he could've he would've been another Bill Cody, another cowboy Indian fighter. Roosevelt loved the west. It'd be no surprise if he had an Indian scout or brought along some well known local chief to regale him with stories of the land and times past when he traveled across Wyoming. Hell, he could've even given one of 'em an eagle from his jacket, or maybe the one on his hat. He might've even laughed when the same Indian turned it into an arrowhead, a rather sly barb aimed at the bespectacled Wasicu. Bully for him.

Everything fit together like the pieces of the puzzle it'd been from the route to the era. Wyoming was still considered the Wild West between 1900 and 1915. The population was small, primarily scattered and most who lived there were either dirt poor sodbusters, drifters or itinerant cowhands. Outside of the Gem City or Cheyenne nobody woulda owned much unless they lived on one of the wealthy ranches and even fewer had more than one set of clothes. Indoor plumbing was unheard of and indoor water pumps were equally rare. Needless to say, turn of the century Wyoming was an era when pretty much everybody either lived in a Soddy or inside a split log cabin chinked with mud and old newspapers. Travel was limited and nobody wandered far from the ol' homestead unless they had to. Nobody traveled by train and cars were all but unheard of. Even having more than one horse or a mule could be a luxury for some.

As such, Sears and Roebuck were considered luxury and even the catalog itself could be put to better use chinking the walls than using it to order from. Besides, you could always rip out a page or two and use 'em for pictures afterwards.

More than a few Wyomingites did.

Needlesss to say, Limoges was not only impracticle in a land of tin cups and Tunstall, but unheard of.

Whoever left 'em was wealthy and traveled in style. Extra weight didn't matter to 'em and extremely fragile and seemingly useless items could be carried into a rough and tumble setting where they didn't belong.

Nothing was Tunstall. Nothing was tin.

Nothing was reused and nobody cared to.

Yep, seems ol' Roosevelt or somebody like him, stopped for lunch, broke a Limoges plate, threw away a Morey medicine bottle after they ate too much and either lost, or had a button torn from their army jacket sometime around 1902 and one of 'em was a Colonel to boot.

Needless to say, Roosevelt followed the Telegraph Road in 1903.

I picked up all of the pieces of the plate I could find and after stuffing 'em into my Columbia vest pocket, took 'em home and glued 'em back together.

While not quite whole, they comprised the pieces of a story that mighta been true.

A story that'd been caught in the spiderweb of illusion, time and space.

Somewhere a crow cawed once, twice, three times.
I heard Caleb laugh.
"Tonweya. Tonweya wakan."
And so the circle was complete.
From Loma Linda to Wyoming. Never kill a Mockingbird.
All it wants to do is sing.

In affectionate Remembrance
OF
KEARSARGE

FRANKLIN
GEARING
MAJOR C.S.A.
1840 — 1921

Driftwood

Stories are the legends we tell ourselves while sitting around campfires early in the morning, steam rising in coils from coffee cups scented with wood smoke, dripping fog wet beyond the rim of what we see; the creations of myths told and collective extrapolations remembered, limited only by our vision. Yesterday and today blend and twine into one, only to be pulled apart as the dichotomy of their existence is merged. Spiraling ever outward, their memories are carried on the Ohlone wind, carried to the west, the south, over the edge of the world and back. The winds of spirits gone and of those yet to come. What we dream today, we dream tomorrow for their existence is the same. There is no contextual difference between the two. No separate language. And so the Esalen winds of Pfeiffer mix with those of the Ohlone and Soberanes Whalers who followed the currents below Partington, their recollections dancing as they do so through the night. A night of songs and dancing. A night of dreaming and distance. A night wherein the ghosts of all commune as one, forever seeking dissolution from the boundaries of the civilized world beyond.

"We're all driftwood, you know."

My ears perked up.

"Always drifting along with the tide. Always hoping to find a shore to land on."

Say, what?

"Always looking for a place to rest. A place to call home. A place to escape the constant battering of the waves and tide; the constant ebbing and pull."

And...?

"If we're lucky, we find it. Most never do. We just drift along until we rot."

One can hear a lot of strange things while sitting in a bar. Most is inane. Some is absurd. More often than not it's just alcohol induced blabber and bullshit.

Every once in a while though, it's different.

Sitting in the corner of the bar where Henry Miller used to perch while oggling wannabe Rita Hayworth's, Nepenthe always seemed different. While the stories one might hear could be bullshit, more often than not they were esoteric and rather canny in what they revealed.

Driftwood.

Was that what we were?

Was I like the rest, nothing but driftwood? Drifting with the tide and looking for a shore to land on? Looking for a home?

It struck a nerve. It was as if Caleb had suddenly materialized out of thin air and was sitting at the opposite end of the bar drinking Bloody Mary's, but if he was, he'd changed into just another middle aged escapist hippie chick searching for nirvana, or maybe trying to escape her Hollywood producer husband down the coast in Laguna.

Driftwood.

Colorado, Wyoming, Nebraska, and now the Big Sur coast.

Was that what I was, driftwood?

Damn long drives between Colorado and Wyoming.

Why can't I just enjoy the scenery.

The mind jumps, the spirit wanders.

Was that all that humanity was, driftwood?

If so, America was certainly filled with it. You could see it everywhere. Nobody stayed in one place long and even fewer seemed attached to anything. Hell, the land itself said that much. So many unmarked graves. So many wagon tracks heading into the unknown. So many migrations. Hell, we were no different than the buffalo, wandering from Texas to Alberta and back. Just one great big herd of drifting bison going nowhere.

Driftwood.

A bobcat crouched under a scrub manzanita in the dunes above Molera, it's green eyes only a few inches from mine as I talked to it. The tufted ears twitched and the jade eyes blinked, but it didn't move.

It simply sat, listened and watched.

Hell, even the wild things listen. They're just as curious as we are.

The bobcat didn't wander far. Probably came down from Pico Blanco. It knew where it belonged and it stayed there.

It'd found its place.

Driftwood.

While it was true that some who wandered were simply drifting and crashing with the tide against an unknown or uncaring shore, others weren't. Some things just needed more range. A larger home. A bigger piece of sky. But then again, some just needed to wander.

But were they driftwood?

I never found out and Caleb couldn't say. He was gone.

The bobcat blinked while the middle aged hippie chick simply babbled on.

Nobody listened except old Henry and he was gone now too. No more Orson. No more Rita.

The hippie chick ordered another Bloody Mary.

Think I'll have another as well.

The mind jumps and the memories unravel, uncoiling like so much smoke below Partington Ridge.

Along Pfeiffer Beach and up Sycamore Canyon. Molera and Bixby. Pico Blanco and the Little Sur.

Damn long drives.

I'd never pole jump the perimeter or see Vedauwoo again and it was a long drive home.

Broken Wings and Damaged Souls

Dan loved the mountains. Loved everything about 'em. Every day after work he'd come home and change into his running gear and hit the road where he'd run until dark. Not a simple jog, mind you, but a run that'd take him from Hyman Street to the Slaughterhouse Bridge and on up into Smuggler and Red Butte. From there if he had a mind to he'd head for Woody Creek and run along the Frying Pan. Sometimes he'd head for Snowmass and the Bells. Other times he'd run up toward Independence and back, or maybe just to Hunter Creek. It was a far cry from where he grew up in Moline and Rock Island where the rivers were dirty and the skies an endless humid gray. The mountains around Aspen were cleaner and the skies were bluer, and the rivers had magical names like Crystal, Roaring Fork and Frying Pan.

Dan loved the Valley. Loved everything about it. It was a place where he could run free and unencumbered by the starkness of the world outside.

For him, the Roaring Fork was paradise and the home he'd always wanted but never had.

It was a far cry from the Quad Cities.

Dan. He always reminded me of Woody Allen. Woody Allen the hipster. Looked like him too. Same outdated black horn-rimmed glasses, but with a black beret and ponytail. Hipster Woody. He never took either off except when he slept or showered. He even wore 'em running. They defined him.

He was the first person I met when I moved to Colorado. Both of us were transplants from someplace else and both of us came for the mountains. Seems nobody we knew was born there. Most were California ski bums who decided to stay, escapist hippies or were simply trust fund babies and Hollywood wannabes with a few Texans thrown in for good measure.

Needless to say, we were the anachronisms.

The mountains were magical in those days and like the Coureur des bois who came before, we were drawn to 'em.

Truth be told, I'd been listening to too much John Denver music back in high school, but then that was back in '72. A lot of kids moved to Colorado after that, myself included. Dan, on the other hand, simply wanted out of Moline. He never cared much for old John Dusseldorf anyway.

Either way, it didn't matter, the Roaring Fork Valley beckoned and the Rocky Mountains were now home. Dan moved to Glitter Gulch and I was drawn to Bonedale.

Aspen and Carbondale. Puns on a cocktail napkin.

But then everything to Dan was either ironic or a pun, a joke to be written on a cocktail napkin while drinking a beer in one happy hour bar or another. He'd do both while we sat in the Cantina or Funion.

Puns were a potent metaphor for life in high mountain Februaries when the sun'd go down by two and the days'd be so short and cold that you thought you'd go crazy. Come February, everything was a joke no matter what and if you didn't have one you'd simply go nuts from the lack of daylight.

Hell, nobody even wanted to ski Ajax in February.

It was the worst month of the year. Even the ski bums preferred to wait for that time of year just before mud season, say late March or so, when they could sport shorts and sunglasses and race the gondola down Ajax to the Little Nell.

But then, that was Colorado.

By Saint Patrick's Day and the first hint of spring everyone would have cabin fever and not even the jokes could keep you going. Once Highway 82 was free of ice and you could make the run from Aspen to G Wood you could head for Highway 70 and D Town. It was part of the spring ritual. Time to load up the Scoobydo and head for Eisenhower, assuming that is, that you didn't spin out on whatever black ice was still on the road between The Edge of Hell and Woody Creek. If you did, it'd be hello Frying Pan, welcome to the Roaring Fork. More than a few SUVs did so, but they were mostly from Texas anyway.

Once past Eisenhower, you could simply slalom your way downhill all the way to Georgetown and after that coast into D Town. Dan and I'd do that; cut the engine outside the tunnel and coast all the way down until, after reaching the bottom somewhere around Silver Plume, Dan'd pop the clutch and slam the Subie into gear, whereupon the engine'd resume it's internal combustion groaning and we'd roar into Denver. We lived dangerously in those days. On the way back we'd do the same thing on the other side of the tunnel between the chain up station and Frisco, but that was a bit more dicey given the multiple S turns and steeper grade. Oh well, the Scoobydo didn't seem to mind and we both lived to joke about it over cocktail napkins and beer afterward. A lot of semi's bound for LaLa land didn't though and they had air brakes.

Either way, once past Arvada, Dan and I'd almost always head for LoDo or Jefferson where we'd nosh on "real" food. After that, we'd head for Capitol Hill and stock up on vinyl.

Seems WaxTrax was always on our bucket list.

After stuffing ourselves with ear candy, we'd head for Cherry Creek where Dan'd hit the Runner's Store and I'd hit the Tattered Cover.

Dan always seemed to need another pair of Saucony's and I was ever hopeful that I'd run into Jimmy Carter or someone like him again in the book store.

Hell, did so once so there was hope.

No matter what, Denver called and it was time to get outta Dodge. Time to get away from the snow and head for the Front Range. Time to coast down 70 from Eisenhower to Georgetown and slalom into the city. Time to see some daylight.

After staying the night in Boulder, we could head back to the Roaring Fork satiated with good food and loaded with enough vinyl to ride out whatever remained of the winter, ready for another round of irony and cocktail napkin humor.

Dan'd find his Talk Talk and I'd find my Electric Prunes.

"I had too much to dream last night, too much to dream…"

All the way past Copper and the Glenwood Canyon beyond we'd sing "Rocky Mountain high, Colorado…"

Somewhere John Denver was laughing.

Even Dan'd sing along at that point. John Dusseldorf be damned.

Colorado. It was a different place in those days.

On another luge run down Eisenhower, Dan dropped me off between the Mint and Capitol buildings in Denver and headed for Boulder. He wanted to see Pearl Street and hang out at Listen Up. Maybe pick up a new subwoofer or Planar turntable. Dan loved to live large even if his pocket book didn't. Seems he was always looking for that perfect audio fit, that perfect stereo addition to bring home to Hyman Street where, when not running the Frying Pan or up Red Butte, he'd sit for hours in his sweet spot and listen to Supertramp or the Soundtrack from Glory. Occasionally he'd throw on an opera or two. Dan loved Pavarotti. I couldn't stand him.

Dan could have Pearl Street for that matter as well, too many wannabe hippies for me. Too many trust fund babies pretending to be something they weren't. Too many kids with nothing better to do than sit on the courthouse lawn all day and smoke pot. None could imagine going up Boulder Canyon for a hike. None seemed to ride a mountain bike anywhere. They'd simply hang around and do nothing until, after putting in another hard day at the office, they'd wander home by bus to an apartment off Valmont or out off the Diagonal that Mommy and Daddy paid for. None seemed to know what a job was and none seemed to care. Other than the art galleries, coffee houses and bookstore, I had little use for Boulder, besides, I wanted to see the museums in D Town.

So off we went. Dan and I could hook up later on Sixteenth Street in front of the Brown Palace. Maybe the clock tower.

I'd get to see the history museum and Dan could hang on Pearl. After going there, I could check out the Capitol and maybe see the Mint. Maybe check out the art museum afterwards. All were within walking distance of each other and Sixteenth Street was nearby.

Sitting on a hill and looking west as it did, the gold dome of the Capitol building all but drew me in. From it's steps you could see the entire Front Range from Long's Peak to Mount Evans covered in snow and the flowering cherries around it were just beginning to bloom. Across the street was the Mint and in between was one of the largest lawns I'd ever seen. Needless to say, I wanted to see the inside as well so up the marble steps I bounded.

Closed.

Oh, joy. Maybe it's like Sacramento. Maybe ya gotta go in the side entrance. Maybe the front one's closed.

After looking for one I found an open screen door and walked inside.

I didn't get very far.

Shortly after stepping inside a sunglass wearing suit came down the hall and stood in front of me.

"What are you doing here" he barked.

"I came in to see the capitol and was hoping to meet Roy Romer, maybe shake his hand".

"The front door was closed so I looked around to see if there was another way in. Saw this one and assumed it was the entrance."

"Well, it isn't and you can't just see the governor. You're trespassing. I can arrest you, you know," the suit said.

"Shit, you should put up a sign. I sure as hell didn't see one. How was I to know this was a special entrance?"

"Well you should've. It's the kitchen and you don't look like staff. The front door said closed didn't it?"

"Yep, but I thought it might be like out in California where you had to use the side entrance. The front door didn't work."

"Well it isn't and you'd best be on your way."

As I turned to leave I couldn't help but thinking "Smart ass. Why was it all suits were the same, even down to the sunglasses."

Hell, they even wore 'em inside.

I kept my mouth shut, but as I turned to walk downhill toward Sixteenth where Dan and I'd planned to meet, I couldn't help but thinking, hell, at least I tried! That's more than most people'd do. Nobody takes any chances anymore.

"What's up, Ouzel?"

"Tried to meet Roy Romer. Went inside the capitol building to see if I could."

"You velly funny man, Ouzel. Velly funny"

Dan was on a roll and he was doing his best Hey Boy in the process.

"Okay, so you think I'm Paladin. Velly funny yourself, Woody. I simply went in through the kitchen door and got busted."

"Velly funny. You a velly funny man, besides, It's time ta go. Gotta get up over the pass before it ices over."

"You velly funny. Velly funny man".

"Velly funny."

As we drove in the Subbie down Speer I couldn't help but thinking about what a story it'd make. A perfect story to tell over cocktail napkins and beer. A perfect end to a perfect trip into D Town and back, no pun intended, to Dan's sweet spot on Hyman Street, Supertramp and Glory, Pavarotti and the new subwoofer he'd acquired.

To the Roaring Fork Valley and home.

By late March or early April one could sense spring coming. The days'd be getting longer and milder while the ski runs would become more crowded with trust fund babies who, after a tough day on the slopes, would spend Mommy and Daddy's tuition money on alcohol and hook ups in the Cantina and Funion. Hollywood'd leave town, while those who stayed behind would have Aspen to themselves. Unfortunately, with early spring came the inevitable hard freezes and broken water pipes.

Once again, it would be time to seek a bit of sanity and one last something before winter was gone and the high country turned to goop. Time to remember why we were there. Time to remember the mountains.

There would be plenty of time for mud season.

It was midnight and the spring moon shown down through a cloudless sky onto the valley below. It was as if one were in

Alaska in winter. You could drive from Carbondale to Aspen without headlights and on occasion even see the Northern Lights, the aurora borealis. Perpetual half light.

It was time to wake Dan up and take him for a hike. A full moon midnight hike up Independence.

Something he'd never do. He'd run everywhere, but he'd never go for a hike, let alone at night, full moon or not.

You had to stick a cattle prod up his ass just to get him to go to the old ghost town below the pass itself.

It was a miracle when he agreed to go to the Grottos and look for where John Denver had his picture taken for the album jacket of Rocky Mountain High. We sang the song the whole way up. It was corny, I know, but it was Colorado and it was spring. Columbines were beginning to bloom. It wasn't late February, midnight and cold.

"What's up Ouzel?"

I never knew why he called me that. It was a joke, I suppose, as I was neither a small fat waterbird nor gray. Maybe it was because I used to spend so much time in Penny Hot Springs. Coulda been because I'd ride my mountain bike up to Hanging Lake and back with a backpack loaded with French bread, wine and cheese, park the bike, hike up top, eat lunch and then hike back and resume my ride through Glenwood Canyon. Always following the rivers. Seems I spent most of my time around water. Hell, I'd moved to Colorado from water. Used to live in Santa Cruz. Maybe he saw it in me.

Maybe too, he thought I was just another cocktail napkin caricature, not unlike his Woody Allen persona, something that always seemed a bit out of context. A comic bird in a comic land.

Everything to Dan was funny.

"So, what's up Ouzel?"

"We're going for a hike."

"Now? It's midnight."

"Yep. Put your pants on and cowboy up. It's time to "Ride The High Country.""

And so Randolph Scott, or maybe it was Joel McCrea, crawled out from under his goose down and put his clothes on, while all the while grumbling ala Dan.

After that we could drive up Independence and head for the Lost Man Trail.

Once we parked the car we could hike.

It was amazing. It was midnight and clear as a winters day in Alaska.

Perfect for a hike.

The Aurora Borealis twinkled to the north, it's ribbons of blue green light moving back and forth as we walked.

12,000 feet up. It was hard to catch your breath even when you were used to it. The cold air didn't help. Your eyes'd glaze over and your nose'd run, but after a few miles you didn't need a coat. You could take it off and carry it.

We hiked in our shirt sleeves, Leadville and the Arkansas to one side, Aspen and the Roaring Fork to the other.

We followed the aurora north.

"Continental Division."

What's that?

"Continental Division."

"Did you hear something?"

"I thought I did."

Just then, but still a ways off, an apparition appeared. An old gray haired man in a Larry Mahan with his hair tied in a pony-tail was heading our direction.

He had on a red flannel shirt and wore 501s and walked with a bit of a rolling gait, somewhat stooped and bow legged.

"Continental Division. You're following the divide ya know. Ya gotta keep your balance. Watch your step. If ya don't, you'll slip. You'll fall. It's a long way to the bottom ya know".

"Walking in balance is the hardest dance you'll ever do. Walk with the land. It keeps you grounded. Tells your feet where to step. Helps your toes know what the rest of you're doing".

Dan and I looked at each other again.

"Did you hear that?"

"I thought I did."

"Me too."

As the apparition got closer it spoke again.

"Name's Caleb. Caleb Cutbank. Be seeing you boys again."

As the apparition walked past us we turned to follow him with our eyes but he was gone, vanished in the light of the full moon.

"What the hell?"

"Lost Man", I said.

"Let's go, Ouzel. This's weird. It's late and I'm dreaming. Let's go home."

So back to the Roaring Fork, Red Butte and Old Smug we went. Back to the Valley and our goose down beds.

As was always the case, it'd be several years before I saw Caleb again. By then I'd be living in Denver where we'd hike along the creeks and out onto the plains together, search for the past and talk about what it meant to be in the present. We'd walk the land together and talk. Talk about tomorrows and of dreams yet to come.

Dan'd stay in Glitter Gulch, but we'd drift apart. Except for semi annual trips to Denver, Dan never liked to leave Aspen. He was attached to it.

Years later I'd read in a Moline newspaper that Dan'd died in G Wood.

Suicide.

Aspen had killed him. It had become too Hollywood, too Tinseltown and Dan couldn't keep up.

He never was very good at pretense.

"We're all driftwood you know."

"Ever drifting with the tide and hoping to find a shore to crash on."

"A place to call home."

Dan was buried in the cemetery below Red Butte where he was free to run the rivers he loved. Free to walk the divide between what we want and what we can never have. What we choose and what we leave behind.

"Continental Division."

Dan made his choice.

He would stay in the valley.

I cried, but nothing heard. Not the wind, not the sky, not the land.

A tree fell in the forest, but nobody was listening. It didn't make a sound.

Damn long drives.

Why was home always so far away?

Dan found his.

I was still looking for mine.

Thirty-four years and I'd only gotten to Virginia Dale.

It was a long drive.

Thirty-four years long.

Not a long time if you're a Sequoia or Bristlecone Pine. Hell, Sequoias can live to be a thousand years old or more, Bristlecones longer than that. Christ, even the desert tortoise down in Mojave can live well over a hundred years.

Thirty-four years. Not very long in the scheme of things.

I never met Skylar. It was said he had my eyes, my nose, his mothers cheek bones and build. The paper said that he loved to listen to songs, tell stories and quote old movies he'd seen. A lot like me.

Thirty-four years.

He seemed to love the mountains, Timpanogos, Provo Canyon and the Wasatch beyond.

Like me he'd wander. Whether he walked the land or not I never knew, but at least once he went beyond his comfort zone. Beyond the Wasatch Front and out across the redrock country that seemed to stretch like a mirage between Green River and the Uintas. He wandered all the way to Eisenhower and coasted down into D Town. All the way to Denver.

How he died, the paper didn't say. Rumor had it that it was in a car crash.

He'd gone to Denver looking for something, or so Caleb said, when we talked about it.

For thirty-four years he'd been looking.

He died not far from the creek Caleb and I used to travel along while we talked of life, the land and the mysteries of each.

"Wakan Tanka", Caleb would say.

"The Great Mystery."

Skylar had died in the wrong mountains. Too far away from the protection of the Wasatch and his mother.

Thirty-four years.

I never met him but I'd had a son.

I wandered off, his mother never telling me she was pregnant before I did.

Maybe she knew something I didn't. Some people were meant to wander. She knew in time I would. She was grounded. I wasn't.

There was something about the Rockies that sucked people in. Something that drew people in who were either looking for something they couldn't find, or were running away from it when they had. It was as if the entire range were nothing but a giant vacuum cleaner that picked up every piece of windblown detritus it could find and dropped it there to be either lost or found again.

It'd drawn Dan in and it'd drawn me in. And now it had drawn Skylar in.

Were we all running away from something or were we looking for something we hoped to find, but never would, a place, a land and identity to call our own?

The land didn't say and I couldn't tell.

"I think he was looking for you", Caleb said.

"All beings need to connect. Everything needs to know where it comes from, where it belongs."

"We all know that place even if we don't always see it. Sometimes it's right in front of our eyes."

"Sometimes we see it, sometimes we don't. Sometimes it takes years to find it. Sometimes a lifetime. Some never do."

"It's all a part of Wakan Tanka."

"Mitakuye oyasin oyasin."

"All my relations relations."

To the point of the infinite.

"Skylar needed to know where his relations were. Where he belonged. Why he was the way he was."

"He needed to find you."

As Caleb spoke, I couldn't help but think of Ralph Waldo Emerson.

"Dream delivers us to dream, and there is no end to illusion. Life is as a train of moods like a string of beads, and as we pass through them they prove to be many colored lenses which paint the world their own hue, and each shows only what lies in focus."

Life indeed was an illusion and like Dan, Skylar and now myself, we all lived within that journey each of us took in order to discover who we were.

Why it was never easy, I didn't know and Caleb wouldn't say.

It'd been a long time since we talked, but his words struck a chord and I can still hear his voice...

"The land has the power to heal. It doesn't care if you're rich or poor, weak or strong, good or bad. Everything is equal if you meet it as it was given. It asks for nothing more than balance. If you can't walk in balance, you don't belong. It'll chew you up. We all must walk the land for ourselves. We all must learn what balance means."

"Skylar found that out. He was walking in balance, the balance that comes from the knowledge that one has completed the circle, the journey. He was free to sing his songs and dance his dance."

"You were each a part of the other although neither of you knew it. Your spirits did, and that's all that matters."

I'd had a son I never met and now like Dan he was gone.

So many unmarked graves.

Both had seemingly perished before their time yet both were drawn to the same place as I was and for the same reason.

We were all looking for something. In order to find it, something else had to be left behind, something given up.

Nothing worth having was achieved without sacrifice, or so I'd heard it said.

Dan and Skylar had both sacrificed in search of what was worth having; what they were looking for.

Had they found it?

I never knew.

And what about me?

What was my sacrifice?

For that matter, what was I looking for?

I'd had a son and his mother had lost one.

Each of us shared the land we walked, the mountains and plains we loved but could never hold, the dreams we could never seemingly realize and for what?

Was it all just an illusion as Emerson had said?

Dan was free to run with the wind above the Frying Pan and Skylar, like the comicstrip bird he'd been named for, was free to fly over Timpanogos and the Wasatch, maybe even the Roaring Fork Valley and beyond.

They'd found their destiny.

But what was mine? What was I free to do?

To walk the land and remember. To celebrate their lives and tell the story of their passing. To sing songs and dance around campfires while recounting the story of our shared creation, myth and illusion...

Share them until they became legend.

To remember.

Broken wings and damaged souls.

I'd had a son.

Thirty-four years.

Not very long in the scheme of things.

Damn long drives. Denver was still a long way off and I hadn't even made it to Fort Collins.

Migratory Passages

Every year the deer would traverse the anticline, sometimes in groups of two or more, sometimes in herds that numbered into the tens of dozens, sometimes even the tens of hundreds. Generational deer, they'd cross over the shale oil and talus slopes of the Winds and migrate onto the sage lands where they'd continue on toward the Red Desert, crossing over the Green and Henry's Fork as they headed for Brown's Hole. Big deer, little deer, two points, four points and six. Every year they'd traverse the anticline, dodging as they did so the pump jacks and flare tops of the methane wells that constricted their route, bottle necking and sometimes blocking the thousand year genetic memory of feed spots and water holes at every turn. The antelope did the same thing. Two prongs, single prongs and unpronged, they too would traverse the down slope from Jackson to the Green generation after generation, moving with the season, first in one direction, then the other, but always in search of a better place; a seasonal home.

The bison that roamed the plains were little different, bison antiquus, bison occidentalis and bison bison migrated from their ancestral homes in Alberta, the Dakotas and Nebraska, some traveling from as far east as Missouri and crossed over the alluvial fan between the two forks of the Platte and headed for the Red Desert. Along the way they'd cross the continental divide twice and eventually make it as far as the Salt Lake Valley, only to be stopped by the Bonneville Salt Flats beyond.

It was in their genes. Genetic memory. Each succeeding generation would build upon the one that'd gone before and repeat the process.

Humankind was little different. When not following the

Rocky Mountains or hugging the coastline from the Aleutian Islands to Tierra del Fuego, he'd follow the rivers and streams, and like the bison, deer and pronghorn before him, travel with the seasons from one place to another. In time, whereas some populations would settle and stay in one location or another, an equal, if not greater number, would simply wander the map, repeating in kind what had come before until they too covered everything from coast to coast and everywhere in between. Given enough time, even those who'd settled would then migrate for the same reason or reasons the animals had before 'em; resources'd fail, populations would become unsustainable, ecosystems would collapse and all too often places'd simply become too crowded. Add to that the constant natural calamities that'd occur and the uniquely human propensity for war, and it'd be time to move.

Genetic memory. It was in our genes, our DNA.

The only difference between man and the animals was the reason and purpose, if there was one.

Sometimes it was hard to tell.

Never mind the suitability or choices where and if they could be made.

The graves of the mistaken were everywhere.

The old Subaru, looking like some disemboweled potato, chugged northwesterly over the hogback between the Poudre and the plains, the out sized U-Haul it was towing swinging from side to side behind it like some flirtatious 1940's pin up girl. To hell with the CV joints and tie rods. They were shot anyway. Too many Nebraska dirt roads and Rocky Mountain two tracks. What was a little more wear and tear?

Looking in the rear view mirror I could see the cement plant where it stood north of La Porte, stark and gray like some neolithic monument over my shoulder, it's usefulness lost to the limestone it'd destroyed. Another Midwestern Stonehenge. Beyond it the sun was beginning to rise through the red orange haze of eastern Colorado as the half light of another day began. A day where I could already see La Porte to the south and as far east as Ault and Keota. The Buttes were still lost in the muck, but I knew they were there.

The Buttes. They'd been ruined. The Eclipse and Dempster windmills that Caleb and I 'd seen on our hikes into the badlands were gone, replaced by sleek multi story turbines with rotors the length of a semi. Gone were the iconic views. Gone were the tipi rings, Arapaho and Cheyenne hunting camps and buffalo grounds, replaced by megawatt producing behemoths that clawed at the sky and chewed up and spit out any hawk, eagle, migrating goose or Sandhill Crane foolish enough to come within their reach. Giant raptor chewing, megawatt producing rotor bladed eyesores blocked the view of the buttes. They obliterated everything. Petrified wood and dinosaur bones were buried. Roads were built where none existed and all for what?

Mega mansions in Windsor?

Politically correct homes for the Croc wearing Birkenstock crowd in Boulder?

It sucked.

On truly windy days they had to be shut down. Useless. They couldn't operate in high winds. Unfortunately, some engineer in some megalopolis forgot that high wind days were all too common in the grasslands of the northern plains. Just ask the dust bowl farmers that'd been blown away. There were far too many Star Windmills that were already broken, their tail rotors and blades scattered over the landscape to not know otherwise even if they hadn't drilled deep enough into the shrinking Ogallala. Tell the Greenies that. Besides, the damn things killed a disproportionate number of migrating birds and raptors. Be sure to tell the Sand Hill Cranes on their way to Nebraska. No more prairie potholes for them.

No more eagles, hawks and falcons.

And what about the transmission lines? They had to go somewhere. Another power plant? A relay station? Multiple relay stations? More roads?

Guess somebody forgot about those.

Ill planed, ill sited ecologically friendly power was in and of itself an oxymoron. Just ask the desert tortoise in the Mojave. Displaced for city sized solar farms that'd sell their energy for electric gadgets and whizbots nobody needed in LA and Vegas. LaLa land.

Never mind that any one tortoise could live to be over a hundred years old. In another hundred years even the techno green absurdities and false promises of the turbine and solar panel industry'd become extinct. Lithium's finite you know. Toxic. Poisonous. And what about everything THEY destroyed? Gone the way of Keota and so many dry farm homesteads bought up by so many eastern yokels in order to fatten the UPs pockets.

Credit Mobilier.

While not exactly the same, equally egregious and now abandoned.

Future grasslands for the government.

A buffalo commons.

Where was Ed Abbey when you wanted him?

It made me sick.

Why these same self styled, so called Greenies couldn't put solar panels on top of their own homes was beyond me.

It was such a simple solution.

Unfortunately it might spoil their views and their HOA's might not like it. Xcel Energy might not make a profit from 'em.

But worse than that was the fact that it never occurred to them that they might, just might, make do with less. One less cel phone. One less garage space. One less RV. One less unused bedroom in an otherwise disproportionate mansion.

WTF.

Colorado'd been ruined.

It'd become nothing more than California with a mountain view, San Francisco in the Rockies.

And it was time to leave.

After cresting the hogback the Subaru, Jean Harlow in tow, followed the highway north, continuing on as it would in it's migration toward Laramie.

The Subaru like me would never see Colorado again.

As the former stage stops along Highway 287 began to recede from view, the Subaru continued northwest past Bellvue, Ted's Place, Livermore and Virginia Dale. Eventually Tie Siding disappeared from view as well. Each vanishing in the rear view mirror as we passed it, never to be seen again.

How many times had I driven this road, traveling both directions and migrating like the deer between Vedauwoo and Caleb's Creek?

How many springs, summers, falls and winters?

How many years?

The mind jumps. The thoughts wander and images come and go only to be replaced by new ones.

Memories.

At Laramie I turned the Subaru west and like the Union Pacific before me, the emigrants who came earlier, and the fur trappers, Indians and mountain men before either knew where they were, I followed the bison bison west. Like the deer following the anticline in fall I migrated away from the mountains and into the desert. We all followed the same path.

Metaphor.

Genetic memory.

As Vedauwoo disappeared in my rear view mirror I couldn't help but think of the aspens and Sherman Granite, the beaver ponds and tallgrass meadows, the hoodos and Arapaho spirits.

They were gone now too.

I'd never see them again either.

Although I could've lived in Laramie, there were few jobs. Wyoming in general was even worse. Either you worked in one or another of the extractive industries or you worked for the University, served in the military or worked for the state. Beyond that, you were either a retired politician or a Hollywood transplant living in Jackson. As someone who loved the land I couldn't abide the first and as a human being I couldn't understand the later. Everything in between was already sewn up. It was pointless.

There were too many trailer parks and the cowboys were gone.

Somewhere Jim Beckwourth rolled over in his unmarked grave and Bill Pickett cried.

The Fort Laramie Treaty had been broken.

Not once, mind you, but twice.

The Lakota had lost the Paha Sapa and the Mahipiya-luta, Sahiela and Susuni were relocated. Only bison bones remained and even those were turning to dust.

As in all good westerns, I headed into the sunset.

It would be the last time I saw Wyoming.

The sun had set and night was coming on.

Night.

The mind awakens at night. It's even worse when driving. Thoughts long buried come to the fore and the ghosts of things both real and imagined commingle until the difference between the two is unknowable, distinct yet different. Often one cannot tell them apart.

Such is time and distance. The lines between what's real and what's not blur. Yesterday is today, is tomorrow, is what's yet to be. It's all the same.

The mind jumps while the time and miles pass. Minutes become hours and the miles, simply so many feet.

Long drives can play havoc with your memory. Nights can steal your thoughts. Combine the two and you're in uncharted territory.

Welcome to the X Files.

Traveling cross country at night is like traveling blind. You can't see the future and you can't see what you left behind. You can only see what your headlights show you. What's all around you is simply a void. You can only see so far. The past is a nothing and the future unknown. Can't tell what you've missed and can't predict what's to come.

Even cheap metaphors don't help.

Never mind the car lights heading toward you even if you can see 'em. They're heading in the wrong direction. The red ones going in the other direction are like you, simply fading away. Fading away until they're gone.

Gone with the wind.

Que sera sera.

Where's Doris Day when you needed her?

Maybe just beyond your headlights. Lost in a space and time.

Transition Zones

Hawk circled lazily above; she was in no hurry for breakfast. It would appear soon enough. Late summer and the Cuiyui Ticutta were still asleep, safe in the knowledge that today would begin as it always had and always would. Life was a constant, immutable as the mice that seemed to follow the camp everywhere no matter where the Numa went. As with the ebb and flow of the seasons, they too were a constant. Set up a karnee and the mice would simply appear. Theirs was a symbiotic relationship.

After a few moments one was spotted and Hawk dove. Breakfast was served.

It was dawn, that time just before sunrise when all things come to life. Hawk had resumed circling and the Mountain Sheep began to appear on the basalt ledges that surrounded the Numa camp. Antelope grazed in the grassy bottoms around the margins of the dry lake at the center of the basin where it was located and the abundant deer were already feeding on the desiccated clumps of rye and bunchgrass that the pronghorn ignored. Sunflowers were in bloom as were Mexican Hats and Corn Flowers, each with their petals pulled back and already drooping. It was late summer and the heat still lay heavy with the morning mist in a translucent gauze within, sucked up as it had been from the river beyond the southern rim of the valley.

August, maybe September, but the season was fading. Soon it'd be time to leave the mountain camp and travel down the canyon to the eastern lake below. Time to make winter camp and once again eat Cui-ui and live beneath the cottonwoods and willows. There would be no more journeys to the Sky Lake and the

Olivella Trail would close until the following season. The women would have to make do with what beads they already had. Hopefully there would be enough to carry 'em through the snow times when all the men did was sit around and talk and the women wanted to be left alone.

Some things never changed.

As the haze lifted and the sky became lighter the camp began to stir. First came the women to start the cooking fires and then the camp crier.

It was time to begin the day. Time to greet the dawn. Time to thank Father Sky for smiling on the Paviotso. Time for the Numa to renew.

Little Brother circled one last time. No more mice. They'd already retreated with the sounds of the women.

Soon the children would follow. Not a good time to be a mouse.

With the sound of the waking camp, the Mountain Sheep disappeared. Soon there would be two legs in their country. Time to move higher up. Time to once again be on the lookout. The deer would soon follow but at a slower pace. Unfortunately for them, they could be a bit too trustful. Too curious. The two legged were often never a threat until it was too late.

Too many missing deer.

The prongs didn't care. The two legs seldom got close. One jump and they were gone.

Very few two legs could catch one even with a trap.

That being said, the game traps and blinds were everywhere. Why the prongs never saw 'em, even they couldn't say.

In the end they too were hunted, albeit not so successfully.

Coyote howled once, twice, three times. His woman was gone.

Looking for the leftover mice Hawk had missed.

Crow had yet to wake and Lizard was still underground. Dragonfly was still safe in her nest.

None cared much for twilight. Crow simply liked to complain like an old woman and the other two didn't like the cold. All would wait until the sun was well up before beginning their day.

As the camp crier walked from one karnee to the others in the camp, those not at the cooking fires would begin to stir, get dressed and follow him in his rounds. First the men, then the women. No children were allowed. There'd be plenty of time for them to learn the ways of adulthood, chores not withstanding. They could help with the cooking fires and clean up the camp.

The crier was a tall man. Taller than most, he was thinly built and had a long nose. Almost ascetic in appearance, he wore his hair on top of his head with a solitary hawk feather stuck into the knot where he'd twisted it. A pair of Olivella shell earrings hung from each ear where they'd sway with every movement he made as he passed between the karnees. When he walked he held his hands upward, palms out and forward, fingers splayed as if he were caught by surprise or was amazed by something he'd seen.

This was his way. He was a Holy Man.

"Say, what?"

Musta been dreaming. Damn long night drives. Can't see anything so all you do is drift in and out of la la land.

Jeez.

Don't even need gas yet.

Another few miles and you'll simply nod off again.

You shoulda fixed the Subies radio. At least then you woulda had something to listen to, but then it'd probably be nothing but the Gospel hour anyway. All the way from Nebraska to California.

Rock and roll?

Nope.

Country?

Maybe if you're lucky.

Wolfman Jack?

Gone.

Yeesh.

As he walked the camp the Holy man told the Numa to follow him to the sacred stone.

The one that faced the rising sun and was shaped like the island in the lake down below.

Little Brother to the great rock in the lake, it too was placed by Father Sky and Mother Earth so that the people would remember how all of creation was sacred and in turn connected, place to place, one thing to another, one being to the next. Lose the connection and you were lost.

It had been there forever and was a Grandfather Stone. Like it's big brother in the lake, it watched over the Numa and was a part of the land.

It belonged.

With the men of the camp in tow, the Wicasa Wakan led them to the Grandfather Stone where each took a seat on the lesser rocks that surrounded it. Arranged in amphitheater fashion, the smaller rocks were placed by Father Sky so that they formed an open C which surrounded the western side of the sacred stone with the open end nearest the center. Important men were seated closest to it and those who were less important, farther away. The women followed their men and stood behind. There were no children.

The Holy Man stood in the center.

All was quiet.

When the sun broke the rim of the valley the seated men rose from the circle and along with the Wicasa Wakan, greeted the dawn, each saying a barely audible prayer as the sun ascended over the horizon. The women behind either chanted, sang quietly to themselves, or hummed in call and response fashion as they did so.

The oldest known form of communication; call and response.

Their belief system was that old. That rooted. That grounded with all that was, had been and would be.

That connected.

Once the last of the rising sun broke free from the constraints of the rim, the Wicasa Wakan spoke, the men sat and the women became silent.

All faced the petroglyph on the stone where the image of the rising sun, rays extending outward, had been incised into its surface and spoke one last silent prayer.

Celebrate the sunrise.

Mitakuye oyasin oyasin.

We are all related. We are the land and the land is us.

It was time to start the day.

Damn if that guy didn't look like Caleb. Musta dozed off again. Sounded like him too.

Damn long drives.

At least the old Subies holding together though, even if I can't stay awake.

The lights atop the stacks of the Fort Bridger Power plant glowed red, blinking on and off in the distance.

No planes allowed, even if it was Flyover Country.

Damn Greenies. They hated dirty energy, but they'd take coal from Wyoming, fire the biggest power plant west of the Rockies and build an entire grid of high tension power lines from there to god knows where all so some sonofabitch in Marin County could heat their jacuzzi and sip champagne.

NIMBYs

Bridger was the Buttes all over again.

Flyover Country.

And why they could never do with less was once again beyond me.

Not my country. Not my state. Don't have to look at it. My Range Rover won't drive there so I don't have to see it.

Christ, and I'm heading in that direction.

Well, they killed California a long time ago and now they've done it to Colorado.

What's next?

Megawatt solar and wind farms, again in Flyover Country, with the same damn grids and infrastructure they wanted to get rid of in the first place?

More lost land. More animals. More sacred sites and petroglyphs.

Who cares?

NIMBY.

Fire up the jacuzzi and pass the champagne. Swimwear's optional. We don't walk anywhere anyway.

The land doesn't matter.

Green River, or was it Sinclair?

God they all looked the same.

After that, Bonneville, Wendover, Elko, Battle Mountain and every other shit stop nothing of a town from Salt Lake to the coast. Hell, even Reno wasn't much of a prize.

Elko. The most right wing place I'd ever seen. Home to Jarbidge and the Sagebrush Rebellion. No Hunter S like back in '72. No Gonzo Party National Convention with Thompson as the self appointed nominee. Not a good place to be passing through while driving a beat up Subie with Colorado plates and pulling an outsized U-haul trailer, especially one with a Jerry Garcia decal in the window.

Might be a pothead. Might be running dope. Might be a hippie. Hell, might even be a commie.

The list went on and on.

Yeah, Hunter, you shoulda stuck to throwing smoke bombs into the Woody Creek Tavern and taking pictures of yourself shooting up television sets with that .44 auto mag of yours. Maybe ol' Stranahan wouldn't mind and Don Johnson was too far down the road to care.

Hunter S.

Maybe you can steal the stuffed boar from the roof of the Woody Creek Tavern again and send another ransom note to the Aspen Times along with a picture saying that it was being held for ransom on the Golden Gate Bridge. Maybe put another Santa hat on it.

More puns for cocktail napkins.

Rocky Mountain humor.

But then again, guess I'll miss your hanging around on Galena in your El Dorado and chatting up ol' Sheriff Braudis; two partners in who knows what this time. Will probably miss seeing you drunk in City Market and doing the ol' bob and weave up and down the aisles as well.

Yeah, Hunter. Even inside you kept your shades on. Kept that damn cigarette holder in your mouth too. Nobody ever stopped you from doing exactly what it was you wanted to.

Coulda been a suit in the Capital Building in Denver for all you cared.

You had a lot in common.

Fear and Loathing in Elko.

And what about Bonneville? Hell, even the playa didn't want it.

Then there was Wendover?

Stayed in a motel there once. What a dive. Cockroach heaven.

The Jack Mormons in Salt Lake loved it. They'd flock in over the state line on weekends to do whatever their bishops didn't want 'em to; have a little sex with somebody elses wife, maybe a minor, and drink a beer or two on the side. After that they'd gamble everything away in the Red Lion, safe in the knowledge that they'd never be caught. Unfortunately, too many of the bishops came along for the ride as well.

NIMBYs.

Christ, it was becoming the American way.

Even the land didn't want the land in some of those places. Just the "Bunny" ranches, and to think, when I was a kid I actually thought somebody raised rabbits there.

Cotton Tails? Jack Rabbits?

Who cares.

Better stop for gas. Still got a long way to go.

Sinclair gas station. Well past midnight. Probably closer to three. Shoulda fixed the clock too. No watch. God, you plan ahead.

Giant green plastic brontosaurus out front. Same green brontosaurus on the pumps. Wonder if they're trying to tell me something?

Fossil fuel.

Shoulda had a giant asparagus looking tree fern for a logo. Most of their oil comes from that anyway. Not as appealing though, I suppose. Who wants an asparagus for a logo?

Not some marketing genius in New York or San Fran.

A Colorado pun. Christ, even those are gone now too. No long snowbound winters without sunlight and stuck in some high mountain valley with cocktail napkin humor.

Sorry, Dan. The Range Rover class's won and you're dead.

Hell, you always hated Wyoming anyway, especially Baggs and Sinclair. You'd probably find the giant green Bronto funny though.

A state stuck in the past and being gobbled up by big coal, oil and methane.

Unfortunately Wyoming wasn't the only place hell bent on trashing the land. Colorado was now on a roll too from the Roan to Rulison. No more Flat Tops.

Guess it doesn't matter much. I miss you anyway. You, your beret and Woody Allen glasses. Your Thanksgiving Turkey for all of us rootless drifters and ski bums. Dead Man and Leadville. Ajax and Woody Creek. Everything.

85 octane.

Fill 'er up.

Damn if this place isn't the quietest place I've ever seen. Nobody but some old geezer with an ancient International Harvester 4X and a brain dead clerk.

"No Rezervations", now isn't that a funny bumper sticker.

Kinda fits though.

Beat up I H Scout, Dakota plates. Wyoming well past midnight.

"Be seeing you kola."

"Say what?"

"Be seeing ya."

Damn if that geezer didn't look like Caleb.

Same worn out 501s. Same bandy legged stance. Same red flannel shirt. Same Larry Mahan.

Too many coincidences.

Must be too tired. Better get some coffee too.

"Waste', kola. Be seeing ya."

"Caleb?"

The old man simply finished pumping his gas, smiled and got back in the truck.

"Caleb?"

As the 1960 Harvester turned over the old man hung himself out the window and waved a solitary good bye, fading as he did so into the Wyoming night.

"Nice bumper sticker. Great pun!"

As he turned and drove off I simply followed him with my eyes.

"Waste', kola. Be seein' ya..."

"Gotta go. Gotta find Daggett. Gotta head for Golconda."

"And remember, walking in balance is the hardest dance you'll ever do."

No Rezervations.

Double entendre.

The mind jumps, the thoughts ramble. Yesterday is today, is tomorrow. I'd lost my way. I needed to find it again.

Koyaanisqatsi.

How soon we forget.

In the meantime we simply drive on. If we're lucky it's forward. Often it's in reverse. Sometimes it's into the night. Frequently it's into the unknown even when we think we know where we're going.

Sometimes we drive blind.

Sometimes we don't know the difference.

And what about Caleb?

Was that really him?

And why was he always heading west? Why was he always there even when he wasn't?

And why all the riddles?

I started the Subie and as it pulled out of the Sinclair station and passed the giant green brontosaurus with the U haul once again sashaying into the night all I could think of was cheap metaphors and 1940s pin up girls.

I still had a long way to go as I turned onto I80 westbound.

Colorado, Dan, Skylar and now Wyoming were gone as the red lights atop the Fort Bridger power plant receded in my rear view mirror.

Ahead?

Who knows.

None of us really does.

Via con dios.

Virginia City

"Fare thee well
My own true love
Farewell for a while
I'm going away
But I'll be back
Though I go 10,000 miles

10,000 miles
My own true love
10,000 miles or more
The rocks may melt
And the seas may burn
If I should not return

Oh don't you see
That lonesome dove
Sitting on an ivy tree
She's weeping for
Her own true love
As I shall weep for mine

Oh come ye back
My own true love
And stay a while with me
If I had a friend
All on this earth
You've been a friend to me"

Mary Chapin Carpenter.

I couldn't get the song out of my head nor would the visuals in Fly Away Home leave my thoughts.

All the way from Green River to Lovelock the images spun in my mind as if they were being played in a continuous loop, a constant rewind.

Had I really seen Caleb at the Sinclair station in Wyoming and if I had, what was he trying to tell me when he drove his International Harvester off?

Christ.

10,000 miles.

Coulda been 10,000 lifetimes.

1950s California? Gone. Destroyed by Silicon Valley and Hollywood. No more orchards. No more Loma Linda.

No more Molera, Sycamore Canyon, Partington Ridge, Tassajara, Cachagua or Arroyo Seco.

Nothing but a sea of greed.

And what about Colorado?

Fly Away Home continued to play in rewind as the Subie headed west on I80.

Fly Away Home.

Christ if that movie wasn't what'd been like in Carbondale and the Roaring Fork Valley when I was there.

Mountain Fair, the Crystal River, the Roaring Fork and Frying Pan.

Redstone and McClure. Penny Hotsprings and Hanging Lake.

Seems everybody was either an artist or a musician, a seeker or a visionary.

Everybody either walked or mountain biked the land.

Fly Away Home...

But in the end it too had changed.

Aspen had moved down valley and the uber wealthy had moved in.

Aspen killed Dan.

He couldn't keep up.

I simply moved to Denver.

Denver.

It had changed as well.

The Maginot lines were drawn all over the map from Castle Rock to north of Fort Collins.

Oil wells, methane fields, wind farms and solar cities. Suburbs springing up everywhere.

Mini mansions and trophy homes. A new Range Rover class of citizenry that claimed to love what they moved to Colorado for, but simply took everything over and destroyed it in the process.

Californication.

Silicon Valley and Palo Alto with a mountain view.

Almost nobody explored Caleb's Creek. Even the bike trail was seldom used. As for the Buttes?

Useless.

Keota?

Meaningless.

Anything east of Metro Denver and Boulder was simply Fly-over Country.

Unimportant.

Denver and Boulder in particular had become Aspen light.

Nothing but a transplanted California middle class that'd make F Scott Fitzgerald cringe.

Too many Gatsby's, and none were great.

Nobody got dirty. Nobody went for a hike and nobody gave a shit for the land.

They simply took selfies up in Estes and drove over Trail Ridge in their land yachts.

Another Bimmer in the mountains moment.

I moved to Laramie.

Shane, Owen Wister and Jubal. Where the west was still wild.

Wyoming.

None of the Coloradans I knew could stand it.

Guess that's why I loved it, warts and all. Nobody else seemed to want it beyond Jackson.

It was everything Colorado wasn't, but then again, it was everything Colorado'd been in more ways than any Coloradan I knew would admit.

In so many ways it was just a more conservative and traditional version of the pre Starwood Roaring Fork Valley.

Everybody spent their free time out on the land and everybody talked about it. If you weren't either sunburned or wind burned you weren't squat.

Passing cars would wave at you on 287 and nobody drove a Range Rover.

Vedauwoo. Gods country.

Endless skies and vistas that would roll on as far as you could see.

Nebraska, South Dakota, Montana. Hell, even Colorado before the Californians bought it up.

Clean air. Clean land. Abundant wild life and a place where character mattered more than the money you made.

No mini mansions. No trophy homes. No private jets. No Perrier. Outside of Jackson, the Californians, and by extension, the new breed of Coloradan, didn't want any part of it.

Flyover Country.

Never should've left.

"Though I go 10,000 miles...."

Fly Away Home.

Shoulda hunkered down. Shoulda rode it out.

Shoulda shown more character.

So many coulda, shoulda, oughtas.

I simply moved away.

Fly Away Home.

Gone.

Just past Lovelock I turned south on Highway 95 as the sky turned from black to gray in the dawn of another Nevada day. The twinkling stars were beginning to fade and the ghosts of the Numa were stirring.

Caleb chuckled.

The Sacred Stones were waiting...

Virginia City

"10,000 miles
My own true love
10,000 miles or more
The rocks may melt
And the seas may burn
If I should not return"

10,000 miles.
Fly Away Home.
I landed in Virginia City before noon.

Where's Hoss

Take two parts post 1940 Hollywood fantasy, add one part myth, a dash of truth and an equal measure of purely concocted fiction, stir robustly, and voila, you've got Virginia City.

No actual events needed.

Simply heat and serve.

Yep. Virginia City. I alternately loved and hated it. As with most loves, it left me conflicted. On the one hand I was drawn to it, while on the other, it pushed me away. In the end, however, it ever so slowly not only changed how I thought about myself, but it did so by chipping away at the quartz veneer I'd created around who I thought I was while exposing the bedrock beneath. Not always silver. Not quite gold. Too much pyrite and decomposed granite, but always just enough color to make me hang on and dig for more of what I was hoping to find.

And what was that?

I didn't know.

And why Virginia City when I could've gone any place else?

It was a riddle.

A riddle I couldn't answer.

I'd lost Colorado. The love of my life. The place of my dreams. The place I'd never have. I loved it, but then, as with so many other things in life, everything changed. Colorado fell in love with flash cash, the dream of endless California vacations and Hollywood and needless to say, I was neither rich nor an actor.

In the end she'd shack up with SoCal and I'd move to Wyoming where it was still okay to be a dirtbag.

Needless to say, Wyoming and I had a lot in common. Neither of us cared much for money and neither of us made much. We both loved the land, but life was always a challenge. Wyoming wanted to live as she always had, and although I wanted to live like her, I couldn't. I got tired of eating Top Ramen every day and I'd never been good at hunting. If nothing else, I needed stability. To know where my next meal was coming from. To eat something more than noodles. To pay the rent.

In the end, for all of her Vedauwoo sunrises and boundless dreams Wyoming couldn't provide either. She too was a myth. A fantasy of her own creation and not wholly of mine.

Needless to say, she didn't want me to leave and neither did I, but I had to go. The Merrell's were worn out and the soles were falling off. I needed another pair and there was no money to be made.

And so I ended up in Virginia City.

One part Wyoming. One part Colorado before she grew tired of her lifestyle and two parts 1950s network Television.

Virginia City.

Still cheap, but like Wyoming stuck in the past. Not overly crowded except when the tourists'd pile into town, and surrounded by enough unused, unoccupied open space to get lost in. Yep, I could point my car in any direction and simply disappear.

The tourists as well as most of the locals didn't like to get dirty let alone go anywhere beyond C Street. The former simply wanted to get drunk and wallow in the fiction the local businesses created and the later simply wanted to get drunk and hide out.

Storey County had the highest rate of alcoholism in the state while I was there. Probably still does.

Yep, Virginia City had more bars than anyplace I'd ever seen. In winter it had more bars than people.

No matter what, around it was a land I could wander. A land to explore. To live in. Untrammeled. Unfettered. Unbothered.

Simply left alone.

Maybe that was why I chose it. I could hide out myself and be left alone to do what I wanted.

Nobody cared.

Besides that, I was not only independent, but reasonably self sufficient and the entire community was nothing but a collection of idiosyncratic escapists anyway. Nobody'd notice another one.

But why Virginia City?

There were certainly other, better places I coulda gone, but love hurts as they say and sometimes ya gotta simply move as far away as ya can from the loss and chose a place as unlike what ya left as ya can.

Maybe it was all of those fishing trips to Kamloops during my pre teen summers. Summers where, during my fathers all things fishing years, if we weren't siiting around a campfire at night, we'd sit in the living room and watch Bonanza.

Bonanza, popcorn and Lorne Greene. It was a ritual. The Canadians loved him. Lorne was a Canadian and the Ponderosa looked alot like Kamloops.

We simply went along for the ride.

Dum, didah dee, didah, dum, dummm...

After that whenever Sunday night rolled around we'd simply saddle up again and imagine like so many others across the country that we were riding with Hoss, Ben and Little Joe as they charged across the meadow next to Stateline or past Spooner Lake. It was like watching your family, or at least the one you wanted.

Dum, didah dee, didah dee, didah, dum, dum, dehhh...

Unfortunately Adam was almost always missing and Hop Sing'd moved on. Nobody missed Adam and 'ol Sing was merely a pleasant anachronism. Just another Hey Boy.

If you followed the storyline, the Ponderosa woulda been on the west side of Washoe Valley near Franktown, pretty far away from the fictional Lake Tahoe where the Cartwrights spent their summers charging across the meadow behind Mt Rose, and just as far away from Virginia City. Never mind that Hoss and Little Joe always seemed to be chasing girls in town. They lived too far away. Virginia City was across a valley, over a seasonal lake and beyond a mountain away. Two if you counted the Sierra. Never mind that aside from Sand Harbor the Cartwrights never got closer to Tahoe than the movie set east of Incline. Never mind that even on the burning map, Reno didn't exist.

It was Lake's Crossing, but who cares. Nobody'd heard of it

anyway, least of all NBC.

And so in true Hollywood fashion, Virginia City created its own mythology. A mythology of celluloid heroes, Errol Flynn and Randolph Scott. 1950s television and artificial constructs. A city populated with characters that never existed and cowboys who woulda been more at home in Dodge City than mining for silver on the Comstock. A city where those same cowboys'd spend hours walking up and down the boardwalks along C Street dressed in their slickers, Dan Post's and Stetson's. A city where, if you couldn't live in the real world, you could always create another one. But then, ironically, Virginia City'd always been that way. Always been an island of misfits and castoffs who'd drift in from over the hill in California, where after failing to make it in the gold fields or anywhere else in the state for that matter, would simply wander over the Sierra and dream of striking it rich along the divide.

Yep, they could be just like ol' Crocker, Sharon, Huntington and Stanford.

Some things never changed.

Unfortunately, while some made it, most didn't.

Their abandoned carpetbags were everywhere.

But people loved it. They'd sit in the bars for hours on weekends and suck it up. Christ, they'd come into town and walk up and down C Street and ask where the Cartwrights lived. Nobody knew fact from fiction and too many bought into the later.

Maybe in a sense I did too.

God knows I'd been raised on the Western mythos.

It was who we were.

Hollywood simply capitalized on what we thought about ourselves to begin with and reinforced what was already there; the need for escapism and a larger than life reality.

"Go west young man".

West into your future. West into the land of milk and honey.

West into the land of Horace Greeley and Ransom Stoddard.

Ever westward,

After all "This is the West, sir. When the legend becomes

fact, print the legend."

I always loved The Man Who Shot Liberty Valance.

Virginia City took it to heart.

Needless to say, Ransom Stoddard never existed, but neither did the Virginia City John Ford helped create.

"Print the legend."

Not unlike the legend of Billy The Kid, it'd created a myth of its own making. A self made fiction that over time became real and spoke to the fact that we were all hiding out or running away from something. That we all wanted something for nothing, or with as little work as possible, and that few, if any of us, would ever find what we were ostensibly looking for. In the end, we'd either cart off what we found, simply take it back to where we came from or create a new reality. After that we'd transplant the framework of the house we thought we were building onto yet another weak foundation and the same thing'd begin all over again.

And so for me, Virginia City became a compromise. A fall back position. A line of defense. A place where I too could hide out, but most of all, a place where I could live my life on my own terms and nobody cared.

A place where I could simply disappear into the unknown as frequently and often as I wanted to. Free to wander the Virginia Range, Pine Nuts, and Pah Rah. Free to wander the Sierra, White and Sweetwater mountains. Free to explore the Mono Basin, Buttermilk's and Alabama Hills. Free to follow the Fremont Trail, the Olivella Trail and Caleb's Trail. Free to become sunburned, wind burned, salt covered and at times, stink like hell.

Free to live in the constancy of the here and now and the grounded moment between place, space and time. Free to stand where others stood over a thousand years before and see for myself what they'd seen; the changing seasons, rain storms, hail storms and blizzards.

Free to greet the sunrise.

To live like Muir and tie myself to a tree if I wanted to.

To wear out another pair of Merrell's. Followed by another, followed by another still.

Ghutta percha for another time.

Free to live as I chose in a world I could no longer live in nor cared for.

A self absorbed world obsessed with greed, consumerism and conquest where nothing mattered but money and vanity.

It'd do.

"So, where's Hoss?"

Just over the next hill.

Just across the ridgeline.

Up On The Roof

"When this old world starts getting me down
And people are just too much for me to face
I climb way up to the top of the stairs
And all my cares just drift right into space
On the roof, it's peaceful as can be
And there the world below can't bother me
Let me tell you now

When I come home feelin' tired and beat
I go up where the air is fresh and sweet

(up on the roof)....."

Up on the roof.

On a clear day, which most fortunately were aside from in mid summer when the heatwaves'd radiate up from the ground in the valley and playas below, sucking up what little moisture they'd find and making the mountains appear as if they were suspended over the skyline, one could see forever down Six Mile and out over Sugarloaf. Well beyond the Virginia Range, Misfit Flats and Stillwater. Fox Peak and Grimes Point. All the way to the Wasatch and Uinta. All the way to the Roan Plateau and Flat Tops. The Roaring Fork Valley and Eisenhower.

It was as if you were sitting at the center of the universe, but hell, the Numa knew that long before silver was discovered on the Comstock by "Old Virginny" Finney, the Grosh brothers and Henry Comstock.

They used to camp along the creeks in Gold Canyon and up

Seven Mile where they'd carve petroglyphs of Mountain Sheep into the basalt and burn cedar and sage in the hills surrounding 'em after a successful hunt. From Barrel Springs to Lagomarsino, Lousetown to Johntown, Brunswick to Como, the mountains were their home. It was said that Old Winnemucca, Numaga and Winnemucca's daughter Sarah preferred the area to any other place they knew. They loved the Virginias and Como that much.

When walking the land they'd arrange stones in S patterns at various places. Medicine wheels by any other name. "S", the sign of the snake. The sign of the Shoshone. The sign of the Paviotso. They marked important locations long before the idiot miners and tunnel builders came along and threw up rock cairns everywhere to mark their so called claim boundaries and tunnel tracks, and all on land that'd once belonged to those who'd gone before.

And then there were the unmarked graves. A lot of stones piled there as well. Afterwards it'd be the occasional backcountry explorer, who being too stupid to know where he was, let alone read any sign beyond Starbucks, or follow a deer track anywhere their quad couldn't reach'd simply place stones in little alien piles everywhere they went in order to mark the trail they couldn't figure out to begin with.

Boy Scout 101.

Those I knocked down. If you didn't know where you were you didn't need to be there.

They detracted from the Medicine Wheels, S and Balancing Stones and allowed more idiots to follow their path.

They didn't belong.

Hell, even the old retaining walls the miners built along their wagon tracks above the canyons as well as the foundations where pit houses and rock shelters had been belonged. So did the campfire rings and stove hearths. They were a part of the landscape and a part of its history. They fit.

Boy Scout 101 was simply an abomination.

Best to remove 'em.

Up on the roof...

From where I'd sit with my feet hanging over the Wyoming

edge, everywhere I looked had either been Paviotso or Washo land at one time or another.

Wa She Shu It Deh.

"This is Washo land."

That was until the Numa came along and stole their women and horses. Once that happened the Numa'd end up with most of what'd once belonged to the Washo and the Washo wouldn't own any more horses until after the white man moved into the neighborhood. Never did find out what happened to their women.

Used for breeding stock, I suppose.

And then there was the white man; by the time he came along, he simply carved up what wasn't already taken and then threw the rest in for good measure. To him, everything was his no matter the circumstance or reason.

Despite everything, each of the parties involved maintained a rather uneasy alliance with the other, because after all, mankind's always been a somewhat symbiotic creature. He can't survive without acquiring something from somebody else and usually does so by claiming that whatever occurred was of mutual benefit to the other. While sometimes the results could be questionable and the benefit was more in the eye of the beholder than not, at other times it'd be the other way around and the entire concept would become moot.

Pointless.

Man. What he couldn't acquire with the benefit being on his terms, he'd take.

When that failed, he'd steal.

Mankind. Ever needful.

Ever deceitful. Even unto himself.

When the Paiute could no longer live in a degraded environment they simply packed up and followed the Sierra and lesser mountain ranges within the Basin and Range landscape north into places where other people already existed. The Shoshone did the same thing when they island hopped their way across the various mountain ranges in the Great Basin as they emigrated from the Rockies to the Eastern Sierra. When it was all said and done both'd end up in the same place and each'd be the dominant culture within the area they occupied. An area that extended across most of the western United States from the Rockies to the Cascades as well as to the Esalen coast beyond. Their trade routes'd create the Olivela Trail and their pictograph and petroglyph memories 'd dot the landscape.

The Paviotso Confederacy.

Never mind the Modoc, Mojave, Maidu or Washo. The Miwok, Tenino, Yana or Klamath. All would either be alternately displaced or have their territory reduced by the wandering Shoshone and Paiute bands once they moved into the area. Man was man. What he couldn't live with, he'd either leave behind or simply acquire as needed. Strength, and in the end, technology always won out. Theirs too were uneasy alliances.

The Paiute bows were stronger than what the Washo, as well as most of the sub Sierran and Cascadian tribes used, and compound shafts were virtually unheard of. Likewise, both the Shoshone and Paiute were greater in number than those they encountered. Both were hunter gatherers and each had warrior societies while most of those they ran into were either semi agrarian or fishing cultures. Some didn't even know what warrior societies were.

Needless to say, the whites and their technology as well as their numbers, were stronger still.

Afterwhich, the results were inevitable.

We simply followed in their footsteps.

All the way to Los Angeles and the Esalen coast.

But getting back to the roof.....

Everywhere I looked was Caleb's country.

Yep, I could simply step off the hillside along the back of the house, stand on the roof and look down on a porch that sat several feet above the ground that ran downhill beneath it.

But then everything in Virginia City was that way. Everything ran downhill. Place a marble on top of the kitchen counter and voila, it'd roll toward Dayton. Leave a garbage can outside on a windy day and after blowing half a mile away, it too'd continue to roll downhill toward Six Mile where it'd inevitably end up in the dump or come to rest next to what'd been a karnee. A karnee that'd been erected by the Pavioto who, after having been reduced to timber harvesting on Peavine or swamping the bars on C Street built 'em below the dump in the "outside district" where they'd live alongside the Chinese.

Ever resourceful, both'd scavenge the dump for whatever Virginia City threw away. Damaged tents and threadbare tarps'd become karnee walls and broken doors'd once again be used for what they were designed for while discarded lumber of any kind'd make for a new shanty floor. Used bricks were once again turned into fireplace hearths and broken pieces of marble would be used to cut leather on. Nothing was wasted.

Scissors, an unknown, and seemingly useless implement had their tips broken off and were used for arrowheads while the remaining pair mighta simply been tossed and broken bottles'd be broken down even further and have their pieces mixed with white "milk" glass to create speckled marbles for the kids in town. Marbles that'd been made by the Numa on the ridge above Fort Homestead.

And what about Fort Homestead?

Built by the miners above the Crown Point Trestle, it was supposed to protect 'em from the bad nasties up north after they got their butts kicked by Numaga but failed in it's purpose when nothing happened. Yep, seems the good citizens of the Comstock who, fearing revenge attacks from their swampers on C Street, simply decided to fortify Gold Hill, whereupon, in true military fashion, they built a gun emplacement that woulda been more at home in South Carolina than in Nevada Territory.

Ironic how the guns pointed toward Gold Hill though. Pointed straight at the Crown Point Trestle. Guess they were afraid ol' Numaga might take the V and T next time he visited.

But getting back to Fort Hill…

During its heyday it sported at least two Naval guns at one time or another as well as a possible quaker which was nothing more than a tree stump painted to look like a canon. One blew up when a miner overloaded and tried to fire it and the other ended up in someones front yard well into the twentieth century. As for the quaker, it coulda ended up as firewood for all I knew, if it existed at all.

Radiating out from everything were multiple rock walls

and rifle pits. Seems Richmond and Petersburg had nothing on ol' VC. Needless to say, once it was determined that no threat existed and the bad nasty swampers had returned to their bars, Fort Homestead was abandoned after which the local Paviotso simply returned to where they'd lived before.

They'd remain there well into the 1880s.

Irony.

The Numa were nothing if not ironic.

It was if they were saying "Neener, neener. We're still here, even if you left your rifle pits and breastworks all over the place."

Maybe they were.

But getting back to the roof...

From up on top every building in town that couldn't be seen as either slumping toward Dayton or collapsing onto the one next to it could simply be seen as supporting the one beside it. Like everything else, they existed in true symbiotic fashion. Some tilted left, some tilted right. Some tilted forward, and some tilted back. A truly politicized town. No centrists. No balance.

No Feng shui.

"Walking in balance is the hardest dance you'll ever do."

Not in Virginia City.

Hang a picture on the wall and square it to the doorframe and it'd look crooked. Level it to the ceiling and it'd tilt sideways, or simply realign itself every time a Harley'd rumble by.

Everything in Virginia City was cocked one way or the other. Nothing was level. The citizenry included.

It could be a strange place.

All of the lettered streets ran north-south while all but two of the named ones ran east-west and were named for individuals who, at one point in time or another, didn't care much for Indians, Numa or otherwise.

Stewart and Howard.

One had an Indian boarding school named after him and the other founded a Freedman's university.

The first was emblematic of the west. The other, a bit of an anomaly.

Otherwise, it was the same story from the Missouri to the Sierra. Build a city and name the streets after war heroes, politicians and Indian fighters.

From Wyoming to the Dakotas, Colorado to Nevada and points beyond the story was the same.

So many Grants, Sherman's, Sheridan's and Custer's. Far too many Crook's, Harney's and Taylor's.

At least Oliver Otis was a bit better. Founded a non industrial university for the education of freed slaves and ran around quoting the bible. Even spoke well of Chief Joseph despite chasing him over the Lolo and into Montana. Even lobbied for his return to Walla Walla. Quite a rarity in those days by some measure.

Hell, even old Ulysses S wasn't as bad as Harney or Custer. At least he named Ely Parker Commissioner of Indian Affairs. Yep, Donehogawa the Seneca was the first Native American to hold such a position even if history has subsequently forgotten. Donehogawa. He was a Lieutenant Colonel in the Union army too.

Collective amnesia.

Wrote Lee's surrender terms at Appomattox and stood by Grant's side when Lee had his sword returned.

And what about Robert E Lee?

When it was all over he supposedly turned to Parker, shook his hand, and said "I'm glad there's one real American here."

To which, Parker reportedly responded "We are all Americans."

How soon we forget.

Maybe there shoulda been a Parker Street in VC. Maybe even a Grant.

Wonder if there's a Parker Street anywhere?

Grant visited Virginia City once ya know, where, along with his wife, he went down into the Savage Mine, or at least part way.

Yep. Old "part way" Grant. Took forever taking Vicksburg. So long that Lincoln considered replacing him with yet another in his ever expanding list of General failures. McClellan, Burnside, Meade, Fremont......

There was no end in sight. The South coulda won. They certainly out Generaled the North and Lincoln had a hard time with his general staff anyway.

Wonder if he got drunk in one of the saloons on C Street when Julia wasn't around? Wonder if he smoked a cigar while riding the hoists down into the Savage?

And then there was Julia Grant. Sure as hell wasn't a Julia Bulette.

And what about Julia Bulette?

She was the Patron Saint of the Virginia Engine Number One Fire Brigade. Hooker, madam, philanthropist and the Comstock's own Florence Nightingale.

Julia Bulette.

Murdered under suspicious circumstances even by Virginia City standards, she was reportedly buried in an "unknown and unmarked" grave when in fact she was interred in what's come to be known as the Pioneer Cemetery outside of town. Yep, the ol' Pioneer Cemetery was built above one of the Comstock's many mining claims on the northwestern slope of a hill located east of town and stands within the shadow of everything; mountains, mines, sunlight and people. Well removed from C Street, it's a colloquialism and all but hidden from sight. A place where the criminals, miscreants, illegitimate and societal castoffs could be buried without having to spend their eternities next to one or another of the fine upstanding citizens of Virginia City who were firmly planted above the dynamite houses of the Mexican Mine.

The true Pioneers.

Seems kinda ironic though, given the fact that they were little different from those who'd spend theirs residing in their own segregated cemeteries along the Silver Terrace or up Seven Mile Canyon.

Yep. There was one for the Catholics. One for the Protestants. Another for the Jews and yet another for the "Celestials". One for the Firemen, another for the Masons and yet another for damn near everybody else.

Needless to say, the cemeteries were little different than the city itself, no matter what the intro to Bonanza showed. Whereas damn near every culture on earth mingled together in town, they did so in a frequently less than egalitarian manner. Everything was stratified from the bars to the housing. The wealthy lived at the top of the hill on Howard, Stewart and A

Streets or simply carted their loot off to Nob Hill, while the upper middle class merchants and quasi professionals lived on B. After that came the average citizens and boarding house residents who resided on C and below them the hookers and immigrant families who lived on D or still farther down hill in the Outside District. The rest, low class, no class, Chinese, Indians, or otherwise, lived either on D or still further downhill or out in the surrounding hills and gullies in either pit houses or tents that ran all the way to the Shanty Towns that covered the hills and Dayton beyond.

Why should the cemeteries be any different?

Hell, even the bars were stratified. One for the Cornish, one for the African Americans. One for the fraternal order of this, and one for the fraternal order of that, and as always, one for something else.

No Indians allowed in any unless they were swamping. No Celestials. Ah Sam could walk back and forth from Dayton to Virginia City every day to peddle his fish for all they cared.

While there could be exceptions, no Hop Sing's were allowed.

And what about Julia Bulette?

Enclosed within a newly painted white picket fence, hers is the only grave one can see from town.

Julia Bulette.

The last time I was there someone'd left a plastic Fireman's hat and a pair of red silk slippers on top of it. Still no headstone though.

Probably never will be.

"This is the West, sir. When the legend becomes fact, print the legend."

Coulda been Samuel Clemens or ol' Mark Twain, but that's another story.

The west was nothing if not a myth of its own making. Some created it. Some added to it. Some embellished it. Other's simply perpetuated it.

Virginia City was all of that, but to me it always seemed that the truth could be stranger and more interesting than the fiction it'd created.

Take the Chinese for example. They came onto the Comstock fresh from laying the tracks for the Central Pacific and built the V and T afterwhich they erected one of the tallest trestles of it's day over the Gold Hill ravine and for what? Nothing. Nobody even remembers 'em anymore. Many carried with 'em Chinese "cash". Cash that, unlike American and European coinage, was cast in bronze and attached to sprues like "trees" which'd then be broken off and have their coins removed. Once removed, the cash'd then be sewn into the linings of whatever clothing the railroaders wore when they sailed from Shanghai or Hong Kong for America; San Francisco, Sacramento, and eventually Virginia City. While nothing was dated, the name of the emperor du jour would be cast into one side while the name of the issuing bank would be cast into the other. Needless to say, some of what ended up on the Comstock was produced between 1661-1722 by Emperor Sheng Tzu while other pieces were cast between 1736 -1795 by Emperor Kao Tsung, already ancient offerings in a new land that neither wanted nor cared for 'em.

In the end, some would be lost while others would be simply thrown away.

Useless.

Before doing so, however, some'd be cut apart like "pieces of eight", whereupon quarter and half cash sections'd be formed and traded with the Numa or other Chinese in and around the mines for whatever their owners wanted, but never with the Gweilo. The Numa and the Chinese had a symbiotic relationship. The Gweilo were simply devils.

Never trust a Gweilo.

To them you were nothing. Best to avoid 'em.

A hundred years later a piece of three quarter cash'd turn up next to an obsidian bird point. Fragile reminders of what'd come and gone.

Wonder what they were traded for?

Roughing it

"According to custom the daily "Washoe Zephyr" set in, a soaring dust-drift about the size of the United States set up edgewise came with it, and the capital of Nevada Territory disappeared from view. The vast dust cloud was thickly freckled with things living and dead, that flitted hither and thither, going and coming, appearing and disappearing among the roiling billows of dust, hats, chickens, parasols sailing in the remote heavens; blankets, tin signs, sage-brush and shingles a shade lower, door-mats and buffalo robes lower still; shovels and coal scuttles on the next grade; glass doors, cats and little children on the next; disrupted lumber yards, light buggies and wheelbarrows on the next, and down only thirty or forty feet above ground was a scurrying storm of emigrating roofs and vacant lots..."

Yep, old Sam Clemens resided on the hill for awhile and managed to live long enough to talk about it.

Sam Clemens.

History recalls that he blew into Virginia City fresh from Missouri like just another Washoe Zephyr, and after landing in town with his carpet bag in hand, assumed, like damn near everyone else who'd done it before him, that all he had to do was wander around the hills, stick a spade into the ground now and again, and he'd end up rich. Rich beyond belief. Rich no matter what. After that he could retire early and skeedaddle for San Francisco where he'd build a mansion on top of Nob Hill and become another Sharon, Stanford or Crocker. Maybe a Huntington or Ralston.

Nob Hill was getting a bit crowded what with all the Comstockers flooding into town, but no matter, it'd do.

Unfortunately, like so many others who called Virginia City

home, the carpet bag'd become lost, tossed or thrown away and end up little more than a rotted mess where only the frames would survive.

Needless to say, some of 'em are still there. From Dayton to Como, to Fandango and back their skeletal remains cover the land.

Solitary reminders of what'd come and gone.

Carpet bags.

Along with Oyster shells, Worcestershire Sauce bottles and buttons, they were one of the four most common pieces of detritus on the Comstock. Everybody ate oysters smothered in Worcestershire Sauce and everyone lost a button now and again. Hell, the oysters were packed in ice and shipped in via the V and T from Pugeot Sound and sheep were brought in from Dayton where they too'd become dinner entrees or bar snacks that'd be drowned in London's finest. Everybody lost a shirt, a pair of pants or a union suit. Buttons made from whale bone, wood, milk glass, fancy-cut glass, steel and pewter as well as ghutta percha, not to mention the ubiquitous oysters themselves were everywhere as were their shells, and those frequently had button sized holes in 'em.

Another tossed bar snack where somebody too poor to afford a new set of mother of pearl simply made do with what they had.

And then there were the occasional Chinese buttons that'd been made from ivory and were shaped like miniature straw coolie hats as well as brass military buttons. Occasionally a dome shaped officer's button'd pop up. Sometimes even a militia button, but by and large most were simply of the general enlistment type.

Seems few officers ever made it onto the Comstock.

Hell, on one occasion I found a Civil War era Naval Officer's button right next to an Army Officer's. Both obviously came from the front of one jacket or another and each was within inches of what'd once been a campfire. A campfire that had obsidian and flint debitage scattered all around it. Yep, damn near every Indian from the Missouri to the Carson loved their military uniforms, the Numa included. Hell, even old Poito had one. Probably got it from Fremont, but who knows.

Those not given Mexican War cast-offs simply acquired 'em

by other means, or when that failed, used what others no longer cared for.

Same thing happened on Caleb's Creek.

Whether the owner of the army button came from Fort Churchill or not, I never knew. While it was well documented that more than a few enlisted men deserted from there to seek their fortunes on the Comstock, officers seldom ran away and few seemed to have ended up in Virginia City anyway.

More likely than not, whoever owned 'em had traveled overland or around the horn and then either lost, tossed, or discarded their jackets once they reached Virginia City. Then again, maybe they were simply traded for something the campfire sitter had or the jacket owners wanted.

No matter what, whatever they had to say was left unsaid and their stories were left untold.

Lost.

Yep, somebody camped where I found 'em, cooked dinner and possessed two non related military buttons. Both were acquired shortly after the Civil War and each came from someplace else. There probably wasn't a jacket associated with either by the time I found 'em and more likely than not, each'd been used as either a form of payment for services rendered, or were simply traded for what their original owners wanted. Then again, they coulda simply been gifts. Even after a hundred years, neither of 'em were dented or tarnished. Neither'd been in the campfire and neither'd lost any gold on their surface. To me it seemed like whoever left 'em either had second thoughts about their value or couldn't decide what to use 'em for. Kinda hard to make anything with one button, let alone two mismatched ones. Then again, they mighta simply been forgotten after eating roasted rabbit and getting a good night's sleep.

Needless to say, it was a mystery.

Who did the buttons belong to and how did they end up on the Comstock?

What'd they seen and where'd their owners been?

Aboard the Kearsarge? Maybe somewhere near Appomattox? Not even my rather fertile imagination could tell.

So many stories.

And then there were the Kepi and Forage Cap buttons as well as those that'd once been attached to one coat sleeve or another as well as a California Militia button. You could still see the word Eureka on the front of that one.

The California Militia. They came over the hill to save the miners from the bad nasties after the Pyramid Lake Paiute War and all because a pair of rednecks at Williams Station couldn't keep their hands off the Paiute women, let alone their girls.

The California Militia. Seems either somebody stuck around after it was over or simply jumped on the V and T afterwards and returned to where it all began.

So many stories lost.

Gone.

Gone with the wind.

No matter what, Scoville Manufacturing was a busy company in those days. They left their calling cards everywhere.

And then there was the anomaly of anomalies, an Army Officer's button of the same vintage, but manufactured in England. That one still had it's gray threads attached to the back and was probably, like the others, either accidentally torn from the jacket it once belonged to, or was intentionally removed.

Another story for another time...

Virginia City.

Nothing was what it seemed.

Kids too young or small to work in the mines'd compete with the Numa and Chinese in the dump or below the tailing piles for usable leftovers while playing with porcelain dolls and ceramic marbles in between.

As such, doll heads, arms and legs'd turn up all over the Outside District as well as ceramic and milk glass marbles, some with their hand painted and crisscross stripes still on 'em and some with speckles of colored glass inside.

"Strange how so many of the arms had their hands missing though. Seems every time a head, arm or leg'd pop up wherever the hands were missing obsidian and flint debitage would be all around 'em."

Numa campsites? More likely than not. Coexisting with the

Chinese? Probably so. Both lived in the Outside District and both did so side by side.

Neither the Celestials, as the Chinese were called, nor their Numa counterparts were much cared for on, or above C Street and neither were allowed in town at night during much of the Comstock's existence, and then it was only to perform some menial task the white population didn't want to.

Theirs too were symbiotic relationships.

But getting back to the dolls...

Their arms and heads were always made of white porcelain while their legs were sometimes porcelain, sometimes bone. All had hand painted eyes on 'em and all had their lips and cheeks rouged. They wore Gibson Girl hairdos and button up high topped shoes. Never could find a body. Never found any clothes.

Some of the dolls were bigger, while others were small, but all could fit into the palm of a child's hand. Maybe the smaller ones were cheaper than their larger cousins. Coulda been more affordable on a miner's salary. Then again, the big ones we usually think of when we talk about the Victorian era were more likely than not kept safe inside a curio cabinet in one or another of the homes above C Street and simply didn't end up with their bodies broken in the dump or thrown away in the Outside District.

By and large, none of the dolls were children, infants or toddlers, but rather full grown twenty somethings. The ideal women du jour.

No bodies though. Seems all of 'em were nothing more than Raggedy Ann's. Raggedy Ann's that wore miniature cloth outfits and were attached via cuffs to porcelain arms, legs and necks and then stuffed with cotton, horse hair or straw.

Yep, all of the dolls either had their clothing made by hand or on some treadle sewing machine back east or overseas in Europe. Needless to say, It was easy to imagine that more than a few ended up in Numa hands and had new outfits made. Outfits with blue quill beads on 'em.

After all, blue was the color of Father Sky.

But what about the missing hands and why were almost none of the feet or arms broken?

The arms on the larger dolls were hollow, those on the

smaller ones weren't. Neither had hollow wrists and none of the legs were hollow at all.

Too many had their arms broken at the wrist. Too many for coincidence. Too many broken at what shoulda been the strongest point.

It was as if they'd been broken intentionally.

None of the break points were jagged. In point of fact, all of 'em were clean.

Needless to say, it reminded me of how, when a person died in more than a few traditional cultures, their belongings would either be ritually broken to set the spirit within the object free or to release the owner from their creation. One could see it in far too many metates and manos, pestals and points around far too many campsites where one or another'd turn up cleanly snapped or broken in two as opposed to being impact fractured or simply broken. It was the same story from Colorado, to Wyoming, to Nevada and westward. Far too many lithics were broken where no logical use breakage should've occurred. Likewise, most of it seemed to have happened simultaneously. By and large, nothing was older than the mid to late 1800's. Too many coincidences. Too many for a single death.

But why the hands, and not the feet?

To me it seemed obvious.

What do you do when an entire culture dies?

How do you mourn?

Maybe, as in the case with an individual, you simply break everything and set their collective spirits free.

Hell, history was full of examples where that was the case and some of 'em were recent. Made me think of the riots in Watts, Oakland and Detroit during the 60s. None of the destruction was directed outward into the surrounding communities where the grief could be externalized, but rather, all of it was directed inward into where the people who were rioting lived. As such the loss was always internalized and what was destroyed was what the people themselves had created.

They could set their own spirits free. Control their own narrative.

As perverse as it sounds, often when one feels powerless, it's easier to blame ones self for whatever perceived deficiency is imagined than to blame another. As such, it's a way of taking control over a situation in which you have none. The powerless become powerful and they're able to dictate and tell their own story on their own terms. To determine their own outcome.

The Numa, like those who lived in Watts, Oakland and Detroit were simply trying to set their spirits free and to do so on their own terms.

All of the dolls were made during the 1880s and all had their wrists broken within the same decade. The same was true with the lithics. Damn near every tool that appeared as if it'd been ritually broken was either made or broken during what would've been the end of an era, the end of the Great Basin lifeway.

To me it all added up.

By the late 1800s the Numa were losing their way. The men no longer wore traditional clothing, preferred Spanish Vaquero hats to buckskin and the women wore cotton dresses and covered their heads in scarves. Karnee's were made of canvas and the willow was gone.

Same with the deer. Same with the pronghorn, the mountain sheep and the pine nuts. All obliterated by the emigre onslaught.

It was the beginning of the Fry Bread Culture, all commodity lard and whatever else the government'd otherwise throw away in payment for what they took from the Indians to begin with; their land and their dignity.

Yep, by the 1880s damn near everything the Numa used had been replaced by whatever the white man no longer wanted for himself. Why should the food be any different? But then the same thing was happening all over the west. Simply make a ball of commodity lard and flour, work it into the shape of a pizza then throw it into a pot of boiling oil and voila, dinner'd be served. Good luck finding any commodity honey or powdered sugar though. Neither seemed to make it into the commodity system very often.

And so, with their lives upended, it was easy for me to imagine the existence of a universal grief wherein everything that was known had vanished. It was easy to imagine the dolls having their hands ritually broken because those were what created everything. If you couldn't create anything, ya didn't need 'em.

By 1880 an entire generation had lost its innocence and the Numa were no longer in control of their own creation.

They were now living in the white man's world.

They'd become dead. Best to set their spirits free...

But then not everyone was Numa.

Damn near everybody else simply wanted to be rich, and more often than not, with as little work as necessary. While most never found what they were looking for, they'd nonetheless act out in true F Scott Fitzgerald fashion that they had.

Hell, it was the American way. Let the Celestials do the work. Maybe those who frequented the Boston Bar. Maybe a Numa or two. For the rest, it was make a penny, spend a dime.

After that they could wander into town and hang out in any one of a dozen or so bars on B and C Streets and drink a Bass, smoke a Glasgow, eat an oyster drowned in Worcestershire Sauce and bullshit about whatever they believed themselves to either be or not be, and all while pretending to be something they weren't.

Rich.

Virginia City.

At least they got some of it right.

Yep. Old Sam Clemens.

History recalls he christened himself Mark Twain after his riverboat days on the Mississippi where the leadsman at the front of the paddle and stern wheelers'd call out the depth of the riverbottom beneath 'em by swinging a knoted rope with a lead weight attached to the end and then counting the number of exposed knots between where the weight hit bottom and the waterline.

Mark one. One fathom and six feet of draft. Mark twain. Two fathoms and twelve feet of draft and so on.

Local legend, however, held that Clemens, ever the do as little as possible freeloader and bullshitter he was, would simply wander into the Corner Bar next to Piper's and order whatever it was he was drinking and assume it was free or that he could pay for it later after which he'd have the bartender check his name off on the chalkboard behind the bar to indicate how many drinks he was in the hole for and then skeedaddle someplace else.

Mark one for Clemens. Mark two for Clemens.

One could almost hear the response...

"Hell, when I was a captain on the Mississippi we used to say "twain" instead of two."

"Why don't you do that?"

Ever the smartass at somebody else's expense.

"Mark Twain."

Has a nice ring to it. Think I'll change my name.

He certainly wasn't the first to do so, nor would he be the last.

Some things never changed.

Well, pick your poison as they say. Believe what you will.

Either way, ol' Sam Clemens was now Mark Twain.

Mark Twain.

Everybody knows the story.

It's part of our social fabric. American lore.

But there was a time on the Comstock when ol' Sam was anything but popular, or for that matter even famous.

In point of fact, there was a time when he was downright despised.

Despised because, more often than not, ol' Clemens, or Twain as he now called himself, would simply make up a story or tell a yarn about somebody he knew without changing their name, or when he did so, simply veil it behind an all too translucent facade. A facade wherein the skinniest guy in town would become "Scarecrow" or the fattest, "Professor Corpulent". Hell, Clemens couldn't even call 'em "Skinny" or "Fatty", he had to reduce 'em even further by giving 'em an even more outlandish moniker. Reducing 'em even as he did so to an even more comedic parody with each retelling. And so the stories grew. Seems every one he told was at somebody else's expense. Never his.

None of the locals liked it and old Sam was threatened at least once with being tarred and feathered, tied to a rail and run out of town via the Devil's Gate.

Ol' Sam.

Used to bitch about the walk from the bars on B and C Streets back to his cabin in Gold Hill when he was drunk.

Christ it was only a mile, maybe two, and if you couldn't take the Toll Road, you could simply follow Gold Canyon down the divide. Either way, you'd end up just below Gold Hill and it was an easy amble back into town. Easy even for a drunk. No hills, no steep grade.

Yep, even walking for ol' Sam could be too much work. Rather bitch about it.

Probably wished he were Huck Finn. Probably wished he could simply laze away the days and drift with the current.

No doubt that thought came to mind more than once during Sam's days along the divide. Hell, Huck Finn mighta been a Comstock creation for all I knew.

Ol' Sam.

Nobody much cared for him in Gold Hill, Virginia City or for that matter in the Outside District.

Even the bullshitters couldn't stand another bullshitter, especially one who was so good with words that not even the brunt of his stories could tell that it was them ol' Clemens was talking about.

Gossip.

No gossip, no Sam. No Sam, no Twain.

Hell, it wasn't until people living in San Francisco, Chicago and New York began reading his stories about the Comstock, Jumping Frogs and runaway kids that ol' Sam became famous. Nobody knew about Virginia City or Calaveras County first hand who hadn't been there and almost nobody floated down the Missouri on a raft. Sam was safe in the fiction he created. So safe, that in time the fiction became fact.

Nobody questioned it and the city slickers swallowed it whole while in time even the tar and feather crowd came to love him. After all, they too were now a part of his stories and by extension, as famous as he was. Now they too could wander into any bar on B or C Streets and claim, "See, that was me! I knew ol' Sam. Gimme one bar keep and be sure to mark it on the board."

In the end, everybody loves a bullshitter.

Sometimes an entire town.

Yep, ol' Sam Clemens.

At least he got the weather right.

Hell Winds and Hurricanes

The winds that'd blow over the Comstock more often than not did so every day, all day, every time of year when they'd come roaring down off Mount Davidson and scatter everything in their path.

One year they blew my chimney down, blew so hard that the garbage can took flight, not once, mind you, but damn near every week where after doing so it'd sail to points unknown and beyond if it had a mind to. You had to walk into winds like that. Had to lean into em' at damn near a forty-five degree angle to keep from blowing away yourself. If you turned and walked with 'em, they could send you flying. Thankfully, more often than not, the winds always came from the same direction, straight outta the west which meant everything'd head along the same path. Downhill. All the way to the dump. All the way to Dayton.

All the way to Glenwood.

Non windy days were rare on the Comstock. As uncommon as daylight in winter in a town where the sunshine would be gone by two.

It always amazed me how, unlike Wyoming where every tree pointed eastward, most of whatever grew on the Comstock did so straight, but then nothing on the Comstock was very tall.

Nature's way of adapting I suppose.

Thank god I never got blown off the roof. Couldn't tie myself to the chimney like ol' Muir did with that Ponderosa in Yosemite.

Virginia City.

Everything was "gone with the wind."

Virginia City.

Sure as hell didn't look that big when you drove into it, but by the 1870s Virginia City and the surrounding Outside District held roughly 25,000 individuals, most of whom either lived in pit houses, lean too's or tents. Where they didn't, they'd simply curl up on the ground next to a pot bellied stove if they had one, or sleep cold if they didn't and eat oysters, drink a Bass and smoke a Glasgow. When not digging for silver, they'd sit around and play checkers. Beds would be either the hard ground, preferably close to the stove, or if one was lucky on a box spring mattress that'd been dragged in from town. In every case, carpet bags made for great pillows whether anything was still inside 'em or not.

Virginia City. Nothing was what it seemed.

Eleven hundred people when I was there. Houses of wood and brick. No tarps, no tents, you'd never know unless you walked the land. Hell, even some of the locals didn't know what was in their own backyard let alone over the ridges and out of view.

Before gold and silver were discovered in the canyons and quartz outcrops above the creeks and springs of the Virginia Range the Numa used to build their summer karnees above slightly hollowed out circular depressions in the ground whereupon a woven frame of willow and foliage in the shape of an igloo would be crafted and either placed over the pit, or simply built above it.

Sometimes these would be anchored with foundation stones, sometimes not. Either way, they were rounded and low to the ground. The wind, more often than not, would simply pass over or around 'em. It was rare when one ended up in Dayton.

Once gold was discovered above Johntown, those newcomers who moved into the area simply emulated the indigenous population they encountered. They dug a pit, covered it with a canvas tarp at ground level or slightly above, anchored it in place with whatever loose rocks they could find, and voila, they too had a place to call home. The only exception to the rule being that most of the miners built pit houses that were both deeper and rock lined as opposed to what the Numa had. Likewise most of 'em added fireplaces, a rarity in the indigenous pits where the fire ring was outside.

After that came the rock shelters which were built into some of the canyon and ravine sides. As with the pit houses, when not built into the entrance of a cave, they too were usually low lying and close to the ground. Unlike the pit houses though, these new structures could either be rectangular or some meandering shape that corresponded to the hills, gullies, caves and enlarged cracks they were built into. Whereas a karnee could house an entire family, the newcomers shelters were more often than not only big enough for one person to curl up in. If you could sit up, you were lucky. Standing room wasn't an option. One person was plenty. Two a crowd. Any more, unheard of. Beyond the caves everything was low to the ground and half buried.

No Washoe Zephyr was going to blow any of these folks away.

Pit houses and rock shelters, the Anasazi of the Comstock.

Both were ubiquitous in the otherwise semi barren landscape that surrounded 'em. That is unless you counted the Glory Holes and failed diggings that were everywhere.

So many gophers, so little silver. Forget the gold. The placer'd already been hauled off.

Needless to say, the wood and brick structures one sees today along C Street didn't come until later, but even then, the pit houses endured, expanding ever outward with those who occupied them well into the early twentieth century.

Like the boarding houses in town, they too were occupied by different individuals and more than once.

A far cry from the C Street gunfighters and slicker wearing faux cowboys one sees today.

The real deal.

Life on the Comstock wasn't all glitter and gold no matter the pretense.

Wealthy?

Absolutely.

Hell, the beer came from England as did the Gilbey's they drank. Pipes were imported from Glasgow and more than a few fancy buttons were made in Paris.

Everything was imported. What wasn't was repurposed. Very little of anything was manufactured locally.

Wealthy yet simultaneously poor, Virginia City was an oxymoron wrapped in a conundrum, a city of extremes. We remember the one. We forget the other.

A city of broken dreams and failed realities, artificial constructs and imagined personages.

A city where Edward Hopper would've been right at home. Nighthawks.

And so many discarded carpet bags.

The Battle of Worcestershire Flat

Old Joe Scramblefoot drifted into Virginia City from California where he blew in like a Washoe Zephyr over Jumbo and down Mount Davidson before taking up residence in the Chapin House and later in the Outside District southeast of the divide.

Joe never made it big in Mariposa and Bear Valley was a bust no matter what John C Fremont said. So were Hangtown and Tuolumne for that matter and after those Frenchman's and the Dry Diggings. Hell, Joe never found more than a few ounces of gold dust anywhere at anytime and beans were getting old. So with no mule, no horse, no train and no prospects for anything at hand other than more hot sultry days living in a patched Sibley tent, Joe packed up his carpetbag and trudged over the mountains between Jackson and Woodfords.

Shit, if Old Snowshoe Thompson could do it in winter with a hundred pound mail sack on his back and ol' Hank Monk could do it while driving a stage team of pissed off horses over the granite and scree passes along the way, then he too, ol' Joe C Scramblefoot, could do it with nothing more than a carpetbag.

If nothing, Joe was tough. A bit dimwitted, but tough. And so after several more weeks of dried beans and weevil biscuits Joe stood on top of Fandango and stared out across Six Mile, Misfit Flats and Stillwater. All the way to Glenwood.

He'd made it.

At last he was going to strike it rich. Gonna be another "Pancake" Comstock. Another Hosea Grosh, another James Finney. Never mind that Hosea was dead, killed by the dream, or that Henry Comstock was an alcoholic do nothing who simply scammed his way to wealth, which he immediately pissed away on warm beer and whiskey. He, Joe Scramblefoot, was going to be different.

Gonna be rich even if he wasn't the first.

And so after landing on C Street, Joe, along with the other 20 odd thousand people like him, began to dig.

At first he'd find a few copper sulfides. A piece of quartz crystal here, an agate there. Maybe some topaz or an amethyst or two. Nothing spectacular. But then he began to turn up a bit more, but like so many others, it always seemed to be farther away from town. Out near Sugarloaf. Off near Sutro's Folly. Even down near Johntown. But never in Virginia City, or for that matter even Gold Hill. Silver City? A bust. American flats? Best leave that to the cows and the Jones boys.

The Jones boys.

Hell, they froze to death looking for their father's cows on Christmas eve. Old skin flint. Not going to happen to ol' Joe. Scramblefoot knew better.

Yep, for awhile ol' Joe did alright. He wasn't rich, but he was living in the Chapin House. He made enough to toddle down C Street and wander into a bar or two. Made enough to occasionally head for B Street and the Corner Bar where he'd grab an oyster on the half shell, drown it in Worcestershire Sauce, then grab a Bass, smoke a Glasgow and eat a lamb chop or two before heading home. If he stayed in his room, he could always throw the leftovers out the back door where they'd either slide, roll, or blow away downhill toward Mackay's place, the V and T or China Camp below that. All the way to Six Mile and the dump. All the way to Dayton.

What didn't blow away, Ah Sam could have. Maybe a Numa or two.

Hell, when I lived below the Chapin House, the garbage pile was still where ol' Scramblefoot'd left it. A pile replete with the usual obsidian chippings and Henry .22 cartridges.

Guess one of the Numa had a derringer.

Joe Scramblefoot. He made it in true VC fashion for a while. Penny rich, pound poor. But as with everything else, nothing worth having seemed to last for long, especially in Joe's case.

In short order out the door he went.

After that, it was onto the divide and down the Occidental whereupon Joe ended up on a small spit of a hill surrounded by a few scraggly pinyon pines. Some of the very few that hadn't been cut down for the Ophir, the Gould and Curry, the Savage, the Chollar or the Mexican. The Potosi, the Crown Point, the Hale and Norcross or the Yellow Jacket.

So many mines, so few trees.

Yep, between Virginia City, Gold Hill, Silver City and all of the mines in between, almost all of the Virginia Range had been stripped of every tree in sight. Gone were the cedar, the juniper and the pinyon pine. Gone the way of the antelope, deer and bear.

Gone with the wind.

So gone, that in the end, Virginia City, being the ever resourceful city that it was, simply moved on to the Tahoe basin where the hill drillers did their damnedest to clearcut that as well. They could use the same flumes their drinking water came from, or if not, simply follow the same routes and send the lumber down from Glenbrook, Spooner or Marlette. When that wasn't possible, there was always the Carson River where the trees that'd been clear cut from the valleys above Markleeville and Woodfords could be sent downstream to Empire before being turned into so much cordwood, assuming there was enough water in the river to operate the Mexican ditch and drive the mill. Sometimes there wasn't. After that it'd be up over the grade above the Washo camp and on into Silver City, Gold Hill and the mines above.

Yep. Ol' Scramblefoot was lucky. He found a hill with shade to live on. Another rarity on the Comstock, except of course in winter when nobody wanted it.

A hill with sunlight. A hill where he, Joe Scramblefoot, could look out, gaze in any direction, and observe what was going on. A hill where he could look down on the head frame of one mine, look up the hill at three others and across multiple ravines in between. Hell, he could see all the way to the Pine Nuts, all the way to Como, all the way to Sunrise Pass. A hill where he could watch the wagons and mule teams coming and going on the

Occidental, look out on Sutro's Folly, or when he was fortunate enough, watch the same teams as they made their way across the gypsum fields between Rag Town and Carson. All the way to Brunswick Canyon and the charcoal kilns, El Dorado Canyon and still more mines.

Yep, ol' Scramblefoot had landed at the center of the universe.

Unfortunately, it wasn't long before the neighbors moved in.

First it was Sam John. Then it was Louie Woo. After that it was god knew how many others. It was the same all over the Comstock. Get rid of one neighbor, and another'd show up. And as always, they all wanted to be rich.

Sam John.

Like ol' Scramblefoot, that wasn't his real name, but everybody called him that because nobody could pronounce his first name, which because he was Numa, was his only name. And so in true Virginia City fashion, ol' what's his name became Sam John.

Nobody knew Scramblefoot's real name either. Not even Scramblefoot himself. Hell, he'd been called Scramblefoot for so long that it simply stuck. It suited him.

Why every male member of the Paviotso had to be named Sam or John though, was beyond Sam's comprehension. But then, so was everything about the white man except for the Spanish Vaquero hat he wore on his head and the denim Levi's and calico shirt that covered the rest of his body. He loved those. But ol' Sam would be damned if he'd ever give up his blue quill moccasins and bone beads.

They came from somewhere up near Como. He never did say exactly where.

And then there was Louie. Like Sam, nobody could pronounce his first name either so after meeting a Frenchmen named Louis while working on the Crown Point, he simply changed his as well.

Woo, however, preferred "Louie" to the French "Louis", because after all, he was American now.

He wasn't living in France.

Yep, ol' Woo renamed himself. After all, that was the Comstock way. Change your name, change your identity. Sam on the other hand, wasn't so lucky. He was just another John.

But then ol' Joe wasn't always a Scramblefoot either. He started being called that back on the Motherload when he was too poor to afford boots, or at least new ones, so everybody called him that owing to the fact that he tied the ends of his boots together with twine because they were always falling apart. Seems his toes were always sticking out and, because he could never afford a new pair, whenever the old ones finally gave up the ghost, ol' Joe'd simply rummage the dumps and tailing piles nearby for another, that more often than not, were little better than the ones he'd had. Seems nothing ever fit

Joe Scramblefoot. No shoes Joe.

Henry "Pancake" Comstock. Ate nothing but pancakes.

And then there was "Old Virginny" Finney. Came from Virginia.

Everybody in the mining camps had a nickname or changed the one they had. Some stuck. Others simply changed the ones they had or were renamed by others.

It was a new world.

In any event, it wasn't long before Joe, Louie and Sam fell in together. None of them made it big in the mining business. More often than not they'd simply hang around one or another of the several pot bellied stoves that appeared on the hill along with the other denizens that blew in and played checkers, the American kind. After all, Louie was now American, Sam enjoyed it and Joe was able to cobble together an old bone set of pieces and Sam made the board, black and white, he knew what he was doing even if the checkers were all the same color, bone ivory. Cow bones. Horse hooves. Not even Chinese ivory.

Nothing was wasted.

If they were lucky enough to find any significant ore or dig it out of the ground, they'd smelt it down and separate the rock from the silver they found, gold was pretty much gone by then, using cyanide and mercury. The Quicksilver came from New Almaden as did the bottled mineral water they drank while playing checkers. That was until the Quicksilver mine collapsed and contaminated the spring nearby. After that it'd be Tahoe water carried in from town.

New Almaden Mineral Water.

The same thing happened with the Comstock. Dig a mine and the underground aquifer, springs and seeps around it would collapse or became contaminated, not that there was much of an aquifer to begin with. After that, it'd be Tahoe water, which like the timber was gravity fed and pressure driven by way of flumes and hand riveted iron pipes up over Spooner, down into Franktown, and then over Jumbo Grade after which it'd flow downhill again into Virginia City.

Unfortunately for Sam, Joe and Louie, whatever cyanide and mercury waste they created eventually made their way into the ravine below the hill as well as into the small springs and feeder creeks around it. After that it'd be the Carson River and Dayton.

Theirs, and all of the other mines and mills south of the divide, most notably the ones on American Flats.

In the end, Dayton would become the worst toxic cleanup site in all of North America; directly adjacent to the high school.

Go figure.

Once, every twenty years or so, when the so called century storms would roll through the area the rivers and creeks'd flood, leach fields and catch ponds'd breach and everything from Silver City, Gold Hill and south of the divide would end up in the Carson River or Lake Lahontan.

"No Fishing" signs were posted everywhere, but did it stop people from fishing?

Hell, no. You can't teach a hillbilly anything.

The damn idiots would eat everything they caught, bottom feeding catfish and all.

There were, and still are, alot of purposefully stupid people in the area, but that's another story.

William's Station anyone?

Yep, right next door to Lahontan and sometimes under water.

For the newly found friends on the hill, however, once the silver was smelted it was then poured into a half egg shaped crucible the size of a person's palm with a small hole in the bottom. Just big enough to carry into town and easy to hide. Easy to conceal when you carried your silver into town and exchanged it for Oyster and Bass money.

Simply place the crucible in the sand next to one or another of the potbelly stoves and pour the liquid silver in. The sand'd keep the metal from oozing out and when done, you could push the bullion out with a small file or nail.

Unfortunately by 1873, that'd become a bust as well. The ore was disappearing all over the Comstock and silver'd been devalued in Europe. Needless to say, it wasn't long before the investments that'd been made before the crash became worthless. Railroads died overnight as did the entire country that was being built by 'em. Businesses collapsed and banks went under. Investments were wiped out and government backed loans became worthless.

Overnight, Virginia City, Silver City and Gold Hill tanked.

There was little, if anything left, and nothing would be the same afterwards no matter what.

On top of that 1873 was a horrible winter. Cold, bleak and snowy. Needless to say Joe and the boys suffered. No more trips into town. No more oysters on the half shell drowned in Worcestershire Sauce. No more Glasgows or Bass Ales at the Corner Bar.

They were slammed, screwed and stuck.

New Almaden Mineral Water and Doctor Bosanko's Pile Remedy bottles were everywhere. Hell, the water was already gone and now the silver too. On top of that, they had the shits.

Joe threw the crucible away. Sam burned his chess board and Louie gave Sam a piece of "cash" that he'd sewn into his clothing when he came over from China as a reward for his effort.

Their lives were broken, but they hung on. Besides where else could they go? Empty carpet bags were everywhere. Folks who came with little left with even less. Best to hang on. Best to hunker down. Maybe things'd get better. Hell, the freight wagons were still running up and down the Occidental. Not as many, but some. Something could still turn up even if the mines had become skeletal.

Gotta hang on. Just a little longer. Just a bit more. But it wouldn't be easy. Joe, Sam and Louie were becoming cranky and irritable. Cranky with themselves. Irritable around each other. Cranky because of the weather and once again, irritable because there was nothing to eat but dried beans and Jack Rabbit stew.

No Worcestershire Sauce. No Lea and Perrins.

Christ it was getting bleak.

Downright depressing.

Hell, even Jack Rabbit stew tasted better with Lea and Perrins on it. Took away the gamy taste.

Nothing could help the beans though.

They made it through Christmas. No gifts were exchanged.

They made it through January and February. Still nothing.

By mid March the snow was beginning to pile up and neither Joe, nor Sam, nor Louie knew whether or not their communal tent could hold any more. All day and night they'd huddle inside and poke at the top with their spade handles to knock it off but it never helped. Get rid of some and more'd simply pile on.

The only time they'd venture outside was to relight the fires in one or another of the potbellied stoves as one by one their neighbors moved away with the drifts that eddied around them. Why they never put a stove inside, they couldn't tell. They just didn't. Beyond that, the only time one of 'em would wander beyond the tent flap was to head for the ravine, Doctor Bosanko's in hand and hope that the by now all bean diet, all of the time, didn't plug 'em up too much, but it always did.

Beans.

Everybody's favorite camp food.

Hell, in the sixties we'd go camping with case lots of canned beans and fruit cocktail. Military Surplus. We'd pack 'em in by mule up near Shaver Lake. C rations. The cans were painted olive drab and were leftovers from the Korean War. Hard to believe, but they were still edible, if you could call 'em that. 1965. Sometimes we'd even take cans of so called biscuits along which were nothing more than stale, flat crackers. Pusan Pain Pills. Why we ate them I never knew. Better than weevil biscuits, I suppose, but not by much.

Bury a Maraschino Cherry in 1965 and it'd still be there a

hundred years later.

So many preservatives, so little time.

Beans. The boys didn't buy 'em canned, but in burlap sacks. Dried beans. Lots of dried beans. Gotta water soak 'em first if you're gonna eat 'em. But what if there's no water?

Hard to imagine.

Better grab the Bosanko's.

By late March the snow flurries would begin to lessen and by early April they'd be all but gone. Afterwards there'd be occasional mud days. Days where you could once again walk into town. That being said, more than a few Mexican Mustang Lineament bottles had their contents emptied on sore calves, ankles and thighs. With or without horses, both Virginia City and Gold Hill were equally distant from where the boys camped but seemed even further if there was snow or when the resultant boot sucking goop that passed for mud would appear after it melted. When that happened it was often easier to simply strike out across the ridges, avoid the ravines, or at least the shaded portions where possible, and jump between the clumps of bunchgrass and rocks that'd appear. Those always melted first. The road was another story. Goop until it got hot and rutted to hell until the goop turned to dust. In either case, you didn't want to take the road anyway. Easier to cross over where nobody'd been.

The boys didn't have any horses, Mexican Mustang Lineament not withstanding. But who on the Comstock did? No place to graze 'em beyond American Flats or out near Lousetown anyway. After that it was either the Truckee Meadows, Eagle Valley or down near Sheep Camp and Sutro. Damn near every other spot was either a mine, rocky or had a pit house on it.

Mules yes. Everybody needed a freight wagon, Horses? Shit, VC was small. Everything was close by and if you wanted to go anywhere you couldn't walk to, there was always the V and T or a stage. Christ, you could even take the train into Gold Hill and avoid the one to two mile hike if you wanted to. Maybe ol' complainer Clemens shoulda stuck around a bit longer. Rather than trudge across the Divide, he coulda simply hopped on the V and T and ridden it home when he was drunk. Besides, there were so many people and freight wagons on C Street that you couldn't get past 'em let alone pay the freight on the hay that needed to be hauled up one grade or another from points ever further away to feed a horse if you had one anyway. It was easier to walk.

Sam, Joe and Louie walked everywhere.

By late April, the teamsters were once again hauling goods between the mines and could head up the canyon through Devil's Gate with whatever the Comstock consumed and the V and T didn't have to plow through as many drifts. By 1874 things were beginning to return to normal. But what was normal about it? The price of silver was still off and the load was still dropping. On top of that, folks were still leaving town.

Virginia City continued to shrink while the boys prospects did so as well. There was no end in sight.

Beans, goop or dust, feast or famine, and no money.

Irritability turned to anger and the boys'd argue, after which one or another'd get tossed out of the tent where he'd have to curl up on the ground next to one of the camp stoves to sleep or walk around all night stamping his feet if he couldn't. Spring may have sprung, but the nights could still be cold April or not. Seems the winner of whatever argument occurred kept the blanket no matter what.

Then one day in early May the boys saw a teamster heading down the grade for the mine directly below their camp. It was loaded with boxes and crates of this, that, and something else, fuller than they'd seen since back in '73. And what was written on the side of one of 'em? Lea and Perrins, London.

Worcestershire Sauce!

Christ, none of them had seen any Worcestershire Sauce, let alone tasted any since the Corner Bar days in town.

It was too much.

They were broke, but maybe they could get some for free, so off they charged.

Once they hit the top of the ravine where the Occidental curved they saw their chance. The wagon would have to slow down not only for the curve, but for the even steeper grade that followed. It'd be an easy attack.

Joe, Sam and Louie simply hid in the arroyo at the top of the ravine, blocked from view of the driver by the hoist works, and waited for the wagon to pass.

Once it had, they sprung into action, attacking the wagon as they did so. The driver was startled and the mules bucked but he held on. Unfortunately though, it wasn't for long. A case of Lea and Perrins was lifted from behind, but broke when the boys tried to toss it out. Needless to say, the entire lot bounced downhill leaving a trail of broken bottles everywhere the crate landed.

When the boys saw this they jumped off the wagon hoping to save as many as possible, but it was too late.

Everything was broken from the case to the contents. Worcestershire Sauce was everywhere.

By then the driver had fallen off the wagon as well, but by some measure of divine providence or godly intervention, stood up unhurt. Even more miraculous was the fact that the mules stopped at the bottom of the grade. Nothing else was damaged after which the bruised teamster got back on, cursed the boys out, and once again continued on to the mine below the hill where they had their tent.

But no matter what, the Worcestershire Sauce was gone. There wouldn't be any more.

And so ended the Battle of Worcestershire Flat. A short and seemingly forgotten episode in the history of the Comstock.

After it was over, Sam returned home to Como and built a karnee next to one of the many springs in the area and close to a spot where one of Louie's Chinese friends had built a berm around another. A spring where he raised koi. A spring that never froze in winter.

Louie settled in Rag Town after the sundown laws were enacted in Virginia City and died shortly thereafter. He was buried near the bottom of Gold Canyon.

Joe? Joe was Joe. He simply wandered off and nobody ever heard from him again. Rumor had it that he'd moved to John Day up in Oregon and was panning for gold there, but then the same thing was said about Pancake.

Nobody knew.

Myths and legends.

Fact and fiction.

What was true and what wasn't.

Years later I'd find the spring where Sam's neighbor lived. The pond he'd built a hundred years earlier still had koi in it and they were huge. Several generations huge. Hundred year huge. When I went back again after that, they were gone. The spring'd collapsed and the slopes that were nearby had been clearcut. Mining had returned to the Comstock.

Thankfully the hill where the boys lived was still intact.

An entire case lot of broken Worcestershire Sauce bottles did run down hill and someone who was Chinese did camp with someone who was Numa as well as someone who was neither. Someone played checkers and poured molten silver into half egg shaped ingots and left behind their Chinese "cash", crucible and checkers after leaving and someone else threw away a pair of Levi's, left a set of rivets and did use Bosanko's Pile Remedy and Mexican Mustang Lineament. They drank new Almaden Mineral Water and Bass Ale. Someone wore blue quill beads on something and someone else owned a bone bead necklace. They smoked Glasgow's and threw away at least some lamb chop bones. A lot of rabbits were eaten. No oyster shells though. Guess they had to go into town for those.

Fact or fiction?

I never knew.

But no matter what, for me, the boys existed.

Maybe not Joe, Sam or Louie, but certainly somebody like 'em.

Their stories were everywhere.

You just had to look and have a little imagination.

Confederate Dreams and Texas Schemes

Franklin Gearing was born in Pittsburgh, Pennsylvania in 1840 where by the time he reached mid adolescence he'd gone into partnership with his father to help run the family shipping business that transported Texas cotton to northern ports along the Mississippi. From New Orleans, to Saint Louis, and eastward along the Ohio river, the Gearing fleet'd transport their loads of southern grown cotton northward where after being unloaded and exchanged for steel and manufactured goods they'd once again head south to repeat the process. Along the way they'd stop at Natchez, possibly travel the Red and maybe even make it to Hannibal.

By all accounts it was a lucrative business.

By 1860 it'd become so much so that Franklin moved to east Texas where he was able to oversee the southern portion of the business more efficiently and in turn, presumably, secure better deals on what was already cheap Texas Cotton.

Between 1860 and 1861 the family business thrived and additional paddle and stern wheelers were added to the Gearing fleet.

Then came 1861 and Fort Sumter. South Carolina seceded from the Union and Texas soon followed after which any commercial activity along the Mississippi between the newly formed Confederacy and their former trading partners farther north should have become suspect, or so we were taught. For the Gearing's, however, it was anything but.

The value of cotton skyrocketed as did the price paid per bale up north while the value and price of manufactured goods did the same thing south of the Mason-Dixon line. Between the two and the increased demand from the cotton gins in England, and the Gearing's made, what was to them, the best choice they could make; they played both ends against the middle and simply expanded their operations to include Cuba, where, after running the Federal blockade outside Galveston, their paddle and stern wheelers could unload their cargo onto the waiting British barks, or should that prove untenable, transfer what they carried at Matamoros. In the meantime they could continue to run the Mississippi as they had and smuggle what they could between Ohio, Missouri and Louisiana, sometimes with help from one side, sometimes from the other, sometimes from both simultaneously. No matter what, the results'd be the same, the Gearing's would make more money and Sumter was of no concern.

From what the record indicated, they did quite well for a while. They could supply both sides of the growing war with what they wanted, and in turn be paid in good ol' US dollars. Never mind the Confederate currency. It wasn't worth a dime. Most of the Confederacy did the same thing.

A nation divided, but still backed by the "yankee dollar".

'Twas ever thus.

Unfortunately by 1862 their enterprises were becoming more problematic both along the Mississippi as well as out of Galveston. The blockades were finally taking hold and it was getting harder to bribe and/or pay off one side or the other while still maintaining a profit.

As such it wasn't long before much of the Gearing fleet was confiscated by the Union and young Gearing was thrown into prison in Pensacola. A Union prison in a Southern state.

Ironic. But then again, history was never what it seemed. Certainly wasn't what we were taught.

Although he tried to escape by cutting his way through the window bars of his cell with a penknife, he failed. Ironically, he was released shortly thereafter and immediately returned to his former ways while simultaneously cozying up to at least some of the Union military commanders up north.

Unfortunately, as fate would have it, Franklin, who after

having been caught in 1862 by the Union side, was then captured by the Southern in Natchez in 1864.

His appeals for help from his northern sympathizers failed and by March 1864 Franklin was mustered into Company L of the 1st Texas Infantry as a private.

Whether he did so willingly or not is a matter of historical debate, but what seems certain, however, is that Franklin was either pushed or prodded into serving the Confederacy given his record.

Either way, F.A.G Gearing was now a private in Hood's Texas Brigade.

By May 6, 1864, he'd be wounded in the Wilderness along the Plank Road where he was shot in the left shoulder by an errant minnie ball. Wounded in the same battle that saw the Confederacy falter, Longstreet and Gregg wounded and Lee stumble backward into trench warfare near Petersburg and Richmond.

1864 wasn't a good year for the Confederacy.

Where Gearing was and what he was doing between then and the dissolution of Hood's Brigade at Appomattox in April of 1865 is likewise open for debate, but clearly his shoulder bothered him and he spent most of his time in and out of one field hospital or another in and around Richmond. Although records indicate that he was issued a new uniform in November of 1864 and released to active duty, nothing is mentioned about where he was sent or what he did between then and April 9th, 1865.

Did he make it all the way to Appomattox along with the remainder of the Texas Brigade? Was he captured and made a prisoner again, possibly somewhere in a trench outside Richmond?

Nobody but Franklin and those who knew him could say, and they were all dead.

No matter what, by June 24th, 1865 Gearing was once again in Texas where he was paroled for his service in the Confederate Army. After that he went back into the riverboat trade; ironically with some of the same boats his family'd owned before the war.

Seems that by one means or another, they were able to reacquire what they'd lost through the courts and questionable legal action.

By 1869, however, Franklin'd grown tired of the riverboat business and went to work as a traveling salesman. Selling what? Again, history was silent.

Whatever he was selling, he did so until 1870.

Between Gearing's return to Texas and 1870, Franklin married and fathered five children. By 1870 he lost one and in 1871, he lost another. Both were daughters. What impact this had on him's unknown, but their deaths seemed to have changed him. He was never the same afterward.

No matter what, by 1873 he'd become disillusioned with his life and no doubt Texas as well after which he abandoned his wife and simply moved away. All the way to Virginia City.

By 1873 the northern industrial machine and the railroads it'd created had finally driven south into Texas and it's easy to imagine that Franklin, having grown tired of Southern living, simply caught the KATY, and once aboard rode the Missouri, Kansas, Texas Railroad into Junction City, Kansas where after having done so, he caught the Kansas Pacific to Denver with carpetbag in hand. After that, more likely than not, he jumped the short line to Cheyenne and caught the Union Pacific where he rode it all the way to Lake's Crossing, Nevada. From there, he coulda taken the Virginia and Truckee all the way into good ol' Virginny. All the way to Virginia City.

A place to hide out. A place to get rich. A place to leave Texas and everything about it behind.

A place to reinvent himself.

What happened to Franklin between his leaving Northern Virginia and parole in Galveston in 1865 is unknown, but what is known, is that once he reached New Orleans, he had his picture taken wearing a Confederate Lieutenants uniform.

The reinvention was beginning.

He'd acquired an officer's uniform and in turn created an identity that he'd keep with him for the rest of his life. An identity that, as concocted as it was, would come to define who he thought himself to be, an officer and a gentlemen.

A Civil War hero.

Unfortunately for Franklin, 1873 was a lousy year to make a move. Especially to Virginia City.

Between 1873 and 1880, what Franklin did was unclear. Seemingly he worked for a while as a Meter Inspector for the new gas lighting system that had gone up in town. No doubt he worked in one or another of the mines, possibly even doing so on his own. Where he lived is likewise unclear. Was he living in town, or outside in a shanty or pit house? The record doesn't say.

Either way, by 1880 when Gearing was counted in the Storey County Census, he was living at 448 South D Street. A block down from where I was. There's no 448 now, just a vacant lot, but in 1880, 448 would've been right next door to Ah Lee, Ah Chung and Ah Sing. Close to the Rosinni's and their immigrant family of seven, and close to at least six other families with children.

Loma Linda anyone?

Hard to imagine. Right next door to the Savage Mine and barely above the Chollar. Right next to the Hale and Norcross. The entire street woulda clanked 24-7 365.

Below that, pit houses and the Numa camp.

A middle class, highly ethnic, blue collar neighborhood immediately adjacent to the Fourth Ward School.

A Virginia City anomaly.

The kids didn't have to walk far to school and they could play with their dolls and marbles everywhere in between. Hell, they could hang out with the Ah's and play with Lieutenant Gearing if they wanted to.

According to the census, private, now Lieutenant Gearing, was employed as an engineer and was single.

Hmm. No mention of the wife back in Texas or that she was possibly living with his parents in Pennsylvania by then.

And an "engineer" for what? Gas Meter Inspection? Mining? Doesn't say.

Lieutenant Gearing was continuing to reinvent himself.

By 1890 when Franklin filed for benefits in the National Veteran's Census, he apparently either exaggerated, changed, or fabricated his service record once again. Although the specifics are somewhat vague and open to interpretation, when doing so he reported that he'd been held as a Confederate prisoner of war in Fort Pulaski, Georgia. He never mentioned Pensacola. If he had, he wouldn't have been a military prisoner anyway, simply a civilian. Whether or not he was held captive at Fort Pulaski remains debatable as no records mentioning him remain.

More likely than not, Franklin was simply once again inventing what he wanted others to believe he'd been.

What's known, however, is that private turned Lieutenant Gearing, CSA would often parade in true VC fashion up and down C Street in uniform whenever the occasion occurred, but by then he'd do so as a Major.

A Major who, by some accounts, had yet another uniform, and a new one to boot.

Yep, ol' Gearing had a new uniform. One that'd never seen action. Never been in a fight. Coulda been a stage prop. Coulda been acquired from Piper's Opera House.

No matter what, Franklin had his picture taken in uniform once again. A picture where the image reflected a man roughly twenty years older than the one who'd been in New Orleans. The picture of a man who was not only wearing a new Confederate Major's uniform, but one that included a pair of brand new leather gauntlets.

Seems old private Gearing not only brevetted himself once again but did so whereupon he charged into battle on a horse. Everybody's Knight in Shining Armor.

Yep, ol' Lieutenant Gearing was now a Major. Never mind that he'd only been a private and a foot soldier. Texas was a long way off and Virginia even farther.

Major F.A.G Gearing, formerly of the Army of Northern Virginia was free to be anything he said he was.

Nobody'd know the difference anyway.

Did Gearing now own a Major's uniform as was supposedly shown in the second graveure? Did he still have the old Lieutenants uniform he'd picked up in New Orleans?

Both were as unknown as where the second picture was taken.

Coulda been taken in Virginia City for all I knew.

Either way, Franklin loved a parade. Loved to play at something he wasn't.

Hell, it was the VC way.

Had he been an ODD Fellow? Maybe one of the Knights of Pythias? Was he a Mason? Who knows.

Private Gearing, Hood's 1st Texas was now free to be a Major, a Major in the Army of Northern Virginia and he could do whatever he wanted to no questions asked.

There weren't a whole lot of retired Confederates living on the Comstock in those days. Just a doctor up the hill and he seemed perfectly content to forget about it.

Franklin was safe to be anything he said he was.

By 1900, the census reported that Gearing was once again married, employed as a miner, but with no address.

Needless to say, there was no wife in VC and where he lived was unknown. Probably somewhere in the Outside District. Possibly in a pit house.

Either way, by 1910 and another census he was living at 73 C Street. Although he told the census taker that he owned the place, 73 C woulda been in the heart of Virginia City's business district. That woulda meant that Franklin either slept on the floor in one business or another, on a billiard table or rented or shared a room with someone else upstairs.

As with everything else in his life, it was simply another fabrication. Why the census taker didn't pick up on it is another story. One I've never known.

No mention as to whether or not his address was on North or South C Street either for that matter. And in yet another ironic twist, there is no 73 C Street on either the north or south portion of C Street in Virginia City today. Not even a vacant lot. The number simply doesn't exist. Whether it did so in 1910 or not is anybody's guess.

Virginia City'd been renumbered at least once, but when, I never knew. Hell, even my place had two different numbers. Played hell with the utility and credit card companies. Neither the phone company nor Sierra Pacific Power could decide where I lived and the credit card companies couldn't seemingly verify my address given that the only way to get mail in VC was to go to the post office.

Twenty-first century America…

Not in VC.

Either way, it was another oops by the not so accurate census taker.

In the same census Franklin reported that he was still married but was working as a carriage painter.

By 1920 he was living in a boarding house at the corner of B and Taylor Street where he shared a room with William Moran. Once again, though, Franklin was single. William Moran was listed as his partner.

But partner in what? Hell, Gearing was eighty. Undoubtedly both he and Moran were living on pensions, but no matter what, he'd made it. He'd moved up hill and was living right next door to one of the step children of ol' Piper, the same Piper who owned the Opera house one block down.

High society.

Major Gearing had made it at last, but it wouldn't be for long.

Franklin (F.A.G) Gearing died in 1921 and was buried beneath a simple polished marble headstone next to the Fireman's section in the Silver Terrace Cemetery.

On it, the headstone proclaims that he was a Major, CSA.

He'd won.

He'd finally made it. Made it all the way to the top.

"Top of the world, ma!"

A hundred years later I'd find a Confederate Officer's button with its gray threads still attached to the loop on the back in what'd once been a pit house below D Street. It looked as if it'd either been accidentally or purposefully torn from the breast of a uniform. A Lieutenant's uniform. Possibly a Major's.

The gold plate on the front was barely tarnished and the button itself looked new. HT&B Manchester was still clearly visible on the back despite the rust.

Yep, the button just like ol' Gearing, had probably run the blockade outside of Galveston. Possibly Matamoros. Could've even done so in one of Gearing's boats for all I knew.

No matter what, it was amazing. Right there in the bottom of the pit. Right next to a child's hightop leather shoe. Right next to a piece of Chinese "cash".

Right down the hill from 448 South D.

Did the shoe belong to one of the Rosinni kids? Did the Chinese coin belong to one of the Ah's? Was it smuggled out of China in someones tangzhuang and what about the Confederate button?

They were all directly below 448 D and only a stones throw away.

My stomach dropped.

Somewhere along the way Private Gearing lost a button on one of his Officer's uniforms.

Virginia City.

Nothing was what it seemed.

Pictures At An Exhibition

The Hut of Baba Yaga.

Living where I did in Virginia City, life sometimes felt that way, or at least the place I lived in did.

Yep, 'ol Modest Mussorgsky musta been thinking about Virginia City when he composed Pictures At An Exhibition. Hell, he mighta even lived on D Street for all I knew.

The Hut of Baba Yaga.

Baba Yaga the gnome. Baba Yaga the guy living downhill on D Street. Baba Yaga, the guy who was always taking off into the hills all of the time and for no apparent reason whatsoever.

Baba Yaga the gnome. The guy who'd head into the hills without a gun. No canteen. No backpack. No compass and, heaven forbid, no cel phone.

Yep. Good ol' Baba Yaga the eccentric, but then almost everybody else in town was anyway, and besides, why go outside when you could get drunk in town? Especially without automatic fire power. Hell, there might be a jack rabbit or two lurking below C Street. Maybe a liberal tourist or two.

Gotta be prepared. Best carry the.44 mag, maybe the SKS. Can't go anywhere without the M16.

Christ, I'll never forget the time when one of 'em reached into the pocket of his Levi's for his trusty six shooter and shot his nuts off. Couldn't even afford a holster.

Idiots. And VC could be full of 'em.

Then there was the time when our local crazy, but then who in VC wasn't, upset a tourist and the local sheriffs department was called in whereupon they gunned him down. Did so right in front of the Wagon Wheel. Right on C Street.

Yep. Can't go anywhere without the proper fire power.

Never mind that the person killed was only carrying a pocket knife.

Never mind that everybody in town knew who he was and that he had his own shack on the promontory south of town. Never mind that he sometimes worked for "coffee" in the local coffee house. Never mind that aside from his occasional rants, more often than not he was lucid and seemingly better educated than most of the tourists.

A tourist felt threatened. God save the effing tourist.

Yep, at times I lived like a gnome while on D Street, but then it was literally hard not to. Unlike most of the Victorian houses in town that had entries that were narrow and tall, mine was set well below building code, Victorian or not. Had to stoop down when going in or out. If ya didn't ya'd hit your head on the lintel. Yep, the door was less than six feet tall.

Once inside, the house itself was little better and it was no stretch at all to touch the ceiling with the palm of your hand. Hell, a kid coulda done it.

Yep, you could touch the ceiling while standing flat footed.

The Hut of Baba Yaga.

The hut where, when it rained, or the snow'd pile up under the eaves on the west side, water'd seep inside and back up around the wood stove. The same wood stove that'd had it's chimney blown down in one of Clemens Zephyrs.

The wood stove that'd had its cast iron top cracked because someone burned newspapers in it. Got so hot that by the time I tried to use it that you couldn't do so without getting smoked out.

The Hut of Baba Yaga.

Smoked cowhippies.

Sometimes VC seemed cursed. No doubt more than a few

folks who'd passed through it thought so.

And then there was the west wall. Over the years it'd gotten so damp from the constant seepage from the hill behind that pictures'd fall off, breaking their glass and springing their frames as they did so.

Virginia City ghosts.

Spooktacular events for the paranormalists who'd flood into town and set up camp directly in front of where I lived.

Sometimes it was an entire film crew, sound men, gaffers and multiple stage, costume and generator trucks.

Other times it was simply groups of idiots who were shuttled around the Mackay Mansion by overly paid, so called guides who were little more than the flim flam artists du jour. Guides who'd tell 'em they'd see something, maybe a ghost, maybe a free floating orb, maybe an unexpectedly cold room. Maybe even a little girl dressed in white.

Yep, they were going to see something and they paid handsomely to do it.

Hell, even the tour buses participated in the game. None of the drivers knew where Julia Bulette was buried, but they sure as hell knew where the ghosts were.

Looking for ghosts. That too had become the VC way.

Ignore the story, print the fiction.

Needless to say, I'd thought about running around the outside of the Mackay Mansion more than once while waving a flashlight and shouting "Whoooooooo".

Yep, the old wavy glass'd make you see things.

"Look, Martha, a ghost!"

Let the idiots see some ghosts, strange lights and orbs. I could laugh all the way back across the street.

Life in the hut of Baba Yaga.

When it wasn't the spook hunters, it was the metal detectorists. Another group of idiots who, with trowel in hand, would simply walk on to any property they chose and create a divot filled golf course. Worse than gophers. Little did they know that the place where I was living was built on top of what'd been a cistern for the Bonner Shaft. Because of that, damn near the entire north side was nothing but sterile infill. They'd never find a thing. Walk twenty feet in any other direction though and it'd be a different story. Dig a hole for a rose bush, and voila, a whiskey bottle'd pop up. Reset a fencepost, and a .44-70 cartridge would appear.

Virginia City.

Nothing was what it seemed.

No doubt living above the former cistern didn't help the leaky wall though The ground was soft, had no compaction and the damn house was built atop a place where the water collected naturally anyway.

No matter what, the metal detectorists left with Vibram soled Merrell imprints on their backsides.

They were trespassers of the worst kind and they didn't belong .

If they couldn't find what they were looking for on their own, they didn't belong there.

Boy Scout 101.

Leave the shit alone.

What's buried's buried for a reason.

It doesn't want it's story told and it doesn't want to sit on your fireplace mantel.

And then there were the camera toting tourists.

While not as bad as the Ghost Busters, it was fairly common to wake up on a Saturday morning, open the blinds, and find one standing directly in front of the bedroom window snapping selfies.

"Look, Martha, I just got a picture of a guy standing in his shorts next to the window."

Another day in VC.

Tourists.

Gotta love 'em.

They were the bread and butter of most everybody in town even if most of the merchants lived somewhere else.

Not too many who worked in VC seemed to live there, but then again, I didn't spend much time on C Street, so I coulda been wrong.

Yep, good ol' Virginia City.

It was a love hate relationship. I loved the history, the hills, and the surrounding uninhabited basins and mountains, but I had a hard time dealing with Deadwood on the Comstock.

Needless to say, there were times when I'd pray for winter, that singular time of year when the tourists'd leave and the gun-fighters'd hide. When the streets were yours and the real ghosts were free to roam.

Winter always brougt 'em out.

After which they were free to roam the hills like me. Unencumbered by the fallacy of their creation.

When I wasn't working, hiking the hills, or sitting on top of Baba Yaga Central, I'd sit in the Adirondack on the porch and drink a Colorado brew.

While I couldn't see down Six Mile from there, it was a place where I could sit and drink a barley pop (a leftover Danism from the Roaring Fork Valley) and simply let the mind wander. And wander it would.

Out past Limoges on the Prairie. Out past the Dead who'd speak in a dead language on Caleb's Creek and out past the Great Gates of Kiev, even if they were only owned by the Devil south of town. After which it could wander over Mussorgsky's Bald Mountain if it wanted to and travel to Loma Linda in 1959.

To hell with Kurt Vonnegut, I had VC.

Schlachthof Funf.

Life imitates art. Aways has. Always will.

Pictures at an Exhibition.

Think I'll whistle the Promenade and drink a 1554. Got the Coyote Chorus at noon.

The Coyote Chorus.

Every day at noon when the fire siren'd go off in town, the hillsides all around VC'd join in ala Handel's Hallelujah and every coyote that hadn't either been shot, trapped or poisoned, would tune up and howl along.

A symphony to keep the tourists at bay.

Life in The Hut of Baba Yaga.

Plant a rose bush, and the deer'd eat it. Put a flower pot on the porch and the deer'd get that too. Move the pot right up against the front door and under the porch light? Same story.

Beyond the psychotic weather and eternal lack of rainfall,

what those didn't kill, the deer would.

Hell, you couldn't even put up a taller fence. Tried that. Eight feet and the damn things'd simply jump over it every time they smelled a rose. Roses. They'd eat 'em thorns and all. Musta been from Ohio.

Christ, I could even go out and yell at 'em and all they'd do was stand there and bat their eyelashes.

They'd never move.

Urban deer. Deer that'd teach their kids where to come back to when they were dead and gone. Multi generational deer. Millennial deer. Deer that'd roam all over town and eat everything in sight.

Worse than the tourists.

It was no wonder nothing grew on the Comstock.

The deer ate damn near everything.

And then there were the black widows, tarantulas, scorpions and rattlers that'd make house calls.

Almost as bad as some of the tourists, but at least the former you could sweep out.

And then there were the ants. Everywhere. Those you couldn't sweep out. One year it was Miller moths. They invaded the place like a scene straight out of Rod Serling's Night Gallery.

Straight out of the Twilight Zone.

Open the door to Baba Yaga Central and hundreds'd fly in. Look down the street toward the Fourth Ward School and all you could see was a cloud that'd collect under the street light. Same with the porch. You couldn't turn the light on without adding to the invasion. Walk a block up or downhill and they'd be gone. It was as if the Miller's only lived on D Street.

Maybe they did. Then again, maybe it was the cottonwoods.

Yep, I used to leave the porch light on to scare the deer off and then I couldn't turn it on for fear of creating moth heaven.

Needless to say, it never fazed the deer and the moths were all over the place anyway.

Worcestershire Flat and the boys had nothing on the Battle of the Miller's. Their corpses were everywhere, but like the Chinese Army at the Chosin Reservoir in Korea, they just kept coming back until one day they simply vanished.

The inside of Baba Yaga Central was covered in their corpses.

More ghosts for the tourists.

Virginia City. Ever the adventure. Probably shoulda put that in the brochures.

As said, it was a bi-polar relationship.

Love and hate.

The cornerstones of modern America.

I loved that porch.

A porch where a convocation of lizards took up residence underneath it. A porch where spring after spring they'd emerge from hibernation below and sit at my feet, in time doing so on top of the Merrels as well.

And that wasn't the half of it. Once the damn things were properly positioned, they'd turn and look up, stare lizard like into my face until they saw where I was looking and then turn and gaze in the same direction. I know it sounds weird, but they would.

After a few years more would appear. Pops'd become Grampops and Mom'd become Gramma and soon thereafter the kids'd follow. And then there were the grandkids. You could always tell who was who by their size and color. The first year there was one. Then there were two. After that there was an entire colony. All blue gray except for the old ones who'd by then turned mostly black.

Needless to say, it was always the first two who'd sit on top of the Merrells. The original two. Never the younger ones.

Pretty human I'd say.

And then there was the chickadee.

Had one land in my hair once and it sat there for what seemed no doubt like an eternity in chickadee time before flying off.

Seems even the animals know what's a threat and what isn't. What they can trust to and what they can't.

Sure goes beyond anthropomorphism.

Hell, even the coyotes followed Caleb around and while hiking in Wyoming and Nevada mustangs'd follow me around. The foals'd come up and nudge me from behind, rub their noses on whatever shoulder they could reach and then follow me around once they had.

The mares never balked and I only got challenged by a stallion once.

Then there were the deer. They certainly weren't afraid of anything no matter the bluster.

Even came across one of the recalcitrant does that'd been in the yard once just minutes after it gave birth and neither it nor the fawn moved.

Both just stayed where they were and I was all but ten to twelve feet away.

And what about that bobcat at Molera?

Except for one time when I was growled at by a Cougar while hiking in the Bodie Hills I never felt threatened. Even the stallion calmed after being talked to.

Treat nature as an equal and it'll treat you the same. That is unless you're either stupid, the animal's sick or feels threatened, or you're on the dinner menu.

Animals seldom attack anything simply for sport. Unlike man, there has to be a reason.

You just gotta know where you are and what you're doing.

Respect.

That's all nature asks for.

Respect it, and it'll respect you.

Never could understand the "lions and tigers and bears" mentality of so many I'd meet.

"Whadda ya mean you take off into the mountains by yourself?"

"Whadda ya mean ya don't carry a gun? Aren't you afraid something'll get you?"

Shit, no.

"Lions and tigers and bears, oh my!"

This ain't Kansas and I ain't Toto.

We're all a part of the food chain and nature's the great equalizer. It doesn't care whether you're rich or poor, ugly or not. You just gotta respect it. Meet it on it's own terms.

Nothing abides either the weak or the foolish, man included, and stupidity is no excuse. Know what you're doing, where you are, and more often than not you'll be left alone. Besides, it's the stupid ones that always seem to make it onto the dinner menu.

Boy Scout 101.

If you don't know what you're doing, you don't belong there.

Think I'll whistle some Mussorgsky and grab another 1554.

The lizards are calling.

Collecting Dust

A hundred miles beyond the point, the farthest point, the most distant point on the horizon. Out past the alkali flats and sinks; Misfit and Stillwater, Humboldt and Carson. Out over the mountains, iceage islands and archipelagos, Ichthyosaur, Columbian Mastodon boned talus slopes and scree fields. Beyond the Saltbush, Bitterbush, Creosote Plants and Rabbitbrush, petrified Redwood forests and Mount Mazama blowouts. Out over the playas, hoodos and springs, koi ponds and basins. Beyond the mustangs, horned lizards, whiptails and rattlers and over the abandoned mines; silver and gold, copper, bornite and cinnabar. Out past the hematite and jasper, chert and agate. Out over Lovelock, Spirit Cave and Wizards Beach. Beyond the grinding rocks, diorite and granitic boulders cast adrift in a sea of sand, dust and wind. Beyond the Rye Grass, Ricegrass and Bunchgrass. Out over the land into the distance and beyond. The distance of a thousand years, a million years, a century, a lifetime. A distance of roads forgotten and graves abandoned, misplaced Iris and Lilac the only indication of a person's passing. Out past Bonneville, Daggett, Donner and Walker. The two tracks, the single tracks, the deer tracks, coyote tracks, lizard tracks and no tracks at all.

Out over the land.

"How many times have we hiked these places ol' compadre?"

No answer.

"You know, sometimes you can be so damned quiet."

Still no answer.

"Jeez, Caleb, we've done it for so long that I've forgotten what it is to grow old, and sad to say, I've become that."

"How many lifetimes have we lived?"

"Think of the things we've seen."

"Shit, if it wasn't for you, god knows, I probably never woulda done half of what I have."

Still no answer.

"No Reservations. Wonder if you had any. Wonder if you made it to Noaha-vose. Wonder if you ever saw ol' Daggett again."

Still no answer.

"Damn if you haven't become the silent type."

"Oh well. C'este la vie."

"You know, the damn knees hurt now. So do the hips and ankles. So does the rest of everything for whatever that's worth. Too much use I suppose. Been a lot of years old pard. How many? Twenty? Thirty? Probably closer to forty. One hell of a lot of dust and alkali. Been so long I can't even remember Vedauwoo let alone the Roaring Fork Valley. Yep, ol' hoss, we've been at this game a long time. Couldn't imagine a life without it though."

The land.

Immutable.

"It is the entire meaning and purpose of Shangri-La. It came to me in a vision, long, long ago. I saw all the nations strengthening, not in wisdom, but in vulgar passions and the will to destroy. I saw the machine power multiplying, until a single weaponed man might match a whole army. I foresaw a time when a man, exalting in the technique of murder, would rage so hotly over the world, that every book, every treasure, would be doomed to destruction. This vision was so vivid and so moving that I determined to gather together all things of beauty and culture that I could, and preserve them here, against the doom toward which the world is rushing. Look at the world today. Is there anything more pitiful? What madness there is! What blindness! What un-intelligent leadership! A scurrying mass of bewildered humanity, crashing headlong against each other, propelled by greed and brutality. A time must come.....when this orgy will spend itself. When brutality and the lust for power must perish by it's own sword. Against that time, is why I am here. And why you were brought (to this place). For when that day comes, the world must begin to look for a new life. And it is (the hope of all who believe in it), that they may find it here."

In Shangra-La.

1937.

How little's changed.

Shangra-La.

Just over that "Lost Horizon."

Damned if it didn't sound like Caleb.

Maybe it was.

Time for one last hike.

One last trip over that horizon...

"Maybe I'll head for Como. See if the old bod'll make it up that road from hell. Pretty sure none of the rocks've moved much. Might even see if that ol' black's still around. Remember him? All protective of his harem and all, but all bluster. Never did challenge him and he sure as hell didn't challenge me. We just nodded at each other and after a bit, came to an agreement. I could go my way, and he could go his."

"Hope he's managed to avoid the roundups and SKS crowd though."

"Too many dead horses out there now."

"Suppose I should take a backpack, maybe carry some food, but how long's it been since I have? Not since back in the Rubicon days. Used to have a bell on it, you know. One of those small sleighbell Christmas types that girls used to tie on their shoe laces back in '59. Used to tinkle every time I'd go up and down the ravine near the No Hands Bridge. Lost the bell and the bridge buckled when the flood hit. Gone now too, I suppose."

Washed away.

"A lot of years. Water under the bridge as they say. But how can you avoid it? If nothin' else, life can sometimes be little better. An oxymoron wrapped in a conundrum. Damned if you do, damned if you don't. If you can't laugh at it, it'll kill you. Still haven't gone horizontal though! Not yet, anyway."

"Wonder if I should take a canteen? Haven't done that in years either. Never liked the weight, or for that matter the incessant bouncing on one hip or the other when walking. Throws your stride off, and besides, the sloshing water in the gut always made me feel sick anyway. Easier to pick up a pebble and suck on it. Maybe carry some mints. Forgot those too. Seem to forget a lot these days."

"May carry some weight though. Needs to be done. Getting old."

"Como it is. Hope the Canadians haven't ruined it. Not enough gold there anyway. Stupid idiots. Just like VC and out near Little Bodie. And to think, I used to love Kamloops even if I got tired of eating trout. Why can't we just leave some things alone? And why is it always the Canadians who're fucking things up now?

As always, no answer. It was like talking to yourself at times where Caleb was concerned.

"And to think, you used to be a chatterbox."

Made it to Dayton within the hour and after packing on the extra weight, headed up Eureka Canyon toward the old Como Road.

It'd be a long hike, but then when wasn't it?

Great views though.

Can always stop at some point along the way if it gets to be too much.

No doubt the extra weight'll slow me down a bit anyway.

Half way up.

Looks like as good a spot as any. Time to unload. Time to rest.

What a view. All the way to the Sierra front. All the way to Wyoming.

Lot's of hawks.

A good sign.

A hundred miles beyond the point, the farthest point, the most distant point on the horizon...

Click, bang.

The 1860 Remington fell from my hand and my head spun as my right hand went slack, dropping as it did the one less chambered black powder .44 into the dust.

The dust of centuries. The dust of a lifetime.

A single white owl feather fell from the sky blotting out an unknown sun that soon went black.

It was a clear day and Caleb was calling me home.

Denouement

"Shoot all the blue jays you want...

...but remember, it's a sin to kill a mockingbird...

...Mockingbirds don't do one thing but make music for us to enjoy. They don't eat up peoples gardens, don't nest in corn cribs, they don't do one thing but sing their hearts out for us..."

Afterglow

Somewhere,
sonorous as a fretted flattop
the sagesky hums harmonic,
hazy vague
on the Panamint wind.

Sounding but a brief riff
a momentary note
suspended in desertspace
until your calling
brings me home.

About the Author

P Edmonds Young is an avid hiker and back country explorer who, after years of wandering the backroads and forgotten byways of Flyover Country, currently resides outside Virginia City, Nevada where he continues to get dirty as much as possible. This is his story.

www.powderriverpublishing.com